Plain of Our Ancestors

Valley

Mountain

BRAVELANDS

SHIFTING SHADOWS

BRAVELANDS

BRAVELANDS

SHIFTING SHADOWS

ERIN
HUNTER

HARPER
An Imprint of HarperCollins*Publishers*

Special thanks to Gillian Philip

Bravelands: Shifting Shadows
Copyright © 2019 by Working Partners Limited
Series created by Working Partners Limited
Map art © 2019 by Virginia Allyn
Interior art © 2019 by Owen Richardson

Library of Congress Cataloging-in-Publication Data

Names: Hunter, Erin, author.
Title: Shifting shadows / Erin Hunter.
Description: First edition. | New York, NY : HarperCollins Children's Books, [2019] | Series:
  Bravelands ; 4 | Summary: With the false leader destroyed, the animals of Bravelands are
  searching for the true Great Parent, but a mysterious new menace is threatening their lives.
Identifiers: LCCN 2018055880 | ISBN 978-0-06-264214-1 (trade bdg.) | ISBN
  978-0-06-264215-8 (lib. bdg.)
Subjects: | CYAC: Baboons--Fiction. | Lion--Fiction. | Elephants--Fiction. | Adventure and
  adventurers--Fiction. | Africa--Fiction. | BISAC: JUVENILE FICTION / Animals / General.
  | JUVENILE FICTION / Action & Adventure / General. | JUVENILE FICTION / Fantasy
  & Magic.
Classification: LCC PZ7.H916625 Shi 2019 | DDC [Fic]--dc23 LC record available at
  https://lccn.loc.gov/2018055880

Typography by Ellice M. Lee
19 20 21 22 23   CG/LSCH   10 9 8 7 6 5 4 3 2 1
❖
First Edition

BRAVELANDS

SHIFTING SHADOWS

PROLOGUE

A *great white moon hung in* a sky scattered with stars; it was so bright, it cast a shadow alongside Gangle the ostrich as he thundered across the dry plain. His splayed talons slammed onto the ground, raising puffs of gray dust as he strove to lengthen his strides, but he was still barely keeping up with Flash. Flapping his stubby wings, he ran grimly on.

Flash, with his long, muscular legs and his glossy black-and-white feathers, had always been stronger and faster. Gangle remembered his friend's tiresome, often-repeated joke: *I don't have to run faster than the lions,* he'd tell Gangle; *I just have to run faster than you!*

In other words, they'd catch Gangle first and be satisfied. Gangle had always laughed, because he knew Flash didn't really mean it. But it didn't seem so funny now, as they raced across the savannah under the unforgiving moon. Gangle wasn't sure if there were really lions behind them, but he could make out snarls and the thud of clawed paws. The creatures chasing them were predators, and they had to be led far away from the flock's shared nest—and the precious eggs that lay inside.

Dust from Flash's feet stung Gangle's eyes, and as one of Gangle's claws caught a rock, he stumbled and almost fell. Flash was drawing ever farther ahead. Perhaps this would be the night his joke came horribly true.

It doesn't matter, Gangle told himself. *This is part of our job. We owe it to the chicks who will come.*

Gangle's breath was rasping now, and his breast felt as if it might burst. He risked a look back and caught sight of dark, menacing shadows and the glittering orbs of eyes. His heart stuttered and leaped as he put on a burst of speed. *What are they?* They were relentless, and he was sure he could hear more and more of them, a horde of intent pursuing paws.

"Hurry!" boomed Flash. "Come on, Gangle!"

"Wait!" gasped Gangle. "Please!"

But Flash didn't. With a burst of new and desperate energy, he sprinted farther ahead.

Oh, Great Spirit, spare me!

Gangle knew it was a hopeless plea. Was the Spirit even watching? Did it care anymore? Bravelands had been without a Great Parent for far too long, and its creatures were on their own.

Including me. From the sides of his huge eyes, Gangle could see the running shadows drawing closer, spreading out to either side, hemming him in. Wildly beating his wings, he swerved, almost crashing into one of his pursuers; he lashed out a foot, catching something hard as bone. The thing tumbled aside with a screech. Panicked and desperate, Gangle thudded on blindly, knowing they were on him now, knowing he couldn't kick away a whole pack, knowing he was doomed. . . .

He could run no farther. He was finished. Slowing, he staggered and lurched. In moments, he knew, savage claws would rake through his feathers, dig into his skin, bring him crashing to earth. Teeth would fasten on his long neck—

No predator sprang. The moon gleamed down on the flat, silent plain. No loping shadows darted across his vision to cut him off.

Gangle halted, his heart racing, his feathers drooping. He was alone on the savannah. No pounding paws, no eager, panting breaths disturbed the quietness. As he recovered his aching breath, he lifted his long neck and swiveled his head, blinking.

Nothing.

Unnerved, he shook out his plumage, letting the cool night air soothe his hot skin. He opened his bill to call to Flash, but his cry caught in his throat.

Distantly came wild snarls and then, horribly, a booming cry of terror. Its notes rolled across the dark plain, frantic at first, before dying to a despairing echo.

Flash! Gangle beat his wings in agitation and began to lope once more across the savannah, toward that awful silence. His heart trembled in his rib cage. Would the shadow-creatures bring him down too?

He had to take the risk. He had to know if Flash was all right, or if the worst had happened.

Terror rippled through him. He could hear the flesh-eaters' triumphant snarls, but faintly, as if they were drawing farther away from him.

As Gangle crested a low rise, the moon's silver light picked it out plainly: a tumbled mound of feathers on the earth. Slowing, Gangle approached his friend, his throat constricting. Flash lay lifeless on the sandy ground, his long neck twisted, one huge eye half open and glazed with terror. There was not even a breeze to ruffle his feathers.

Gangle listened. There was nothing now, not a breath or a pawstep. The crickets and cicadas trilled their constant, monotonous song, but the predators were gone.

Lowering his bill to prod gently at his friend, Gangle ached with grief and pity. Apart from a gash in his chest, Flash's body was unmarked. Uncomprehending anger stirred in Gangle's gut.

Only kill to survive: that was the ancient, sacred rule of Bravelands. Everyone knew what it meant—animals could kill to defend themselves and to eat, but nothing more. Yet Flash lay here, his life ripped away, and those creatures had done it only for the sake of killing.

Does the Code mean nothing, now that we have no Great Parent?

Shaking out his plumage, Gangle bent his head once more

to his friend's. His voice hoarse and cracking, he managed to hiss the traditional farewell.

"Now, Earth-Runner, you will fly. Soar with the birds who went before you." He hesitated, and whispered, "I will miss you, Flash."

Swallowing, he turned away. For all his friend's joking, being faster than Gangle hadn't saved him. Why hadn't the predators chosen him, the weaker of the pair? Perhaps the Great Spirit had heard him after all. . . .

But that seemed a forlorn and guilty hope. More likely, he'd simply been lucky. Luckier than he deserved.

What mattered, he reminded himself as he plodded sadly homeward, was that the nest was safe.

As safe as anything could be, in a world without a Great Parent.

CHAPTER 1

The mango tree had been a part of Thorn's life for so long, casting cool shade over the Tall Trees clearing and bearing its prized fruits each year without fail. *It's always so beautiful,* thought Thorn. New mangoes glowed there now, their red and gold peeping out from the glossy splayed leaves. It should bring him contentment, he knew; but even as he gazed up at the bounty, his father's voice came to him across the years, gruff and wise: *Remember, Thorn—the fruit is juiciest just before the rot sets in.*

Blinking, he turned away from the tree and rubbed his head hard. Last night's nightmare had been the worst one yet; he still felt dazed from its horror, and his nerves were raw.

If only the dreams didn't feel so *real.* This time he'd been an ostrich, of all creatures, bounding across the plains under a stark and brilliant moon, a horde of shadowy predators at his heels. He hadn't been able to see them, he hadn't known what they were, but they had filled him with a bone-deep, heart-freezing terror. He'd barely been able to lift his feet.

And why *should* he be able to lift those hefty, two-clawed feet? *I'm not an ostrich!* Clenching his fangs in irritation, Thorn shook himself. Maybe he should tell Pear Goodleaf about these vivid, strange visions? She was so wise, and she'd seen so much in her life as a healer.

He dismissed the thought with a flick of his paw. No, Pear couldn't give him anything to help. This wasn't a torn tail or a bitten ear; it was a bug that had crawled inside his head.

"I have to get over it," he muttered to himself, "or put up with it. That's all."

He had to think less about his ridiculous nighttime dreams and more about the troop. His fellow baboons weren't strange dream-creatures—they were very *real*, and he should be happy that life had gone back to normal for them. Or rather, as normal as it could be after the Great Battle with Stinger.

Thorn couldn't believe that it was barely a year since he and his best friend, Mud, had set out to complete the Three Feats. All the two of them had wanted then was to rise in the troop's ranks and find their place in the world. Life had been so much simpler. That was before Stinger Highleaf—the baboon he'd thought of as his mentor and friend—had murdered his way to leadership of troop.

Even that hadn't been enough for the power-hungry baboon. As Crownleaf, Stinger had gone on to manipulate Stronghide the rhino into killing Great Mother, the elephant who was leader and guide to all Bravelands. Then he'd talked the poor rhino into replacing her. And he'd done that because he'd *known* Stronghide would be a disaster as Great Parent—and that the Great Spirit's anger would engulf them all. Stinger had foreseen that when terrible heat and floods tormented Bravelands, its creatures would clamor for a new, strong Great Parent—Stinger himself.

Thorn had discovered the truth—and he'd almost been destroyed as he tried to bring down the tyrant. He'd nearly lost everything: his troop; his lion friend, Fearless; his best friend, Mud; and his beloved Berry, Stinger's own daughter.

But Sky Strider, Great Mother's wise young granddaughter, had seen through Stinger too. She, Thorn, and Fearless had rallied the animals of Bravelands and led a Great Herd against the False Parent. And in a final, bloody confrontation, Sky had flung Stinger into the watering hole, where the crocodiles had put an end to him at last.

That terrible battle had been less than a moon ago. Since Stinger's death, Brightforest Troop had been leaderless; they had simply been too busy and preoccupied to hold an election. That was disconcerting for every baboon—but good things had happened, too. The Great Herd's Crookedtree baboons had united with Brightforest after the battle. And it had been a wise decision to come back to Tall Trees, Thorn thought. Before Stinger's reign of terror, Brightforest Troop had been as safe and happy here as baboons could be.

Not that their return had been easy. Before Stinger's downfall, the vervet monkey Spite Cleanfur and his troop had launched an attack on Brightforest. The monkeys had badly damaged Tall Trees—and torn the mango tree so badly, Thorn had feared it wouldn't recover. But over the past few days the troop had worked hard, clearing debris and stripping away broken foliage, and Tall Trees was almost restored. The new crop of mangoes seemed to promise hope for the troop's future.

There were still squabbles, of course—sometimes Thorn thought the original Brightforest Troop and the Crookedtree arrivals would never agree on anything, from the best way to hunt lizards to which trees were safest for sleeping in. He sighed. He could hear some of the sentries now, returning from their duty; their voices were raised angrily and several of them were chittering and snapping their teeth.

Trust Viper, thought Thorn with an impatient roll of his eyes. He remembered the sharp-tongued baboon from the old Brightforest Troop, and she had always been a troublemaker.

"Oh sure, Kernel, you might have been a Highleaf in Crookedtree Troop," Viper was saying, her teeth bared in a sneer as the sentries padded into the clearing. "But you're barely qualified for dung-clearing in Tall Trees."

"You've got some nerve," snarled Kernel. "Crookedtree Troop always had better fighters than you Brightforest baboons. We never let our territory be invaded by *vervets!*"

"Are you calling us soft? You flea-ridden monkey!"

"You're calling me a monkey when you practically invited them in?" Kernel threw back his head in a sarcastic hoot of laughter. "You all deserve to be Deeproots!"

"You take that back!" With a screech of rage, Viper twisted and sprang.

Thorn threw himself between them, only just in time to stop her blow landing on Kernel's snout. They both staggered back, shocked eyes blazing.

"Stop it, both of you!" Thorn glared from one to the other. "You know the last time the troop argued like this? When Stinger was Crownleaf."

Viper and Kernel scowled at the ground, truculent.

"Listen to me, ranks aren't important." Thorn rose onto his hind legs. "They're just a way of organizing the troop, that's *all*. Every baboon has a role, and every baboon should be pulling together for the good of the troop—especially now, while we don't have a Crownleaf. Deeproots, Lowleaves, Middleleaves, Highleaves—nobody is *better* than anyone else, they're just better at certain things."

"Yes, like Highleaves are better fighters," muttered Viper.

"Maybe they are," snapped Thorn, "and that's why they're Highleaves. But Viper, you were here when Stinger appointed some of the baboons Strongbranches and told them that they were more important than everyone else. Remember how awful that was?"

Viper glanced at him slyly. "I remember that you were one of them."

"I was," said Thorn. "And I hated how Stinger made us bully the other ranks, and how scared everyone was all the time. Do you really want us to go back to that?"

Viper had stopped muttering. Kernel was picking at dead

leaves with his forepaw, and the other sentries shared embarrassed glances. They all looked ashamed.

"You've had a strenuous turn of duty," said Thorn more kindly. "Go and eat. You can all take double rations."

"Thank you, Thorn." Kernel hesitated as the other sentries began to slouch off toward the food pile. "You know, there are still hyenas prowling around. They're just outside the border, but some of them are venturing into the trees."

Root Highleaf, a sturdy former Crookedtree member, looked back over her shoulder. "There are a lot of vultures hanging around, too. It's strange, because there isn't any rot-flesh nearby."

"Maybe it's another sign," remarked Grit, an older male. "The Great Spirit is still displeased, after all. No Great Parent has come forward yet."

"Or maybe they've found some rot-flesh that you missed," said Thorn quickly, scratching at his arm. "Hurry up, all of you. You must be hungry."

He watched them disappear into the trees, chatting together now in a friendlier way. As the foliage rustled back into place behind them, Thorn swallowed hard and shut his eyes.

It had been many days since the vultures had spoken to him, yet he still hadn't gotten over the shock of understanding their weird Skytongue. And that had been nothing compared to what they had actually *said*.

Because they'd hailed him as the new Great Father.

Thorn had told himself many times that it had all been

just another fever-dream; maybe he'd gotten it from eating a rotten mango. The birds were *deluded*, because he couldn't be the Great Father. He wasn't up to it. It was too much responsibility. He didn't have the skills. He didn't have the patience. Most importantly of all, he didn't *want* the job.

Thorn hadn't told his troop, and he wasn't going to, not ever.

If I don't say it out loud, it isn't true.

Unease squirmed in his gut. When the branches of the mango tree creaked and rustled above him, he jerked his head up, startled and a little afraid. If that was the vultures, coming back to harass him again—

No, he realized with relief: it was Berry. His elegant, golden-furred mate was leaping purposefully through the branches toward him. He smiled. Her grace and balance were still breathtaking, even though her beautiful tail had been bitten to a stump by the brutal monkey Spite Cleanfur. Springing down to the ground, she rose onto her hind legs and returned his embrace. "Thorn. I heard Viper and Kernel bickering again. They're such a troublesome pair. Did you manage to sort them out?"

"It's fine. They're obsessed with ranks and status, and they're a bit too proud of being Highleaves." He puffed out an exhausted breath. "I told them every rank is important. I *think* they took that in."

To his surprise, Berry looked hesitant. She sucked her lip and gazed at him thoughtfully.

"You're right in a way," she said slowly, "but there is one

rank that's more important than the others—the Crownleaf. And we don't have one. As long as that's the case, there are bound to be fights. We need a strong leader, Thorn."

"We just need a leader." The words *strong leader* made him want to shudder, but he repressed it for Berry's sake. Stinger had been a strong leader; he'd also been a tyrant and a villain who had endangered all of Bravelands.

"You'd be a good leader, Thorn." Berry drew him closer and nuzzled her face into his shoulder. "You've more than proved that."

Unease rippled through his skin. "Oh, I'm happy as I am," he said lightly, and rubbed her snout with his to distract her. "This is all I wanted. Us being together is the best thing that's happened to me."

"And not having to hide that we're mates. My mother likes you very much, you know." Berry drew away, smiling and clutching his paws. "As you know, that's the most important thing!"

Thorn laughed. "For a mother, it is."

"Hey, Thorn!" a baboon interrupted, padding toward them. "Lots of us have been asking—when are the Three Feats going to start again? Everyone misses them."

Thorn looked around. "I don't know, Moss. I—"

"Leave him alone," hooted Lily as she bounded past. "Can't you see he's busy talking to Berry?"

"Ah." Moss wrinkled her muzzle. "Sorry, Thorn." She padded away.

Berry smiled wryly at Thorn, then nodded toward the

empty Crown Stone in the middle of the clearing. "You see what I mean? That seems to be yours by right."

"I told you, I don't want—"

She tutted. "We need a Crownleaf, Thorn! And you would be *perfect*. Every member of this troop looks up to you, respects you. Make it official—call an election!"

Thorn shook his head rapidly. "No, Berry, no. I'm not meant to be the leader. I know they asked me after the battle but—it's not me. Truly."

She shook her head in frustration. "But who else?"

Thorn thought desperately. "Mango," he said, nodding. "Mango's well liked, *and* she's respected. She's got the right qualities."

"I'll do it!" Nut shambled to a halt beside them, grinning. "I'll be Crownleaf—I'd quite like to lounge on that rock all day, being waited on paw and tail. It'll be great—I'll get sun-streaks in my fur, and all the females will love me."

Thorn and Berry hooted with laughter. "Nut!" scolded Berry.

"Hmph! It's no laughing matter. Or it won't be when I'm Crownleaf." Haughtily, Nut tilted up his chin and flapped a regal paw. "My first order will be to exile you both for gross disrespect."

"You, Nut, are a scoundrel." Berry was still chuckling. "I have to go and see Mother now. I'll ask if she has a cure for your delusions, Nut." She squeezed Thorn's paw. "Think about what I said, won't you? *Please.*"

"Seriously, Thorn—I agree with Berry." Nut gazed at him thoughtfully. "You should consider it. I know I'd vote for you."

"There," said Berry. "You see, Thorn?"

"Lots of baboons are on edge right now," Nut added. "Having no Great Parent is unsettling for every animal."

"I suppose that's true," said Thorn evasively. He and Nut used to be enemies, and Thorn usually found Nut's reformed, more thoughtful behavior refreshing—but right now he rather wished Nut would stick to his frivolous remarks.

"Some certainty and authority would be a real positive," Nut went on. "At the very least it would put the troop more at ease."

"I guess they need that," mumbled Thorn. "Have you seen Mud anywhere?"

"Ha!" Nut chortled. "He's probably off on his own again, messing with those stones of his. He thinks he's some kind of Starleaf. Try the stinkwood glade."

"Thanks," murmured Thorn. "I'll go look for him. Berry, say hello to your mother from me."

He scampered away before there could be any more talk of Crownleaves and votes. *Berry and Nut are both wrong. I don't want to hear any more about my responsibilities. I'm not cut out to be Crownleaf any more than Great Father!*

Wrapped in his worries and resentments, he loped over a fallen log and broke out of the edge of the forest to run across the open grassland. The sky above him was an intense blue, cloudless from horizon to horizon, and there wasn't another

baboon in sight. Thorn felt a guilty surge of pure relief and
freedom.

There were black specks in the blue above him, and as he
glanced up he realized they were growing larger. Sucking in a
breath, he put on a burst of speed, but within a few strides he
could recognize the shape of them. They were no longer drifting specks; they had broad, black wings and bald heads, and
they were swooping rapidly lower.

Go away! I don't speak Skytongue, I don't, I don't . . .

One of the vultures tipped its wings and flew lower, its call
a harsh, strange rasp that echoed across the plain's emptiness.
But he could understand it, all right.

"Thorn Highleaf," it cried. "You can't outrun your destiny."

Just give me a moment to try. Thorn sped up, his paws pounding
on the dry yellow earth.

"The Great Spirit is within you, Thorn Highleaf. Listen
to its call." With a sudden banking turn, the vulture was in
front of him. Arching its wings, it stooped down and came to
a lurching, hopping halt.

Thorn scrabbled to a stop, breathing hard. The bird
stretched its wings, folded them, and stared at him with piercing eyes. Behind it, the rest of its flock landed and clustered,
silent.

Thorn glared at them. Then, spinning, he took off at a rapid
lope toward the east. "You've got this wrong!" He paused and
turned back, resentment flaring inside him. "You don't know
everything! Leave me alone. It's not me!"

The leader of the vultures began to hop toward him, half running and half flapping. "Thorn Highleaf. Great Father."

"No!" He twisted and ran faster, glancing over his shoulder. Were they still behind him?

Yes. The leader had lurched into flight, her great wings beating the air, and she was coming after him. Seized by panic, Thorn crashed into a patch of long grass and kept running, his breath coming in rapid gasps.

He didn't dare look back again. *They can't talk me into it if I refuse to listen.* Barely even registering his surroundings, he burst out of the long grass and skidded to a halt at the edge of a small, sharp drop.

Trembling, dry-mouthed, he stared at the shimmering gleam of a watering hole in the distance: a huge, silver lake, its far shores indistinct in the hazy distance. He knew it well—he could make out the jutting peninsula that Stinger had renamed Baboon Island; small groups of animals lingered on the dried mud at its edges, dipping their heads to drink. Through the heat shimmer, he could make out a cluster of zebras, a couple of hartebeests, and a lone rhinoceros; all of them except the rhino were keeping a respectful distance from a single leopard that crouched low, lapping at the water. And beyond them all, their feet submerged in the shallows, stood a herd of elephants.

As he watched, one of them plunged her trunk into the pool and blew a silvery spray of water over her own back. Others were drinking; two calves were splashing and capering as if they had nothing more important to do than play. Thorn squinted hard. One of the elephants seemed very familiar, even at this distance.

For a moment, his delight overcame his worries. Yes, he recognized that young female who stood a little apart from the others. He couldn't make out the creamy color of her tusks, the creases of her skin, or her dark wise eyes. But he'd know her anywhere.

Sky Strider!

CHAPTER 2

At the edge of the shrinking watering hole, Sky waited near the rest of the herd for her leader's decision. There was a palpable anxiety in the air. Sky could feel the tension in her hide and the sensitive tip of her trunk; only the little ones played, carefree, and Sky felt a little envious of them. *I remember when I trusted the grown ones to do the right thing. I never doubted Great Mother would lead us down the best path.*

Feeling the weight of the decision was part of growing up, she understood that; but surely the worries of the herd had never been so agonizing, their faith in their matriarch so shaky? Comet had been head of the Strider family only since the death of Rain in their misguided, Codebreaking attack on Stinger. The truth was, Comet hadn't had long enough to learn the ways of a leader; she was their youngest matriarch in generations. Unlike Great Mother or Rain, she did not have many years of experience and knowledge of the paths of Bravelands. And even those two great matriarchs might have had trouble now, with a landscape so changed by the calamitous weather of the last few seasons.

"It's difficult," said the rangy matriarch now, squinting into the sun. Anxiously, she swung her head and her long, mottled tusks toward the south. "It all looks much the same. But I *think* I know which way to travel."

Swinging her trunk, Sky tilted her head toward her aunts and cousins. They flapped their ears, exchanging nervous glances. The tension was unbearable now. Only the oblivious calves continued to romp in the watering hole. Creek, the youngest male, cantered past, squirting Sky with a trunkful of water, and she started and shook her ears.

"I think," said the sturdy Cloud, blinking her long brown lashes, "we should be quite certain before we set off. Don't you think so, Comet?"

Other elephants nodded, murmuring their agreement. *They're right*, thought Sky. If the herd took the wrong direction it could be disastrous, and it would be the young and the very old who would suffer. They'd all heard tales of whole families wiped out with a wrong turn into drought-stricken wilderness or flooded, muddy swampland. Sometimes, Sky had seen their lonely bones, bleaching under the sun with no one left to take them to the Plain of Our Ancestors.

But Comet's doing her best. We have to support her. "I'm sure you're right about the direction, Comet," she said hesitantly, "but

perhaps we don't have to leave quite yet? There's still plenty
of water here."

"The dry season is coming, and we must move to greener
lands." Comet pounded the exposed mud at the lake's rim
with a foot. "Sooner rather than later, we must move on." Hesitantly, she twitched her trunk toward Sky and gave a slightly
embarrassed rumble. "Sky . . . you're young, but you carried
the Great Spirit for a season, and you seem to have absorbed
some of its wisdom. Do you, ah . . . Do you have any ideas
about our path?"

Sky blew uneasily at the water's edge. No matriarch should
have to ask for advice. But then, these days all the grown elephants deferred to Sky for answers—and they seemed almost
nervous when she gave them. It should be flattering that they
did, Sky supposed, but it made her anxious. It wasn't how
things were supposed to be.

"Just . . . listen for the spirits of our ancestors, Comet. Be at
one with them, and they might guide us."

"I'm sure Sky's right," put in Cloud, "but I have a bad feeling about our journey. Why is Bravelands still without a Great
Parent? The False Parent is dead, his followers defeated. All
should be well again, but no new Parent has revealed themselves!"

"I don't know why there's a delay," said Sky, "but I *do* know
we have to trust the Great Spirit. It's never failed us."

But Cloud had a point, thought Sky: the new Great Parent
should have come forward by now. She had carried the Great
Spirit inside her for almost a moon, but it had left her after the

battle when the Great Herd had beaten Stinger. The Great Spirit had found its home—the new Great Father or Mother of Bravelands.

They might be a hippo, a cheetah, a bushbuck. Sky had no idea what that would be like, but she no longer cared what kind of animal the Great Spirit had chosen. She knew only that Bravelands needed its Parent, and that the creature needed to hurry.

"Sky?" Cloud prompted her. "You seem very distracted."

"We all know why that is," put in Mirage, her torn-eared aunt. She waved her trunk dismissively at a ridge above the dry riverbed.

Sky turned to look, but she already knew what she'd see. Sure enough, there was the massive, dark gray shape of Rock lumbering toward the herd. Sky's heart surged at the sight of his sturdy, broad chest, his deep-set green eyes, those huge creamy tusks.

Cloud shifted back, her ears flapping. A stir went through the other elephants as they tossed their heads and grumbled and raked the ground.

"It's not right," Mirage muttered.

"He shouldn't be here." Comet shot an accusing glance at Sky.

They were right, Sky knew it, and her gut twisted as warring impulses and instincts tore at her. A fully grown male should not be lurking around the herd—but how could she drive him away? He had stood so loyally at her side throughout all her troubles. *What does he want now?*

As they all stared at him, Rock stopped and raised his

trunk. "Strider sisters! May I speak with Sky alone?"

Comet's eyes widened, and she half turned to Cloud. "I don't know about that, Rock. I'm not sure that—"

"I'm sure." Cloud stamped the earth. "Tell him to go away, Comet. He doesn't belong here."

"Lone males are dangerous," agreed Mirage, glowering at him.

Dangerous? Sky almost wanted to laugh, but she didn't dare. The bull elephant she knew was so gentle, so caring, so protective.

But Cloud and Mirage were already pushing forward in front of Sky, their heads high and determined.

"This is unseemly behavior, Rock!" Cloud scolded him. "You know perfectly well that bulls may not mix with us!"

Sky's other aunts were shambling forward now, joining Cloud and Mirage to form a protective line in front of her.

"Leave at once!" trumpeted Mirage.

"You should be ashamed of yourself!" blared Comet.

"Comet, Cloud." Embarrassed, Sky tried to shoulder her way through the line. "This isn't necessary."

"And what if he falls into the Rage?" demanded Cloud, her ears flapping. "We've told you all about it, Sky, about how unpredictable the bulls can be when they're excited! Why, my own mate Ravine used to get into *quite* the frenzy—"

"He's not suffering the Rage!" cried Sky in exasperation. "Look at him, he's calm. And anyway, it's not Ravine, it's Rock, and he's the gentlest elephant I know! I'm not scared of him—"

"You certainly shouldn't be," declared Comet, swinging her rump to obscure Sky's view, "because we'll look after you."

"Times are quite bad enough," said Cloud sternly, "without discarding our prized customs."

"Be off with you, Rock, you rogue." Sky's aunt Timber sounded scandalized.

"Sky!" Rock's thunderous trumpet rose above the herd's voices for a moment.

Desperately Sky lifted her trunk. "I'm here, Rock, don't worry—"

It was no use. Her aunts simply raised their voices, drowning out her cries with their loud disapproval, and as Sky backed away in dismay, they began to stampede toward Rock.

"Away with you! Don't come back!"

Through their huge bodies and the dust they raised, Sky could just make out Rock, turning and making a hasty retreat over the ridge. *Oh, I hope he doesn't think I wanted this!*

The ache in her heart swelled to a fierce resentment. Her family thought they were protecting her—but from what? From the friend who had stood bravely at her side through every battle, who had treated her with nothing but kindness and respect?

Turning abruptly away from Rock and her aunts, Sky cantered along the edge of the watering hole. The compacted mud felt gritty and hard beneath her feet, and the few straggling patches of grass were yellow and parched. To her right the winding course of the riverbed followed the line of the shore until it met the broad sweep of the bay; when she reached its bank, Sky halted, breathing hard.

The edge of the riverbed sloped away sharply at her feet; Sky clambered carefully down it. Rocks and stones lay exposed on the bank, abandoned where the stream had carried them on its way to the lake; miserable and lonely, Sky turned them over with the tip of her trunk.

Not all of them were rocks, Sky realized. Half buried in the silt of the bank lay scattered bones, crusty and yellowed with mud. One of them was round and smooth.

That's no stone.

The recognition came out of nowhere, instant and certain. Sky knew at once what the thing was, and who it had belonged to. Her heart clenching, she stepped closer, circling the skull until she could make out the top edges of the empty eye sockets. Even now, even when flesh and fur had been gnawed away by the rot-eaters, those twin gaping holes held malevolence.

Stinger. Sky's knees almost buckled, and dizzying heat swamped her.

The whole scene came back to her, vivid and awful. She'd snatched the baboon up by the tail as he'd tried to make his escape. She'd swung him up high as his maddened eyes blazed into hers.

It had haunted her since the moment she had made the decision to kill him. Indeed, it had barely been a decision at all: it had been instinct, and rage, and a fierce longing to save Bravelands. She'd tried so very hard not to remember that terrible day.

I could have set him down. He'd lost, it was over. I could have left him to the justice of his troop.

She could have shown mercy, but she hadn't. Instead she had dropped him over the edge of the cliff, into the black water where crocodiles circled.

As the skull glared its hate at her, it all came back in blinding detail: the thrashing, churning water, the reddening foam. Stinger's head, surfacing once, fur plastered against his skull, jaws peeled back in a grimace of rage and terror. Then, at last, he had vanished.

Until now.

Staring into those half-exposed eye sockets, Sky trembled with guilt and shame and horror. *I murdered him as surely as he murdered his victims.* The knowledge struck her with brutal clarity. *I broke the Code.*

Was that why the new Great Parent had not appeared? The Great Spirit had left her that night, it was true—but did that mean it had found the Parent? Perhaps, instead, it had been sickened by her act of violence, so much that it could remain inside her no longer. Perhaps, because of her, it had abandoned Bravelands forever.

Her trunk quivering, she reached for the skull. She could hardly bear to touch it, but she made herself nudge and tug until it was dislodged from the mud. It rolled clear, the empty eyes staring up at her.

She didn't want to read this bone. With all her being, she recoiled from the thoughts and memories and dreams it held.

But I have to. With a deep, shuddering breath, Sky curled her trunk around its smooth bone and raised it high.

*Animals. Animals of every shape and kind, galloping and pounding, flee-
ing in hordes across Bravelands. Sky could feel their primal fear; it crackled
in the air like lightning. Every one of them ran in the purest, coldest terror,
and not just the most timid of the grass-eaters: she saw lions, rhinos, hyenas,
buffalo, their eyes white-rimmed, their jaws foaming in panic as they fled.*

*What could frighten them so? Flesh-eaters, savage horned herd-leaders,
predators that feared nothing! Why were they running as if the ghosts of
every evil creature were hard at their heels?*

*After all, running could not save them. One by one the animals were
vanishing, their bodies spinning into sand and whirling to nothing in the air.
As the front-runners dissolved, the creatures behind them ran on, oblivious
to the fate that awaited them, until they too fragmented and were sucked into
nothingness.*

*Sky could not see what was driving them helplessly to oblivion, but she
could feel it. Not Stinger, but the malevolence that had lived in him. It
drenched the scene like a dark, invisible cloud of evil. And she was sure she
could hear his laughter, high and triumphant, making her heart clench and
wither in petrified horror.*

The skull shattered explosively in her grip. Starting back
to reality, she realized her trunk was squeezed tight around
nothing; shards and fragments of bone lay at her feet. She'd
destroyed it.

What did it mean? The vision had made no sense. Stinger was
gone.

If only, she thought with an inward cry of despair, she had
someone she could talk to.

"Sky?" said a familiar voice.

She spun around, her heart lifting before she'd even laid

eyes on the new arrival. "Thorn!"

He stood before her on his hind legs, wringing his fore-paws, his eyes bright with anxiety. There was no creature she could have been gladder to see. So few animals understood her part in Stinger's death—but Thorn knew best of all why she'd had to do it, and why the survival of Bravelands had depended on it.

Overwhelmed with gladness, Sky stretched her trunk, then hesitated just as the tip of it brushed his fur. She must not intrude on his memories—

But it was too late. Thorn lunged forward and hugged her trunk.

Nothing.

Sky blinked. Not a single memory assailed her as Thorn hugged her. Not a sensation, or an image, or an emotion. *Nothing.*

She swallowed hard, curling her trunk around his furred body.

The power has left me. The gift the Great Spirit gave me—the gift of reading the living—it's gone.

Shock curdled her blood. The Great Spirit had truly gone, then. Perhaps, appalled beyond bearing by her murderous action, it no longer even watched over her.

Oh, sky and stars. It has not left only my body.

The Great Spirit has abandoned me completely!

CHAPTER 3

Sky Strider blew out an aching breath that ruffled Thorn's brown fur. There was a sudden sadness and pain in her eyes, and Thorn stiffened in concern as he drew away from her trunk.

But she blinked rapidly, and the look of torment was gone, or hidden. "Oh, Thorn Highleaf. You've no idea how good it is to see you!"

"And you, Sky Strider." He gave her a rueful grin. "I'm sorry that I'm here to ask for something. Again."

"You can ask me for anything," she rumbled with warmth.

"I need advice," he confessed. "I've got a problem, Sky."

The elephant brushed her trunk across his shoulder. "How can I help?"

Sinking back onto all four paws, Thorn averted his eyes. Then he sat on his haunches and picked at his chest fur.

"I think . . ." He took a breath. "Sky, I think you know more than most about duty, and responsibility, and doing what's right."

She chuckled wryly and lowered her own eyes. "I'm glad you think so, Thorn."

"You *do*. And that's why I need your wisdom." He nibbled his lip, trying to get the words right. "You see, Sky—what if you knew you were supposed to do something, but you weren't ready for it?"

Sky swung her trunk slowly, pondering. At last she looked up. "Your troop still doesn't have a leader, Thorn. I know that." She sighed. "It's only to be expected. Stinger did so much damage, it's no wonder baboons are hesitant about choosing a new Crownleaf." She lifted her head and flapped her ears forward eagerly. "But you, Thorn—I think you'd be the best Crownleaf your troop has ever had. They wanted you to lead them, didn't they? After the Great Battle—I know you said there would have to be a proper vote, but they seemed so enthusiastic."

He frowned, thinking hard. He could hardly tell her that he had an even bigger decision to make than whether to stand as Crownleaf—and luckily her advice could serve for both. "Yes . . ."

Sky fidgeted, swatting a clump of reeds with her trunk. "The truth is, I don't know what to advise. Our herd—we lost two matriarchs so quickly, and Comet isn't ready to lead. She's struggling. So although I think you'd make a wonderful Crownleaf, I understand if you feel you aren't ready. Only you know, Thorn. You have to decide what's best."

"Only I know, and I must decide," he murmured, a little sadly. "Yes."

"I'm sorry I can't make the decision for you. It must be so hard."

"It is," he said. "It is."

For a moment they stood in dejected silence. Then Sky cleared her throat and asked brightly, "How's Berry?"

He gave her a grin. "She's fine, Sky. It's going well. We're happy."

"I'm so glad you two are finally able to be together," she said softly. "Actually, since things have worked out so well, I should ask *your* advice."

"Go on." He tilted his head.

"It's Rock," she sighed. "I want to be with him. I don't feel at home with my aunts and cousins anymore. But it's just—it isn't *done*. Bull elephants live apart, they always have. We have to stay in our separate herds."

"Hmm." Thorn scratched at his muzzle. "Sky, I don't know much about elephant tradition, but if the last few seasons have taught me anything, it's that these are strange times. And maybe strange times mean different answers. Traditions are all very well, but aren't they supposed to help us? If they don't, maybe we need to change them?"

"I feel I should be the one to change," murmured Sky, "but I can't."

"Why should we be trapped by old customs?" Thorn gave her a long, solemn look. "If we'd stuck to old traditions and rules, Berry and I could never have been mates. She was a Highleaf and I was a Middleleaf, remember? I think you should follow your heart, Sky. Truly."

Her eyelashes fluttered closed. "If only it were that simple."

"It's hard," he said sympathetically. "I know just how hard. I'm sorry I can't be more helpful."

"So am I." She gave him a rueful smile.

"Oh, don't worry." Thorn patted her trunk lightly. "As a matter of fact, you've helped me a great deal. . . ."

So that was that, thought Thorn with satisfaction as he loped back toward Tall Trees. He had been certain his instincts were right, and his talk with Sky had only confirmed his decision.

Only you know, Thorn.

The Great Spirit was such a powerful presence. It was everywhere, and it was aware of all things; it knew the hearts of every creature in Bravelands. It must know that Thorn's was not the right place for it to live. The Great Spirit would understand, and it would find another animal to carry its essence—someone strong, like a rhino or a buffalo or, best of all, another elephant. Thorn shook his head ruefully. It would be *ridiculous* for the ancient, wise, esteemed Great Mother to be succeeded by a not very competent, not even full-grown *baboon*.

All he'd ever really wanted was to be with Berry. And now he could be. Yes, he might still put himself forward as Crownleaf; that was different.

But Great Parent? It was nonsensical. Unthinkable. *Wrong.*

Maybe the vultures had come to the same conclusion after

all, because when Thorn reached the fringes of Tall Trees, there was no longer any sign of them. Anxiously he peered into the sky, but no broad-winged black shapes haunted him from above. His heart felt almost light, until Nut came charging out of the forest.

Nut's expressions had become much harder to read—the scars from his beating by Stinger's thuggish Strongbranches had left his face battered and scarred and his snout misshapen—but right now the alarm in his wide eyes was obvious. "Thorn! Where have you been?"

Thorn blinked. "What's wrong, Nut?"

In reply, Nut simply grabbed his arm and dragged Thorn through the woods after him. At a marshy clump of grass between two fig trees, he halted and pointed at something lying on the ground. "That. That's what's wrong."

Two baboon sentries stood before it. Thorn crept between them, unease already growing in his gut. The fur was black-streaked brown, and he recognized it at once as a hyena. *And I think I even know which one.* Its snout was peeled back in death, its eyes wide and glazed, and dark blood clotted a deep gash on its chest.

Thorn crouched and parted the stiff fur to examine the wound. "Is this the hyena that was prowling around the camp yesterday?"

"We reckon so." Tough old Creeper sat down with his back to a tree, picking his teeth.

"We drove it away." Stump, the other sentry, shrugged. "I guess it came back."

"Nobody's tried to eat it," added Creeper, studying the corpse with fascination. "At least, not the creature that killed it. I suppose we can drag it back to the food pile, though."

"Though there might be something wrong with it." Stump elbowed Creeper. "Why else wouldn't a flesh-eater want it?"

"I don't know," murmured Thorn, sucking his teeth nervously.

"Well, we don't either." Nut shook his head. "We don't even know what killed it."

"Probably your breath," said Creeper.

"Yeah, Nut," agreed Stump solemnly. "That could take down a grown buffalo."

"Oy!" Nut twisted his brutalized face into its fiercest scowl and punched the air in front of their snouts.

"You don't scare us." Creeper grinned.

"Except when you breathe on us," said Stump, miming a swoon of horror.

Nut launched himself at them with a dramatic bellow of offense; instead of striking Stump, he grabbed the big baboon's shoulders and panted deliberately into his face. Creeper sprang to rescue his friend, shrieking, "I'll save you, Stump. Hold your breath if you value your life!"

But as the three of them rolled around, wrestling and squealing, Thorn couldn't bring himself to join in the fun. The corpse troubled him, and it wasn't just that a hyena had come this far into Tall Trees unchallenged. *Why wasn't it eaten?*

By the time he had picked at the torn skin around the hyena's wound and searched it for any more injuries or bite marks,

Stump and Creeper were playing dead between the fig tree's roots, and Nut was straddling both their bodies, pounding his chest as he hooted in victory.

"Come on, you lot," Thorn growled, irritably. "The fun's over. Creeper and Stump, why don't you go and check there aren't any more hyenas nearby?"

"All right." Grinning, they scrambled to their feet, and with a last swipe at Nut's head they bounded off.

"What's bothering you?" Brushing off twigs and dead leaves, Nut ambled over to Thorn. "I know it came into Tall Trees, and that's bad, but it didn't attack anyone. I didn't know you'd be *this* upset."

"It's too strange to be natural."

"It's a dead hyena!" said Nut. "The best kind!"

"A bad death."

The harsh screech came from overhead. Thorn jumped, then froze in despair, staring up through the branches.

The vulture cocked its head as it soared in a circle; Thorn could feel its cold eye more than he could see it. "A bad death, Thorn Greatfather. The Code is broken. You must divine the cause."

Thorn shut his eyes tight, feeling his stomach lurch. They'd found him again. And making their crazy accusations and demands in front of *Nut*—

"What are they squawking about?" growled Nut, throwing a twig uselessly at the birds.

Thorn shook himself. *Of course. Nut can't understand Skytongue.* "I've no idea," he lied.

"Well, they're clearly hungry. And everybody in the troop went off hyena meat when you all lived in that abandoned den. Let's leave the vultures to it."

Before either of them could scamper away, the vulture stooped suddenly, its black wings dislodging leaves. It landed heavily, glaring at Thorn, and hopped closer as three more of its flock flapped down behind it.

"Thorn! Accept your destiny!" Their guttural voices filled the glade, resounding from tree trunks and beating on Thorn's ears. "Do not dare walk away from the Great Spirit."

"What the—" began Nut, and snatched up a branch. He advanced on the huge birds, sweeping it to drive them back. "Go and eat the hyena, monkey brains! Not us!"

The vultures flapped away from Nut, screeching angrily. But for Thorn there was no escaping their scolding. "You cannot evade this responsibility, Thorn Greatfather! Do the Great Spirit's will!"

"We should go," he babbled, grabbing Nut's shoulder.

Only too gladly, Nut turned with him, and they bounded through the trees, finding the narrowest gaps and the lushest foliage to make sure the birds could not follow. Pausing to peer back, Thorn shuddered. The vultures were clustered around the hyena now, but they were not tearing at its fur and flesh; they looked from the corpse to him, their black eyes condemning.

"Keep going," he told Nut hurriedly, and they ran on.

Deeply unsettled, Thorn almost failed to register the stinkwood glade as they passed it; it was only a muttered curse from a familiar voice that brought him up short.

"Nut, wait! Mud's here."

"Oh, him and his useless pebbles," grumbled Nut. "What does he think he'll achieve?"

"You go ahead, I'll catch up." Still panting, Thorn ambled into the sun-dappled patch of bare ground between the trees.

His oldest and best friend crouched in the center of it, gathering up his stones in both paws. They were bright and multicolored; some were translucent and smooth, some rough-surfaced and sparkling with chips of silver. Some glowed red or green or gold. Mud's small face was creased with anxiety and frustration as he stared down at them.

"It's not working," Thorn heard him mutter. "It doesn't make sense. . . ."

"Mud!" called Thorn cheerily.

Mud's head jerked up. Despite his surprised grin, the lines of worry did not leave his face. "Hello, Thorn."

"What's the matter?" Thorn sat down beside him.

Mud gave a deep sigh and shook his head. "I know I'm not a *real* Starleaf," he murmured. "But I learned a lot from my mother. I thought I understood all the rules and all the meanings. I've been practicing for *ages*. But it's not working."

Poor Mud, thought Thorn. He wanted so much to be able to follow in the pawsteps of his wise and skillful mother; he longed to be able to honor Starleaf's legacy, after her death at Stinger's paws. "Are the stones saying different things each time?" asked Thorn gently.

"No. That's the trouble." Mud raked at the fur on top of

his head. "Every time I throw the stones, they give me more or less the same message. But I can't get to the root of it! It's so *vague*." Miserably, he added: "I'm sure my mother would have understood at once."

"All right," said Thorn encouragingly, "it's vague, but generally what are they saying?"

"Something about a hidden menace. Coming to Tall Trees, yes, but also to the whole of Bravelands." Glowering at the stones in his paws, Mud growled. "Why won't they be more *specific*? This is useless. I don't know if it's a rogue hyena or—or—or a flood that's going to drown us all!"

"That's not very helpful of them." Thorn risked a mischievous smile, but Mud would not be cheered up.

"It's all because of the Great Parent, that's what I think. Or rather the fact there *isn't* one. Everything's confused!"

Ignoring the niggle of guilt in his rib cage, Thorn leaned closer to examine the stones. He'd seen Starleaf throw them so many times, but he'd never understood what it meant when they fell a certain way. There was more to it than that, anyway; the whole ritual was a lot more complex than some random pattern of falling pebbles. He could only admire Mud for trying—even though his friend's efforts made him nervous. . . .

"Mud. Can the stones, uh . . . Can they tell you who the new Great Parent is? Or where they can be found?" Trying not to let his voice shake, he added: "After all, if there's a menace threatening Bravelands, the Great Parent should surely know."

Mud shrugged. "Let's try, shall we?" He clutched the stones

tightly, then closed his eyes, whispered muted words, and tossed them into the air.

They pattered down like colorful rain, rolling to a stop, and Mud leaned over them. There was an achingly long silence, and Mud's eyes narrowed. He chewed his lip and muttered: "Yes, fine, but *where?*"

"What?" said Thorn.

"Oh, its *nonsense*, I tell you. Something about the Great Parent being nearby, but it won't say *where*. Or if it does say that, I can't read it. Hang on." Mud leaned even closer over the stones, staring at them for an unbearably long time.

"Any more details?" Thorn's heart was pounding so hard, it came out as a harsh squeak.

Mud shook himself and sighed miserably. "I'm sorry. Sometimes these stones talk nonsense. Or more likely it's me. I'll just have to practice more."

Thorn patted his friend's paw. "Let's go back to the Crown Stone clearing," he suggested. His hide felt hot and tingly with relief. "You probably need a break, that's all."

Mud didn't seem to want to discuss the stones anymore, and Thorn was glad. They padded companionably through the trees, making light conversation about Berry and about the troop's progress with the restoration of Tall Trees.

"It's going so well," Mud remarked happily. "The mango tree has recovered, and things can only get even better when we elect a new Crownleaf."

"And when we have Mud Starleaf to advise us," Thorn told him. "You'll soon get the hang of it, you know."

"I hope so." Mud's eyes were bright. "I really am trying hard, and I want it more than anything. Will you nominate me, Thorn? I need support from a baboon from each rank—Highleaf, Middleleaf, Lowleaf, and Deeproot."

"Of course I will." Thorn nudged him affectionately. "I'm glad you have faith in yourself, Mud. Because I *certainly* have faith in you."

As they padded into the Crown Stone clearing, Mud's delighted smile faded to a frown of confusion. "What's that racket?"

From the forest came a torrent of hooting and angry screeching, and a rattle and crack of branches. Other baboons, too, were turning and staring in the direction of the noise.

Thorn bounded forward as the two big sentries burst into the clearing. "Stump! Creeper! What is it?"

"We went to check for more hyenas, like you asked," panted Stump, his eyes blazing. "We weren't expecting baboons!"

Creeper rose onto his hind paws and hooted the alarm to the whole clearing. "Dozens of enemies! They're almost here. Tendril Crownleaf leads them!"

The troop erupted in cries and whoops of anger, and Thorn found himself joining in. Even the timid Mud looked furious.

"Tendril!" shouted Nut above the hubbub. "That crazy monkey!"

"This wouldn't happen if there was a Great Parent in charge," snarled Moss.

Thorn leaped up into the nearest tree and scrambled up the branches until he could make out the savannah beyond the forest. Rising onto his hind paws, he creased his eyes, feeling nervous fury rise inside him.

Stump and Creeper were right; through the shimmering heat he could see brown-furred attackers drawing swiftly closer to the Tall Trees border. Tall Trees was an enviable territory for any baboon troop; now Tendril Crownleaf must think she could grab it.

"It's Crookedtree all right, and they're almost here." Shaking a branch violently, sending leaves fluttering down, he gave a whoop of enraged defiance.

"Brightforest Troop—we're under attack!"

CHAPTER 4

The stink of the bodies made Fearless's nostrils constrict with revulsion.

He and his pride stood on the banks of a muddy, stagnant watering hole, its surface streaked with scum. Half sunk in it were the corpses of a whole family of giraffes, their legs and necks stuck out at absurd angles, their bellies bloated in death. A small giraffe drifted loose, bumping against its mother's shoulder; the rest were aground in the shallow mud. Where their corpses touched the slimy water, their patterned hides were drenched black.

The reek was overpowering. Keen coughed and spat, his clever face contorting with revulsion. He took a pace back on his long legs.

"I'm not *that* hungry," he growled.

"I wonder what happened to them?" Gracious sounded

almost sympathetic. Delicately, she licked one of her slender paws. "Did they just wander in here and get stuck?"

"Giraffes aren't clever," remarked Tough, "but I didn't know they were *this* stupid."

"Really, really stupid." Stocky, blunt-faced Hardy rolled his eyes.

Fearless opened his jaws, then hesitated. He couldn't join in the pitying mockery. There was something very odd about the scene. It was an awful fate for the herd of giraffes, of course, but it wasn't just the deaths; there was something dreadful and sinister in the air here: as if a terrible, unnatural death had struck this herd out of nowhere.

Tough lay down in the dry grass, her rangy forepaws extended. She glanced to the side and opened her mouth to speak, as she'd been doing throughout the hunt: as if she expected to see her pale-furred sister at her side as always. But Rough had stayed behind, nursing the tiny cubs that had been born less than a moon ago. Tough shook herself, sighed, and spoke anyway.

"You know, I saw a warthog run straight off a cliff the other day."

Hardy drew back his lip. "What's that got to do with anything?"

Tough glared at him. "It's *weird*. Obviously. Like these giraffes."

"And now that you're a father, Hardy," suggested Gracious shyly, "you've got to look out for unexpected signs of danger. So you can protect Rough and the cubs."

Hardy snorted, but he looked proud. "I don't think stupid giraffes and sun-crazy warthogs are anything to worry about."

Thoughtfully, Fearless shook his head. "Bravelands still has no Great Parent," he growled. "I guess when animals don't have the guidance of the Great Spirit, strange things are going to happen. And it'll get worse."

No one replied. Fearless turned from the grim spectacle in the watering hole to eye them again. Tough was watching him levelly. Hardy had cocked his head, wrinkling his blunt muzzle. Gracious was wide-eyed, and her elegant features looked startled; Keen licked his jaws and flicked his golden ears.

Oh, he thought. *I forgot again.* No wonder they all looked so awkward. Of course, lions didn't believe in the Great Spirit, and they wouldn't dream of taking their lead from some Great Parent they'd never chosen. Usually Fearless tried not to mention his beliefs; he'd picked them up from the Bright-forest baboon troop who had taken him in as a cub.

Being the leader of Fearlesspride made him fluff up his fur and filled him with protectiveness and affection. *But I guess I'll always be a little bit baboon. . . .*

He raised his head, doing his best to look as noble and fierce and thoroughly lionish as any pride leader. But as the light breeze brought him a new scent, his nostrils flared and his eyes widened.

"Buffalo!" He nodded at the putrid watering hole. "And if I can smell them through this stink, they're close."

Tough angled her pale-furred head and sniffed the air, and

Gracious got to her paws. Keen narrowed his eyes and glanced at Hardy.

"Buffalo?" said Gracious, blinking.

"Maybe we should wait for your sister, Fearless," suggested Tough. "She's the most experienced hunter."

"Valor isn't here," snapped Fearless. "I don't know what's got into her lately. But we can't always wait for her if she keeps disappearing."

Irritation nipped at him, as it so often had in the last moon. Why *did* Valor keep wandering off with no explanation? Maybe she was forgetting that Fearless was her pride leader. Maybe she was deliberately disrespecting his authority. Fearless's muzzle curled in hurt and resentment. Without waiting to make sure the others were following, he set off at a trot into the long grass.

All the same, it was a relief to hear the rustle of their bodies moving quietly behind him. For a moment he'd been afraid . . . *No.* He had to be confident of his authority if he was to keep his place at the head of the pride. Fearless tightened his jaws, refusing to glance back.

Upwind, the thick meaty scent of buffalo was growing ever stronger, and he slowed to place his paws more quietly. *Yes.* There was the herd: a vast, slow-moving mass of black-hided grass-eaters. The sound of their hooves on the dry ground was a low, constant rumble, and yellow dust rose as they ambled, ripping intently at the grass. Fearless crouched, and at last turned to nod at Keen.

I can rely on him. Keen was already at his flank, looking back in his turn at the rest of Fearlesspride. In only moments they were in position: Gracious and Tough behind Fearless and Keen, and Hardy a little to his leader's right flank.

So far, so good. We're getting so much better at this.

The day was dying, and the paleness of the dry savannah looked ethereal against the darkening indigo sky. Fearless narrowed his eyes. The main part of the buffalo herd was blurring into the falling twilight, but a young calf was much closer than the rest; it had strayed a little too far from its mother. The calf raised its head, puffing loud breaths through its big nostrils.

In silence the five lions edged forward, slickly coordinated. Fearless hunched his shoulders low, staying well beneath the top of the grass stalks. The pride's field of vision was limited, but it wasn't as if the buffalo were hard to track. He could hear that youngster now, snorting as it pawed at the ground. *Any moment now—*

A high growling bark split the quiet, and Fearless tensed in horror and swung his head. Hardy was gaping at him in appalled guilt; a dun-and-gray kori bustard was bolting away from the young lion through the grass, crest cocked back, long legs slapping down as it began to spread its wings.

He spooked that bird! How could he not have noticed it?

The bustard was still rasping in alarm, and as Fearless watched, it took off at last, wings beating heavily, and flew low, straight toward the herd. Hundreds of great, black-horned heads seemed to rise at once, and with a sudden thunder, the buffalo turned and lurched into a run.

"Go!" roared Fearless.

The five lions sprang forward, bursting from the long grass and racing across the flat plain in huge, desperate strides. The youngster was galloping now, headlong for the rest of its family; the herd itself was raising clouds of dust as they plunged down a low bank and across a sluggish river.

Fearless followed, his pride with him; they were almost alongside the fleeing calf now. Mud flew up beneath buffalo hooves, spattering the lions' faces and stinging their eyes. The stream was churned to thick sludge, and already the far bank was slick with the hoof prints of the first of the herd. Others slipped and slid as they followed the leaders.

"Hardy! Stay on the right! Keen, pull closer!" Fearless bellowed orders, but he was almost certain his pride couldn't hear him—not over the reverberation of huge hooves, and the suck and splatter of water beneath them. Keen dropped back for a moment, looking confused and overwhelmed, then clenched his jaws and put on another burst of speed.

Ahead of them all, the calf had reached the bank, and it made a frantic leap for safety. But its split hooves went from beneath it on the steep incline, and it toppled backward, crashing on its flank into the mire. Fearless coiled his muscles and bounded on top of the creature, sinking his fangs into its coarse black hide. The taste was more of mud than of blood. Half blinded, he could barely see the vulnerable points in the calf's neck, and it continued to flail and struggle, bellowing in panic and pain.

Grimly Fearless hung on, his teeth and jaws aching. The

desperate calf was plunging on up the bank, hooves biting into the mud, and in disbelief Fearless realized it was carrying him to the top of the bank. With its final spurt, it dragged him over the crest and onto level ground.

On either side of him, Fearless saw black-spattered, tawny bodies rush in as the pride caught up. The calf tipped back its head and gave a bray of terror as Keen and Gracious each seized a leg in their jaws. For a fleeting moment, Fearless thought they had won their meal.

The triumph lasted only until he felt the ground vibrate beneath him. Stiffening, he tilted one ear.

The oncoming thunder was almost on him, and it made his bones shake. Releasing the calf's neck, he twisted to see the herd stampeding toward them, a massive and furious bull at their head.

"Leave it!" yelped Gracious, letting go of the calf's foreleg.

"No, we can't—" Frantically Fearless snapped at the calf again, but Keen shouldered him away from it.

"We have to go! *Hurry!*"

Claws scrabbling in the mud, Fearless rolled and lurched away just as the huge bull crashed in among them. Its gigantic horns swept in a low arc, catching Tough's shoulder and flinging her through the darkening air. Bolting for his life, Fearless heard the yelp and the sickening thud as the rangy lioness hit the ground.

Jerking his head around, he saw the calf scramble to its feet and stumble back into the herd, where it was swiftly lost among much bigger bodies. The massive bull had drawn up, snorting and pawing gouts of wet earth from the ground.

Slowing at last, Fearless limped to a halt and turned to peer back, his heart thrashing.

Tough was lurching toward them out of the gloom, heavily favoring one foreleg. The bull's charge-and-toss had lamed her, then. *But at least she's alive.*

With that immediate relief, a dismal cloud of anger and despair settled over Fearless. They had lost the calf. His mouth sour with bitterness and hunger, he began to trudge back toward their camp.

"That would never have happened if Valor had been here," growled Hardy as the pride slouched homeward together. "She'd have got that baby buffalo, no problem."

"We'd have got the calf, Hardy, if you hadn't spooked that bird!" snapped Keen, sidling protectively in front of Fearless. "We all lost concentration. Fearless was relying on us, and we let him down!"

"All right, don't squabble." Fearless shoved between them, forcing their snarling muzzles apart, and kept walking. "We've had a bad enough day without that."

And he'd had the worst day of all, he thought. Because if they didn't start working together better and forgiving each other's errors, Fearlesspride would be finished within moons.

"She's back," growled Hardy, nodding ahead as the miserable lions plodded back into camp.

"Valor?" Pricking his ears, Fearless stopped and stared. Night was falling, and in the darkness he made out the bright glowing spheres of two pairs of eyes. Now he could see the outlines of two lions, shaded in green and blue.

Summoning his energy, he loped forward to his sister's side. "Where have you been? We needed you!" His voice sounded plaintive, and he hated that, but he couldn't help himself.

Valor glanced up. She and Rough were crouched beside a dead gazelle, their muzzles black with its blood, their bellies already comfortably swollen. Fearless's belly rumbled with longing, but it was nothing next to his anger.

"What's your problem, Swiftbrother? I got us a gazelle." Valor licked blood from her jaws as he stood above her, breathing hard. "Rough needed to eat." She nudged the young mother lioness.

Valor probably hadn't meant it as a criticism, but that was how it stung in Fearless's heart. He bared his fangs in wounded resentment, and for a long moment there was heavy silence.

Then Hardy padded straight past Fearless, lowered his head to Rough's, and licked her affectionately.

"Are the cubs asleep? I'm glad someone provided for you," he muttered to his mate, a little too loudly.

Fearless clenched his jaws, just stopping himself from taking a bite at Hardy's flank. "You haven't told me yet, Valor. Where *were* you?"

The elegant lioness stretched idly and yawned. "Hunting, obviously. Come and have some gazelle; it's nice and tender. Didn't you lot have any luck?"

Keen's head and whiskers drooped. "We tried to get a buffalo calf. And we nearly had it."

"But everything went wrong," said Gracious mournfully.

"Of course it did!" Suddenly wide awake, Valor sprang to her paws and bared her teeth at them all. "You went after *buffalo*? At your age and size? *I* wouldn't take on a buffalo, Fearless, and neither would have our fully grown *mother*! If she was still alive she'd nip your ear!"

"It was a *calf*—" Keen protested.

Valor cut him off with a snarl. "A calf with a horde of grown buffalo to defend it! You're all lucky you weren't killed." She snorted in contempt. "Idiots."

That bit like a fang in Fearless's gut, and it hurt worse than anything else she'd said. *Valor always used to call me an idiot,* he thought, *but I was just a little cub! And back then, it sounded like a joke.*

It hadn't sounded like a joke just now.

"Honestly, Valor," said Gracious timidly as she settled down to gnaw at the gazelle's rump, "Fearless did brilliantly. It was very close. And he was brave."

Valor ignored the young lioness, but Fearless bristled. "I don't need you to defend me, Gracious. I'm your pride leader!"

Gracious flinched and slunk backward, looking cowed and hurt.

"Fearless, she's only defending you because she likes you," Valor muttered to him, ripping off another strip of belly meat.

Feeling a twinge of guilt, Fearless glanced at Gracious. He hadn't meant to hurt her feelings that much, but did Valor mean what he thought she meant? Because he didn't feel anything like that toward Gracious. He hadn't even noticed the growing affection between Rough and Hardy, and had been shocked when Rough announced she was expecting cubs. Yes, he knew he'd be expected to take a mate too in the coming season, but he found it hard to pretend he was interested. "Why does it matter if Gracious *likes* me?" he muttered. "She needed to be told."

Valor sighed patiently. "Come on. Eat something and you'll feel better."

"I'm not hungry," he snapped.

"Suit yourself." Valor licked her jaws as if the gazelle was the best thing she'd ever tasted. Fearless stalked haughtily away, afraid his sister's sharp ears would catch the rumbling of his stomach.

I don't need food. I need a bit of respect.

Turning his back on the pride, he sat down, curled his tail round his rump, and stared out at the darkness of the plain. There was no prey in sight.

Fearless tapped his tail against the ground irritably. As the horizon's last sunset glow vanished, stars blinked and twinkled into life. Herds moved and stamped distantly, he could hear them, but of course no grass-eaters drifted close to him. Hunger nipped and gnawed at his belly. *But I won't go back, I won't—*

"Fearless!"

Keen's trotting paws were approaching from behind him; his friend, thought Fearless crossly, had barely given him time to sulk.

"*What?*"

Keen halted, his flanks rising and falling with edgy

excitement. "I smell a grown lion. Nearby!"

Fearless rose to his paws, his tail stiffening. "A male?"

"Yes." Keen nodded apprehensively as Fearless paced back with him to the pride. "You think it might be one of Titan's cronies?"

"It had better not be," growled Fearless, tossing his neck. "I'll go and investigate."

"Is that a good idea?" Valor was sitting up now and licking her bloodied jaws, her belly distended with gazelle. The others were still stuffing themselves ravenously.

Fearless bristled. "Of course it is! I'm the leader of Fearlesspride, and this is my job!" Resentfully he added, "Don't you have any faith in me?"

"Of course it isn't that," she told him quickly.

"Then I'll *go* and *investigate*."

"I'll come with you," offered Keen.

"No, you won't. Stay here to defend the pride." Fearless stalked off, fuming inwardly.

In only moments, he heard the light thud of paws again, but Fearless knew it wasn't Keen disobeying orders. He'd known Valor's pawsteps all his life.

"Fearless," came her voice at his side, more conciliatory now. "What's the matter?"

"Nothing," he gritted, staring ahead.

"That's not true, Swiftbrother," murmured Valor. "Something's really got under your hide. Let me help?"

Fearless stopped and swung his head, glaring at her. "I don't need your help!"

Her eyes widened in surprise. "Come on, Fearless, that isn't true. We're supposed to help each other. Remember what Mother said before she died?"

It was the lowest of paw-blows. Staring at her pleading eyes, Fearless realized she hadn't meant to hurt him, but he winced at the memory. *Yes, Mother said we were to look after each other. Though that doesn't mean* Valor *always has to do the looking-after!*

He hated fighting with his sister; they were all that was left of their Gallantpride family. The two of them had been separated for so long, and their reunion had been one of the best moments of his life. But they weren't the same lions now. At least, Fearless wasn't.

All his life he'd thought of himself as the cub of Gallant, the brother of Valor. And now he knew that was all a lie. Everything he'd believed had been ripped away after the Great Battle, the death of Loyal, and the revelations that had come to light when Sky Strider touched the great lion's body. Because he wasn't Gallant's cub—he was the son of Loyal, the bravest lion he'd met but an oath-breaker too.

As Fearless watched Valor's glowing eyes, she tilted her head in appeal. "After all, Fearless, we're brother and sister!"

A stab of pure, angry grief tore through him, and he sprang back. Baring his teeth, Fearless gave a shaky growl.

"Are we?"

He spun and walked off into the night. Valor stood silent and didn't follow.

CHAPTER 5

His shoulders hunched in threat, his forepaws driven hard into the leaf litter, Thorn snarled at the oncoming enemy. At his back, the fighting members of Brightforest Troop were lined up in their defensive ranks. The hostile baboons might not yet be in sight, but everyone could hear the rattle and crack of branches as Tendril's invaders approached. Dislodged leaves fluttered into the clearing, and birds flew squawking into the sky. Thorn drew a deep, determined breath and gave a ringing whoop of defiance. Behind him, the rest of the troop joined in, shrieking and hooting, jumping up and down and pounding the forest floor.

But as Tendril finally broke out of the undergrowth and halted, her fighters emerging to flank her, a tense quiet fell.

The lanky Crownleaf of Crookedtree glared at Thorn, her golden eyes brilliant in her hollow face. "You! *You're* the leader of this worthless troop?"

"Hello, Tendril," he growled levelly. "No. Actually I'm not."

Her lip peeled slowly back from her upper fangs in elegant disgust. When she spoke, her voice was as eerily calm and distant as he remembered.

"I should hope not. It can't be good for any troop to be commanded by a traitor. You and your crony Nut—you made me a pledge to stay in Crookedtree Troop. You broke it." The serenity cracked, and Tendril slammed a paw onto the ground. "Liar!"

With an effort, Thorn kept his breathing steady and calm. "My paw was forced, Tendril Crownleaf. Perhaps there's a way I can atone for letting you down? A war would damage both our troops."

For a long, tense moment, she stared at him.

"Very well!" Tendril rose onto her hind legs—Great Spirit, she was tall!—and gave him a cold sneer. "Surrender your territory to me."

Thorn's eyes widened. "All of it?"

"*All of it!*"

Thorn shook his head slowly, almost amused. "You know I can't do that, Tendril. If you made a more reasonable request . . ."

"I make no request!" She slammed both fists into the earth, her rage erupting. "I *demand*!"

"Oh, you do, do you?" Berry stalked forward to Thorn's side, her fangs casually bared. "Then this is *our* demand: leave now, or face the consequences."

"Come now." Berry's mother, Pear Goodleaf, bounded forward, shooting anxious glances from her daughter to Tendril. "Let's not rush into a terrible fight."

Tendril looked nonplussed. Her snout twisted, and she glanced at her second-in-command before turning back to Pear; for a moment her eyes softened with respect.

Pear pressed her advantage. "Tendril, I've known you your whole life." She gave the Crownleaf a gentle smile. "Do you know I saved your life once, when you had a fever?"

"That was your job," spat Tendril, gathering her brittle dignity. "Of course you did."

Pear seemed not to have heard her; her smile was still in place and her voice was soft. "I knew your mother and grandmother well. What noble baboons they were. They'd be proud of you, Tendril, for all you have done for your troop!"

"All I have done for my troop?" Tendril's voice was smooth and soft once more. "Oh, Pear, yes. How I have tried to protect them! I kept them safe within Leopard Forest, I swore no invaders would ever threaten us. My troop would remain secret, confined within our perfect, beautiful territory; why should we ever leave?" She pointed a thin, languid paw at Thorn and Nut. "Why, I even took in two lost baboons, offered them companionship and shelter. They vowed their loyalty. And what did they do? They betrayed me." The level sweetness of her tone grew sinister. "My authority was challenged, Pear! Other baboons now question and defy me, thanks to these two. Many things I will tolerate, because I am reasonable, a kind and patient leader." Fangs flashed in her muzzle again. "But this? *This I cannot stand!*"

Pear hesitated, biting her lip. "But Tendril, taking our forest will not prevent disloyalty in your troop!"

"Let me be honest, then." Tendril rubbed a claw idly across her forehead. "I do not really want your forest. It does not appeal to me."

Berry stared at her, perplexed, then frowned at Thorn. "So why come here?"

Tendril's coolness became a frigid, contained violence; Thorn saw it in her eyes, and he stiffened.

"Because I must demonstrate to my troop that traitors suffer. Is this not quite clear?" She shrugged. "Thorn and Nut must die."

"Tendril!" Pear surged forward, aghast. "Violence is not the answer!"

"Why, Pear, I believe it is." The lanky baboon flapped her paw at the old Goodleaf. "You too betrayed and abandoned your troop, so if you do not want to get hurt, stay out of this. Because the time for talking"—she swiveled once more to glare at Thorn with contempt—"is *over.*"

With a ringing screech, she threw herself at Thorn, her long arms striking out, her hind claws raking at his belly as he fell backward. As his head thudded onto the ground, Thorn saw his own troop as a blur of gray and brown fur; they raced past him, hurtling into the Crookedtree ranks. The angry uproar was instantaneous, filling the forest and sending yet more birds clattering in alarm from the trees. War cries and hoots made the boughs tremble.

Thorn himself was only momentarily dazed; with a snarl he twisted and kicked out at Tendril, dislodging her, then sprang on top of her. Her jaws were open in his face; as she bellowed in fury, he felt spittle fleck his snout. Together they rolled, biting and scratching, into a green patch of lantana. As Thorn briefly got the upper paw, he took his chance and hammered at her face with his fists until she went limp, groaning.

Leaping off her, he spun toward the battle, taking a moment to find where he was most needed. Berry was holding her own, he realized with a surge of pride: she was tearing mercilessly at a big baboon beneath her, who curled and rolled away as he tried to protect his eyes. Creeper was methodically swinging his enormous arms at two enemy baboons, driving them back into the trees; together Moss and Mango held down a huge, snarling male. Nut, no stranger to a beating himself, was punching another's snout, his paws a blur of furious power.

A high-pitched squeal of pain made Thorn snap his head around. Mud—always smaller and weaker than the rest of the troop—had been backed against a mgunga trunk by two thuggish-looking baboons. Mud winced as the prickly bark dug into his skin, but when the bigger of his attackers lashed a fist into his jaw, Mud only shook his head and peeled back his snout in defiance.

"Nut!" yelled Thorn. "Quick, help Mud!"

Turning from his dazed opponent, Nut raced to Thorn's side. The two enemy baboons were snapping their savage jaws into Mud's shoulder and belly, and he was fighting courageously back; the two brutes didn't notice Thorn and Nut till it was too late. With a howl of rage, Thorn flung himself at the bigger one, dragging him away from Mud and pummeling his chest; close by, Nut had knocked the other baboon to the earth and was kicking and raking ruthlessly with his claws. Freed, Mud staggered forward.

"Go, Mud!" yelled Thorn.

"Thank you," gasped his small friend, needing no second urging. All the same, when Mud bolted, it was straight back into the fight; he slammed into a baboon that was closer to his own size, and the two fell to the ground in a snarling tangle.

As Thorn himself bounded back toward the melee, a maddened screech split the air. *"Traitor!"*

Tendril had recovered, then. She was loping toward him, her eyes bloodshot with rage.

Thorn glanced swiftly from left to right. If he led Tendril into the high branches, he decided, it would keep her apart from her main force, and Crookedtree Troop might descend into chaos. Lunging for the lowest branch and hauling himself onto it, Thorn began to climb, paw over paw, swift and determined.

"Get back here, coward." Tendril's shrill voice was only a little way below, and he could hear the crack of twigs as she scrambled after him. "Stay and fight, you wretched Brightforest monkey!"

"I will, then." With a hoot, Thorn twisted abruptly and lunged down, digging his claws into her shoulder.

Tendril gave a shriek of surprise and pain, but she recovered fast, driving him back along the branch till he was pressed against the thick trunk. Thorn kicked her away and dodged to climb higher, then turned again, lashing out as she leaped up to follow him. Gripping each other with their claws, they wrestled precariously but viciously, their snouts so close their fangs clashed.

She's tall, but I'm bigger and more powerful. If he could tire her out, exhaust the energy of her fury, Thorn knew he could land a strike that would finish this fight. Throwing back his head, he screamed another war cry and flung himself bodily at her.

Tendril stumbled back, but she didn't lose her footing. She skipped nimbly aside, then leaped into the next tree, bounding higher through the thickly leaved boughs. Grimly, Thorn pursued her.

All right, I'm stronger—but she's faster. Her brown tail and hindquarters were a blur of speed through the leaves, and Thorn panted desperately as he put on a spurt.

Springing over a branch, he drew up sharply. Tendril stood facing him, elegantly balanced on all four paws, her tail high and waving. Her grin was unnervingly smug.

And no wonder. Above and below Thorn, and crouched on either side of him, waited five of her Highleaf warriors.

They were Tendril's elite; Thorn recognized them from his time in Leopard Forest. With a screech of angry warning, Thorn began to back off, but the Highleaves moved almost too fast to see. He felt powerful bodies crash into him, and as he shut his eyes to protect them from scratching claws, he felt himself topple.

No!

Thorn crashed down through the boughs, snatching wildly at pawholds that were just out of reach. Leaves whipped his snout as he twisted in the air, his limbs and shoulders striking what seemed like every branch on the way down. He grunted as his spine thudded against a broken stump. A jutting twig tore at his fur, leaving spines in his skin; at last, inevitably, he crashed to the stony earth, knocking the air with brutal abruptness from his lungs.

Helpless, Thorn gasped, his body shuddering with pain. The forest spun around him, and in his blurred vision he saw brown-furred figures swinging down from the trees above him. Thorn couldn't even draw a breath to defend himself as they fell on him, biting and pummeling and ripping. One of them shoved his snout into the ground, and he felt the weight of another on his back, making it impossible to recover his breath. Frantically he twisted his head, seeking air.

There are too many. They'll kill me. In his wobbling line of sight, the streaks of brown and gray faded, darkening in his vision; even the pain began to seem distant. *Yes. I'm dying.*

Then his body jerked, his spine arching high, and air rushed into his lungs as he clutched hopelessly at the earth.

No. Not dying.

I'm dead.

He must be. Because suddenly Thorn was weightless, flying, rising up through the dark green of the forest and breaking abruptly into a world that was blue and clear.

My spirit. It's flying to the stars. I'll see my parents again.

His head fell forward and his jaw hung loose; below him

was all of Bravelands, golden and green, with stubbly dark forest where silver streaks of river ran. The whole expanse of it swung in his vision, magnificent and dangerous and beautiful. *Farewell, Bravelands. I'll miss you.*

I'll miss . . . Grief surged in his chest, the first weight he'd felt since dying. *Berry. Berry, my love. Farewell to you, too. And to Brightforest Troop. All of you, please . . . survive. Have long, happy, peaceful lives, all mangoes and cool shade and fresh water.*

Oh, Berry, I love you. Win this battle. Live on, even if it's without me. . . .

It hurt to see his whole world shrink and recede beneath him, vanishing into his past. With a mighty effort, he lifted his head, squinting into the wind.

Before him, in the far distance, lay a blue line of mountains, shimmering in an ethereal haze. His flight was taking him there, straight and true.

Have we all been wrong, then? Did the Starleaves misunderstand? Do we go to the mountains, and not the stars?

It hardly mattered now. As his whole body sagged, his fur rippling with the speed of his flight, blackness and oblivion claimed him.

CHAPTER 6

"It's time." Comet raised her trunk in an age-old signal, her gray eyes bright with determination. At the water's edge, the other elephants gathered behind the matriarch, flapping ears and nodding heads. "I know the way we must travel," Comet declared.

The herd didn't look nearly so confident as Comet, Sky realized; her aunts and cousins did not argue or contradict their leader, but she caught their apprehensive glances. All the same, the young ones were crowding to the legs of their mothers, and the older aunts were shepherding the stragglers into position, touching and caressing them with reassuring trunks. Cloud closed her eyes; Mirage lifted her head and blared a last call.

"Thank you, Great Spirit!"

"Thank you for guiding our matriarch on the true path," cried Timber beside her.

Nervously eyeing the dry grasslands that lay before them, Sky edged closer to Comet. "Are you sure about the way?"

"Of course she is," snapped Mirage irritably, before Comet could answer. "She's the matriarch!"

As Comet took a pace forward, the whole herd moved slowly behind her. Great feet struck the ground, raising clouds of red dust, and with unspoken understanding they began to form a line. One by one, implacable, the elephants trudged up the bank and onto the great expanse of plain, the low rumble of their tread resounding in the still air.

Sky gathered herself, ready to stride after her family. Her muscles bunched, she took a deep breath—

She did not move.

Her heart slammed inside her chest. Her head swam as a vision of a skull filled it: *bone, crushed in my trunk, shattering into fragments.* She gasped in a breath, and her blood buzzed and tingled.

I can't go.

The urge to follow the herd was a powerful one, buried deep in her gut, yet she could not make her feet obey that instinct; they remained planted solidly on the riverbank. And now she knew: she had to stay. There was no choice.

Timber glanced back in puzzlement, her ears flapping. "Sky?"

Another cousin paused, turning. "Hurry, Sky. Don't be left behind."

Impatiently, old Mirage stirred the earth with her foot. "Come along."

"I can't," Sky told her. There was fear and foreboding in her gut, but it was overwhelmed by an absolute certainty.

Timber started. "What do you mean, you can't?"

Cloud too turned, narrowing her eyes. "You mean you won't."

More of them were hesitating now, swinging their trunks quizzically. A small elephant squealed, "Why isn't Sky coming?" but her mother shushed her and hurried her on.

Mirage took a pace back toward Sky, then halted, angling her ears forward.

"You have to put that young bull from your mind, Sky," she said. "Us females must stick together."

"Yes, forget about Rock," scolded Timber. "You can't stay here! It is the way of those stubborn males to live alone. That's not *our* way."

"I . . . I have to stay." Forcing her muscles to stop trembling, Sky took a step backward. She gazed resolutely at the older elephant. "It's not Rock, I swear, Aunt Timber. I can't explain it."

"You can't explain it because it's *nonsense*," exclaimed the old elephant.

"It isn't nonsense," blurted Sky, shaking her ears. Inside her, there was an almost unbearable conflict; it hurt her heart. "I want to be with you all, but something is tugging me back." She stared around them, meeting their eyes. "It's the Great Spirit, I know it is."

"You said the Great Spirit had left you." Mirage's gaze was severe.

"Yes, but now it wants something from me. Something I have to do here," Sky insisted. "I feel it, Mirage. I'm *so sure*."

Even Comet had turned now, and was walking apprehensively back toward her. The whole herd came to a halt, shifting impatiently, blowing at the dust; mothers calmed their infants, shooting annoyed looks at Sky.

"Please," said the matriarch, halting before her. Comet's gray eyes were huge and anxious. "Sky, please won't you come? You're always so helpful, and I'm sure your advice would be useful. . . ."

"I can't, Comet. I'm sorry." Sky looked away, unable to bear the hurt expression on her leader's face.

"But we'll miss you so," lamented Cloud.

"Oh, leave her," snapped Timber. "She's made her decision."

"Quite," agreed Mirage with a haughty glare. "We know how stubborn Sky can be, and we've no time to waste. She's chosen her mud hole, let her roll in it."

Mirage and Timber set off again without a backward glance, their rumps swaying, their sharply flicking tails betraying their irritation. Comet looked agonized, but she turned and hurried back to her place at the head of the line. Cloud gave Sky a brief, sad nod before joining the others; a couple of the young ones looked miserable, and they strained their little trunks toward Sky.

But the herd was moving again, in an inexorable rhythmic sway, and soon Sky stood alone as she watched her family recede into the hazy distance. Her throat constricted, and her heart wrenched painfully, but she didn't move.

The herd's ponderous tread took them away from her with unnerving speed. Before long they were a wobbling blur, their individual shapes lost. Then they were a smear of thin shadow, only just visible. As the quivering horizon finally swallowed them, Sky gave a mournful, longing cry that none of her herd would ever hear.

Her path was aimless; Sky knew Rock would help with whatever the Great Spirit wanted from her, but she didn't know where to start looking for him. She trudged across parched grass, barely raising her head to check the landscape or the position of the sun. A herd of gazelles drifted past in the middle distance, browsing, their tails flickering in constant motion; their leader called out a polite greeting, but she barely heard him. A little farther away she caught sight of a rhino and an adolescent calf, grooming each other, and for a moment her heart skipped, but when she peered more carefully she sighed. Neither of them was her friend Silverhorn. It felt as if she didn't have a friend left in Bravelands.

I thought I might have come across Rock by now. Perhaps my aunts scared him off for good.

That thought was too sad to contemplate. Sky shook her ears and tore listlessly at an acacia branch with her trunk. The leaves tasted dry and bitter on her tongue.

Where is Rock? Sky had no more idea where to look for him than Comet had had about the migration path.

Exhausted, she stopped beside a copse of dense thorn scrub.

It looked no more enticing than the acacia, but she had to eat. Reaching out her trunk, she curled it around a clump of twigs and yanked.

The bush stretched, snapped, and sprang back. Sky's trunk-tip went still, the clump of leaves tickling her mouth. It had been only a momentary glimpse, but surely she hadn't imagined what she'd just seen?

Dropping the twigs, she parted the foliage again and peered down. The sun was high and very bright above her, and the green shade beneath the bush was dappled with sparkling sunspots. No wonder she hadn't been sure.

The two cheetah cubs gaped up at her, trembling. Against the sandy earth, their spotted yellow coats and fluffy heads were blurred and indistinct, but their eyes were huge and bright and unmistakable. They nestled tightly against their mother's flank; she sprawled with her limbs outstretched, her eyes slitted open, her flanks hollow and unmoving. And she, like the cubs, was instantly recognizable.

"Rush," breathed Sky, her heart clenching. "Oh, Rush."

The elegant cheetah had been so swift and so brave; she'd been one of Sky's first allies in the war against Stinger, and she'd fought courageously with the Great Herd. Sky, Rock, and Silverhorn had met Rush on their journey from the mountains, when they rescued her from Titanpride; the brutish lions would have torn the young cheetah apart even though she was pregnant.

And it turns out we didn't save her after all. Sky gave a deep rumble of grief.

"Mother's asleep," chirped a scared, small voice. "She should be waking up now."

"Oh, Nimble." Sky stroked his fluffy head with her trunk, then moved it to caress his sister, Lively.

"How do you know my name?" The cub's eyes narrowed.

"I'm Sky. You're too young to remember me, but I was— I'm your mother's friend. I was there when you were born."

"Oh," he said. "Hello, Sky."

Lively only swallowed, nervously.

Sky's heart ached for them. "Nimble, Lively . . . What happened?"

Nimble gulped and glanced at his sister. "Mother went hunting and she didn't come back, so we came to find her."

"It must have been a hard hunt," whispered Lively, "because she's rested for ever so long."

Sky's throat dried. "Cubs," she croaked gently. "You must be hungry. Why don't you look for some beetles on the other side of the bush? I'll take care of your mother for a moment."

Warily, they glanced at each other, but at last they rose and padded a little way off through the tangled branches. Sky could still make out their dark eyes as they turned to watch her doubtfully, but she couldn't bear to send them farther away. Closing her eyes, she turned back to Rush. Then, very gently, she turned the stiff body over with her trunk.

Hunting. Turning, running. Being hunted.

Sky could no longer read the living, but like all elephants she could still read the dead. The images were more broken sensations than clear memories, and they didn't explain how the cheetah had died. *Rush*, Sky thought, *what happened to you?*

The cheetah's slender rib cage was broken at the breastbone, a single ugly puncture crusted with dried blood. Tensing, summoning all her nerve, Sky pressed her trunk to the wound.

The flashes that raced through her mind were too swift, too blurred and confused to make any sense: they were all color and noise and fear. Sky squeezed her eyes tight shut to focus, but it was no good: *blood and pain and shapeless terrors.* With a sad, shaking breath, she pulled away.

If the Great Mother or Father were here . . . they might understand this. They could help me see how Rush died. Her own grandmother, the wisest Great Parent of all, would have known what had happened here, Sky was sure of it.

But Great Mother isn't here. Like Rush, she never will be again.

What did cheetahs do with their dead? Sky had no idea. Uncertainly, she peered around, then began to tear down more of the scrubby thorn branches. In the silence of the afternoon, the crack and snap sounded horribly loud, but Rush's body was small and lithe, and it did not take Sky long to cover it.

She stepped back, then tugged down another clump of twigs to fill in a few last spaces. It was the elephant custom, but it was the only way she knew to honor Rush. The way the sunbeams speckled the leaves reminded her of Rush's beautiful fur.

Sky did not know the cheetah words, either, but she hoped she could do Rush justice. "May you run forever free among the stars, Rush."

"What are you doing, Sky?"

She looked up, her heart plummeting. The two cubs stood watching her, and Lively sniffed hesitantly at the pile of branches that covered her mother.

"Nimble. Lively." Sky curled her trunk tightly. "Your mother . . . she can't wake up. She has gone to run with your ancestors."

Nimble tilted his head, staring at the branches. "She's gone to the sky?"

"Yes," said Sky hoarsely. "Cheetahs run and run there, and never get tired. And the hunting is always good." Was that the right thing to say? She hoped so.

"That sounds . . . nice," said Lively.

"Your mother will be safe and happy, but she'll miss you until she sees you again." Once again Sky wrapped her trunk around both the small furred bodies. "You'll have to be strong for her and make her proud."

Nimble nodded. "We will."

Lively peered up through the tangle of scrub. "Good-bye, Mother."

Nimble turned to his sister. "We'll have to look after ourselves now, Lively. Till we're grown-up cats. I'm sure we can hunt like Mother taught us."

Sky stared at them both, aghast. *I can't let them fend for themselves. They'll be hyena-food in days!* "Not just yet, Nimble," she said hurriedly. "I won't leave you alone. You can stay with me for now."

"Can we?" Lively brightened.

"Yes." Sky nodded. "Though I can't hunt, you know."

Nimble screwed up his nose. "But you're *enormous*." He shut one eye and studied her tusks. "And you have *massive* fangs."

Sky couldn't help laughing. "It's true, Nimble, I'm sorry. I've never hunted a single animal. But I think your mother had litter-sisters?" She could remember Rush describing them one night soon after they'd met. "Far beyond that dry stream with the mgunga trees, and then to the west? I can take you there, if you like."

"We've never met our aunts," said Nimble with trepidation. "Mother said they lived ever so far away."

"That would be lovely," said Lively, giving her brother a stern look. "And we can walk a *long* way."

Sky blew gently at their ears. She had no idea if cheetahs would even look after another's young, but she had to try. And her own journey could be delayed, she told herself firmly. She did not know what the Great Spirit wanted of her, after all. And her own heart's desire was not as important as these helpless cubs: her search for Rock could wait until she had found them safety with their mother's family.

Perhaps this was penance, she thought, glancing toward the sky. Perhaps the Great Spirit wanted her to make amends for killing Stinger.

"Come along, you two," she murmured, and turned to begin her ponderous trek across the grassland and the dry streambed.

Her progress was slow; she had to let the little cheetahs keep up, and at first they kept hesitating, turning to throw longing glances back at Rush's resting place. The sun was drifting westward, its arc now lowering toward the horizon, and Sky felt a nip of anxiety in her belly. This felt like a tremendous responsibility, and she knew the weight of it would be even heavier in the dark hours of night. It would be good to reach a thick patch of forest before the three of them stopped to rest.

Once again, Nimble had paused to give a forlorn mew at the now-distant thorn scrub. Wanting to distract him from his unhappiness, Sky raked on the earth for a stone and tossed it ahead.

"Would you like to play, Nimble?" she called cheerfully.

He and Lively twisted, their ears pricking up. As the stone rolled and bounced, they both shot suddenly after it. Lively reached it first, pouncing and clutching it, kicking her small legs as if to disembowel it. Nimble collapsed on top of her, and they wrestled in the dust until Sky caught up.

They peered up at her eagerly. Smiling, Sky snatched up the stone with her trunk and threw it again.

It was fun watching them play, and chasing the stone was certainly making their progress faster. Sky found herself feeling far happier as she walked. The two of them must miss their mother terribly already, but they were still only cubs, and she was glad they could have fun to lighten their grief. Ahead of her, Nimble shot up stiffly into the air on all four paws, then landed on his sister, who squealed in delight and scrabbled at his belly with her tiny claws.

But abruptly, Nimble tumbled away from her, his face serious as he sniffed at the ground. As Lively grabbed his rump, he batted her away.

"What is it, Nimble?" called Sky, breaking into an anxious trot.

He turned, his eyes bright. Lively was sniffing now, too, the stone and the scrap forgotten.

"Elephant!" they both chirped together. "We smell another elephant!"

Sky took a breath. Letting the tip of her trunk stroke the ground, she realized the cubs were right. The trail was going in the same direction as they were. And what was more, she could see tracks now, faint in the dust but identifiable: the marks of huge and heavy feet.

Rock!

CHAPTER 7

The warthog gave a screeching squeal, stumbling onto its knees as it turned, but it never had a chance. Fearless struck, sinking his fangs deep into its face, suffocating it with his jaws, bearing down with his full weight. The stocky creature kicked and thrashed, but at last it went limp and collapsed.

Fearless stood over it, panting. It hadn't been a long chase: he'd surprised the warthog where it browsed. But he was still short of breath with fury.

At least he'd taken it out on his prey and not on Valor. The argument with his sister still rankled, especially since part of his anger was rooted in guilt. He might not be Gallant's son, but he was still her brother—at least, half of him was. They had had the same mother. They were both Swiftcubs.

But I can't help being angry. She's the cub of Gallant, and I'm not. Valor's always thought she's better than me.

No, that wasn't fair. Glaring at the warthog, Fearless admitted it to himself.

The trouble is, I've *always thought she's better than me.*

It was the revelation that Loyal was his real father that had made everything worse. He'd always believed he was Fearless Gallantpride, destined to take Gallant's place at the head of the best pride in Bravelands.

No, that's not fair either. It wasn't Loyal's fault, and it wasn't Valor's, and it wasn't Fearless's either. It was Titan's. He had shattered Fearless's shining future on the day he killed Gallant.

The little warthog wasn't exactly the prize a buffalo calf would have been, but it would do—and he'd caught it without the help of his pride. He couldn't have taken down a swift-moving grass-eater alone. Gripping it in his jaws, Fearless dragged it across the grassland as the sun dipped lower on the horizon. Ahead of him, clear now that the heat haze had given way to the cool evening, a rocky kopje rose out of the plain, its stone glowing gold in the sun's slanting rays.

Grunting with his burden, Fearless leaped up the ridges of rock, then crossed the small barren plateau and slunk behind the blade of rock that hid Loyal's den. *My father's den.*

Lichen and straggling thorn had grown down over the den mouth; Fearless pawed the vegetation aside and wriggled into the cool darkness within. Dropping the warthog, he stood and inhaled Loyal's lingering scent.

It was growing stale now, and fading, like his memories of his father's face. *One day I'll forget Loyal,* Fearless realized with a stab of grief. *Because I never really got to know him.*

Loyal had been his friend, his mentor, his protector. But Fearless hadn't known until it was too late that the great, scarred, prideless lion had sired him. *I loved him, but I should have been allowed to love him as a father.*

Opening his jaws, he gave a roar of sadness and regret. "Why didn't you *tell me?*"

Tell me. Tell me. The echoes rebounded from the cold stone, finally dying away.

He knew why, of course. If he thought about it with his head and not his heart, he understood. Loyal had been an oath-breaker, even if the breach had been unintentional. The great lion had taken Swift as a mate when he had believed Gallant dead. But it had still been a betrayal of the vow he'd made to his friend and pride leader, and Loyal's shame had left him no choice but to go into exile alone.

Frustration rose within Fearless, mixed with sadness and anger—and a searing, sudden loneliness.

I miss him.

It was Loyal who had taught him everything he knew, because Gallant had been killed before he could guide Fearless to adulthood. Loyal Prideless had hunted with him when Fearless's incompetence meant he was almost starving. When Fearless was in one of those angry, impulsive moods that could have gotten him killed, Loyal had counseled him and calmed him. The crooked-tailed lion had given him a home, friendship, and, true to his name, unswerving loyalty.

And Fearless hadn't always shown his gratitude. Sometimes,

he thought now with a shudder, he'd been unspeakably mean to Loyal.

Yet he still kept on loving me. When he looked back on it, Fearless could hardly believe he'd missed the clues. Loyal had been his father in everything but name—and then it had turned out he was that, too.

The straggling creepers at the den mouth rustled, and paws pattered against stone. Fearless stiffened, turning, but the face that appeared in the gloom was friendly and familiar—and it was the one he'd been expecting.

"Ruthless," he rumbled, pacing forward to lick the cub's muzzle. "You've grown!"

Titan's son gave him a mischievous look. "Fearless! You say that *every single time* you see me!"

"It's true, though." Fearless studied the young lion. He was rangy now, his legs too long for his body and his paws too big for his legs. Ruthless would never become a massive, imposing male like his father—but he would never become such a murderous brute, either. And he had none of the sly malevolence of his mother, Artful. "You'll soon be growing into those enormous paws, I promise."

"Too slowly," moaned Ruthless dramatically.

Fearless laughed. "But you *are*. You're going to be tall."

"And skinny." The cub gave a loud and mournful sigh.

Fearless rolled his eyes in amused exasperation. "Lean and fast, Ruthless, lean and fast. But that's enough about you. What news of Titanpride?"

Ruthless flopped to the earthen floor, looking entirely at

home. He'd developed a useful habit of sneaking away from his father now and again, to meet up with Fearless and let him know what Titan was up to. All Fearless had to do was check the baobab on the plain for Ruthless's scent mark—or leave his own as a signal. And Loyal's abandoned den was the perfect secret rendezvous point.

"Titanpride is as boring as ever," growled Ruthless. "Is that a warthog? Is it for me?"

"You know it is. Let's eat."

Settling down, the two lions began to tear companionably at the warthog's tough hide. Ruthless was a noisy eater, and for a while there was no sound but the gulping and chewing of two hungry lions. At last the cub slowed down a little and began to chew before he swallowed. He licked his bloodied jaws and glanced at Fearless beside him.

"Father still hasn't got over that wound you gave him at the Great Battle," he said. "He's got a permanent limp, I reckon."

Fearless just managed not to say, "Good." He simply nodded and rasped his tongue across a leg bone.

"But he's still acting oddly," the cub added. "He's always given the pride the weirdest orders, but I swear they get stranger and stranger. He asks for injured prey to be brought to him, still alive. He takes it off and eats it by himself." Ruthless frowned at the warthog's torn belly.

"Really?" Fearless twitched an ear in surprise. "Where does he go?"

"Off to the Misty Ravine. You know, the one at the edge

of Titanpride territory? Nobody sees him till he limps back, licking his jaws. But nobody ever asks him why he does it. Nobody dares."

"That does sound odd." Fearless wrinkled his lip. "But your father's never been a normal lion, I guess."

"That's for sure," said Ruthless with feeling.

Fearless paused, then asked quietly, "Have any new males joined the pride? Any been scouting around my territory?"

Ruthless creased his forehead in surprise. "Funny. I was going to ask you the same question. We've picked up a strange scent on our boundary, too."

Fearless said nothing, but growled thoughtfully as they settled back to their meal. They ate in silence for a little longer, and it was Ruthless who drew back first, rolling onto his side with a deep sigh.

Fearless eyed him. "What's up? You can't actually have finished before me? That's a first."

Ruthless didn't return the banter; he was gazing up at the darkness of the den roof, his eyes sad. Fearless stood up and stretched out his forelegs. His belly felt wonderfully round.

"What's wrong, cub?" he asked more gently.

"The thing is," Ruthless murmured, "I'm not sure I can keep coming to see you like this. I'm raising suspicions already, and some of my father's seconds are watching me."

Fearless nudged him with his muzzle. "You'll get away with it. Titan and Artful think you can do no wrong. The sun shines from your nonexistent mane, remember?"

"I wish that were still true," growled Ruthless despondently. "They've got a new cub, Fearless. She's called Menace, and she's well named."

"Oh," said Fearless. He could just imagine.

"Mother and Father have only got time for Menace, now. And what's more, the other lions know it. I don't eat in my usual turn anymore, because they'll swat me or growl, and Mother barely even notices. She certainly doesn't bother to stick up for me." He buried his muzzle in his paws. "I wouldn't be surprised if they throw me out."

Fearless felt a stab of angry sympathy. He knew very well what it was like to be an outsider in Titanpride; without Titan's approval, survival was almost impossible. How much worse must it be for Ruthless, who had once been the golden son of the leader?

He gave Ruthless a sympathetic nuzzle and licked his ear. "Whatever happens, Ruthless, I'll protect you. Maybe you should leave before that happens. It's time, anyway—you could join Fearlesspride. We'll accept you—all of us. I'll make sure of that."

"Nah," muttered Ruthless, though he gave Fearless a grateful look. "Thanks, but I can't leave. I still love my parents. They'll stop fussing over Menace soon, and they'll remember they love me too. I *know* they will!" There was an edge of desperation to his voice that cut Fearless to the heart, but Ruthless gave a defeated, slightly-too-casual shrug. "Anyway, don't worry. Once Menace stops suckling, Mother might be back to her old self."

"I hope so," Fearless told him sincerely. However much he disliked Artful, Ruthless had always been close to her. "But if you're being watched, you should probably get back to your pride soon."

"I will." Ruthless got to his paws and licked Fearless's nose. "I'll try to see you again, but I can't promise."

"Don't take any risks," warned Fearless, as Ruthless padded out of the den ahead of him. "You've had a lot of courage to keep coming this long. Thank you."

They separated at the foot of the kopje, and Fearless set off toward his own pride through the twilight. Sparkling points of light were blinking into life in the dark blue sky above him; without a moon, the long sweeping crest of stars was clearly visible, stretching up from the horizon. That, he knew, was where lions went to hunt after death: forever pursuing sleek zebras and gazelles along its glittering silver track. Fearless peered up, wondering if he could ever make out the ghosts of Gallant and Loyal and Swift. *Hello, Mother. I know you're happy now. You have eyes again, and you hunt better than you ever did.*

Calmness filled him. *I don't need to be angry with Valor.* There was more to being a good pride leader than hunting, he knew; after all, Swift had been a better hunter than Gallant. Fearless himself had done good work tonight, with his secret meeting with Ruthless Titanpride. He was laying the groundwork for revenge, and one day he would punish Titan, just as he'd always promised, for Gallant's death. But now he had Loyal to avenge, too.

I'll unite the prides. We'll live well, and in peace, without evil, brutal leaders to intimidate lions as if they were gazelles.

One day, Fearless knew, the pride would understand and appreciate all he was doing—and so would all the lions of Bravelands.

Lowering his head, he set out once more toward the camp— and was instantly brought up short. His nostrils flared, and he snuffed the night air.

Lion. That same scent from before, prowling close to his pride. Exposing his teeth, he broke into a trot.

Fearlesspride was not far away; he could smell them. But that strange lion scent was still strong and fresh. Breaking into a run, he bounded over a stretch of dark grassland till he reached the low rise that shielded the pride from view. Hunching his shoulders aggressively, Fearless stalked over the crest.

There he was: a sizable young male with a mane that was already thick. The insolent brute was padding straight for Valor! The stranger looked well built and muscular, but Fearless was too angry to care. Coiling his muscles, he bounded forward, widening his jaws to snap them into the intruder's neck.

"Fearless. No!"

He started, landing on the earth with an awkward thud that made him stumble. Disbelieving, Fearless gaped as Valor came running toward him, her eyes glowing.

The intruder had spun around, his own fangs bared, and he snarled at Fearless—but he made no attempt to strike. Slowing to a trot, Valor halted between them and swiveled her head to eye them both.

"Valor?" exploded Fearless in bewilderment. "What are you doing?"

"Stopping a ridiculous scrap," she told him, flicking her tail at the strange lion. "Fearless, my brother, I want you to meet Mighty. He's my new mate."

CHAPTER 8

The sky was like the sky he'd known in life. It was paler, perhaps, its shade the cold blue of the distant mountain horizon, and thin wisps of cloud drifted impossibly high above him. Thorn blinked fiercely. There was something sharp and hard beneath his spine, and his head pulsed with pain.

So we still feel pain in death? That's not fair.

And do we really have to keep our sense of smell, Great Spirit? The pervading stink of carrion was pungent. Worse than that, eerie voices were raised in a chant around him.

"*Great Father Sleek, Leopard of the Greenforest.*"

"*Hail to his memory!*"

"*Great Mother Cavern, Elephant of the Stonelands.*"

"*Hail to her memory!*"

"*Great Father Ridge, Elephant of the Desert Plain.*"

"*Hail to his memory!*"

"Great Mother Lightning, Cheetah of the Grass Sea."

"Hail to her memory!"

"Great Mother Baobab, Elephant of the—"

"Oh, will you shut up about the Great Parents!"

Thorn didn't know that he'd yelled it out loud, but he must have, because the chanting was silenced abruptly. He shut his eyes, mortified at his disrespect to the spirits. Then he creaked one open again, cautiously.

A chaos of beating black wings made him flinch and gasp. Bolts of pain shot through his limbs as he tried to rise, but the great bird did not attack; it touched down right in front of him, folding its magnificent, tattered wings. Ancient black eyes in a wrinkled face gazed into his.

"Oh no," Thorn groaned, sagging back. "Not you."

"Such ingratitude," rasped Windrider, though her harsh voice was touched with amusement. "Our flock saved your life, Great Father."

"Don't call me that!" Thorn tried to sit up again, but even the air he breathed felt thin and cold in his chest. Dizzy, he reeled back, collapsing onto what he now saw was a nest of twigs and black feathers.

The vulture ignored him. "Your life, Great Father. Restored to you not once, but twice. The Great Spirit speaks plainly through us."

Wait. I'm not dead?

Thorn's head spun with relief and confusion. He put his paws over his face and rubbed his eyes. "You brought me up here? Why?"

"We brought you to the mountain to embrace your destiny."

Thorn peered out between his fingers. The vulture's black stare was unflinching, and he couldn't hold it. Risking a glance around him, he saw dusty, windswept stone rising in steep walls around him. Vultures perched there in shadowy ranks: some were ranged on the valley floor, others high on sharp outcrops of pale rock. If this cold and barren place was not the home of the spirits after all, he was glad. But if he wasn't dead—

"The battle!" he cried, leaping up suddenly. Instant agony shot through his hind leg, sharp as a crocodile's fang, and he collapsed, gasping. "Tendril! My troop—"

"You can do nothing," croaked Windrider. "Your troop's fate is its own to control, for now. You, Great Father, must rest and recover."

Thorn stared down at his hind leg, stunned by pain. "But—"

"A bone in your leg is damaged, perhaps broken." Windrider shook out her wings. "You have no choice."

"You don't understand," he shouted. The leg was unresponsive, as if it didn't belong to him, but Thorn dragged himself forward with his forepaws. "I—"

He couldn't finish. The bolt of pain returned, and he gagged as his head spun. Blackness swept over him, and he had to fight to remain conscious. When he clenched his teeth, blinking, the sky was blue again and the rocky slopes were gray, but it all seemed distant from him, like a dream. Windrider's voice sounded so very far away.

"Rest, Great Father. All is beyond your influence, for now. Even the Great Parent cannot direct the lives of every creature in Bravelands. You can only guide, and advise."

"I'm not . . ."

The walls of rock spun in his vision, and Thorn fell back onto the nest of feathers. His last sight, before his senses left him, was the unremitting gaze of Windrider, glittering and black, piercing him down to his bones.

There was darkness when he woke. The stars were closer than ever; he stretched out a feeble paw to touch them, but they stayed just out of reach. Black wings blotted them out, and he slept again.

A white, hot sun, at the highest point of the sky's arc. His throat was parched. Shade fell over him, and a curled leaf was brought to his muzzle. Greedily he sucked cold water from it. *You are the one. You, Thorn Highleaf.* The whispers around him were like the voice of the mountain.

Pain again, seizing him in its jaws. No, not jaws: talons. An ancient vulture had hold of his leg, shifting its position, jerking it straight. Thorn thought he screamed, but no sound came out. The old vulture muttered and croaked; then its shabby feathers brushed his snout as it took to the air.

Food. They'd brought him food. He tasted a fat beetle in his mouth, then broken chunks of melon, then torn flesh. They made him swallow before they would let him lie back again. *Leave me alone*, he tried to say; *I only want to sleep*. But again, the words didn't come.

There were stars again, a whole river of them, sweeping above him like the path of the spirits. He couldn't see the vultures but he could hear the scratch and tap of their claws on the dry stone, the rustle of their feathers. He didn't try to turn his head sideways; the sky was too dark and beautiful and calming. He'd forgotten about the pain. Perhaps he was used to it. Perhaps it was ebbing.

Food again. Water again. A beak clicked at his ear, and a voice whispered: *Thorn Highleaf. Great Father of Bravelands.* He couldn't protest. He didn't even want to. He felt too serene.

The dreams came in fits and starts, etching themselves on the inside of his skull, and they left his head in excruciating pain. They showed him places he knew he'd never seen. The dark close warmth of a jackal den; the creatures' dusty, sharp scent was in his nostrils. A nest of intertwined branches, high in a pine tree; those smooth, curved objects against his belly were eagle eggs. As the vision changed, he was soaring above a watering hole, and it vanished swiftly behind him; he was heading for the cliffs in the distance. He tilted his wings and plunged down, deep beneath the earth's surface; and now he was scurrying through a narrow tunnel, his tiny claws clicking on unseen roots.

* * *

"It is not unheard-of," said Windrider's hoarse voice. "Not unprecedented."

Groggily, Thorn managed to sit up. He blinked in the sunlight. There was a throbbing ache behind his eyes, but for once his head did not spin, and he did not tumble back into unconsciousness. He felt lucid for the first time in . . . *I don't know. I don't know how long.* Had it been days? It could have been moons, for all he knew. Thorn's leg ached dully like his head, and his ribs showed through his chest fur, but he felt remarkably lively.

"What isn't unheard-of?" The words scratched against his throat, but he'd definitely said them out loud.

"Your dreams." Windrider cocked her bald head toward him. "You've been telling us about your dreams."

"Oh. Have I?" He didn't remember.

"Well," croaked another vulture. "You've been muttering and rambling, but we listened."

"The Great Spirit reveals itself in many ways, Blackwing," said Windrider. "Each Great Parent may sense its power differently."

"Once," rasped an elderly vulture with scraggy wings, "there was a baboon Great Parent who could see through the eyes of other creatures, just as easily as elephants can read bones. Great Father Orchid of the Goldenforest, it was."

Windrider gave the old vulture a nod of respect. "Hail to his memory."

"It seems a baboon trait, then," remarked Blackwing,

with a sidelong look at Thorn.

"Indeed," said Windrider. "Yet another sign that Thorn must accept and embrace his destiny. He must train himself to use this power, to hone it for the good of all creatures."

"I wish you'd leave me alone," mumbled Thorn, but without passion. Tiredness was seeping into his limbs again. "Those dreams—they give me rotten headaches."

"It is natural. But sleep now." A crooning sound rose from Windrider's throat, and the other vultures began to join in; in moments there was a harsh, monotonous chorus that rose and fell in volume. To Thorn it was like giant ants skittering around and around inside his head.

"Vultures sing?" he mumbled drowsily. "I never knew. Horrible racket."

Yet there was something soothing about it, and it eased the pain in his skull. Thorn drifted into sleep once more, but whenever he woke after that, he could still hear it all around him: the ancient, strange song of the vultures.

Thorn's eyes snapped open to a bright, clear morning. He sucked in a breath, realizing he'd grown used to this thin, cold air; it cleared his head, and he needed that. He'd dreamed again, and that pounding was back behind his eyes; he'd been a leopard, dragging an antelope high into a tree.

His nostrils twitched. Headache or no, the gamy scent of flesh was enticing, and he rolled over to see a dead ground squirrel at his side, along with a small pile of marula nuts and wizened figs. Ravenously, he grabbed a random handful of the fruits and began to eat.

He was just picking the last scraps off the squirrel's bones when he heard the rush of wings, and Windrider flapped down to his side.

"You look much recovered this morning, Thorn Greatfather."

"Thorn *Highleaf*, and yes, I do feel better." He glanced at her gratefully. "Thank you."

She dipped her head a fraction. "Now follow me."

She took off and flew low up a craggy slope, and Thorn turned to follow. He'd almost forgotten his injured leg; he lurched and stumbled, but righted himself. It still ached, but the pain was blunted now and much more bearable; the long, fevered time on this mountain must have healed his leg, at least to a degree.

More carefully this time Thorn limped up the incline, his paws slipping on loose scree, his underused muscles stinging with effort. Windrider touched down now and again, hopping across rocks, as if making sure he could keep up.

She vanished over a ridge of sharp stone, and Thorn stumbled after her. Halting, he stared around.

The crater in the mountain's crest was almost circular, its floor covered with smooth white stones and pebbles. Right in the center of it lay a still pool, sunlight sparkling from its surface. As Thorn watched, the water began to bubble, air popping on its surface, and a strange and unpleasant odor drifted to his nose: dank and noisome, like eggs that had lain too long in an abandoned nest.

Thorn felt the fur on his neck rise, and his hide began to prickle. This place felt ancient, and somehow sacred, as if it held unseen spirits. It was far, far older even than the vulture who stood over the pool, his feathers ragged, sparse, and gray.

The old bird raised his deeply creased head and eyed him, but he said nothing. Beside him, Windrider spread her wings. "Come forward, Thorn. Stand with Grayfeather and drink from the pool."

Thorn shut one eye, sniffing skeptically at the air. "Why?"

At last Grayfeather himself spoke. His voice was reedy and harsh. "Every Great Parent drinks from this water. It seals the pact you must make with the Great Spirit."

Shaking his head slowly, Thorn backed away. "Windrider. Grayfeather. I'm sorry." He took a breath, almost choking on the pool's reek. "I don't know how I can be any clearer. You'll just have to accept that I'm not doing this. My duty is to my troop, and only my troop. Do you understand?"

Grayfeather's eyes gleamed, hard and angry. "It is you, Thorn Highleaf, who does not understand."

"I understand very well. I know I'm disappointing you." Thorn turned his gaze to Windrider. "And I thank you for saving my life. But I need to go home now. I've been gone too long."

The two vultures turned to each other, their eyes unreadable. For a moment Thorn held his breath. Then Windrider turned back to pin him with her gaze.

"Then go," she said. "But know, Thorn, that if you do not reconcile yourself to your destiny, it will find you anyway. It will overwhelm you, and the fate it brings you will be a far worse one."

"I'll take the chance," said Thorn.

"Then we can no longer help you." Windrider turned her face to the sun and spread her great wings, letting the breeze stir them. She flapped into the air as Grayfeather turned without a word and hobbled away.

Thorn's eyes creased as he stared up at the vulture. "Does that mean you won't fly me back down this mountain?"

Windrider said nothing at all. Her wings caught a current of mountain air, and the tips twitched. She banked, soared past Thorn, and vanished beyond the barren ridge.

CHAPTER 9

Fearless squeezed his eyes tighter shut, irritation gnawing at his insides. With luck, the pride would be convinced by his pretense of sleep. The late afternoon sunlight slanted beneath his acacia tree, almost as if it was trying to pry his eyes open, and he made a muffled growl in his throat.

His faked slumber had worked, thank the Great Spirit; no other lion had approached him. Letting one eyelid crack open, he peered cautiously around. Yes, there was that awful Mighty, snuggling up to his sister. Valor rolled lazily onto her flank, batting at the big lion's ear with a paw, and he stretched his jaws in a mock bite, gently mauling her muzzle. Valor's tongue came out to lick his jaw.

Yuck. Fearless curled his lip. The pair of them were acting like stupid cubs. It was undignified and *embarrassing.* If they could see themselves from where Fearless was lying, they'd—

As Mighty laughed at something Valor said, the big lion twisted around, and his idle gaze landed on Fearless. Quickly Fearless shut his eye again.

He found himself breathing hard. Had they been talking about him? *Laughing* at him?

"Hey, Fearless." Gracious sauntered past, close to his nose, and swished her tail playfully at his flank. "Are you all right? You don't seem at all like yourself."

"I don't know what you mean," grunted Fearless.

Refusing to pay Gracious any attention, he glared past her slender legs at Mighty and Valor. Mighty was standing up, stretching out his forelegs, shaking his golden mane. He gave a brief, deep roar.

"I want to go hunting," he announced.

Typical, thought Fearless sullenly. *He never* needs *to do anything, he just* wants *to.*

Valor got to her paws, then clawed lazily at the bark of an acacia. "Good idea. I'll come."

Mighty cast an inviting look around at the other lions. "I know a promising bit of ground, and we can easily get there before sunset."

Tough rose eagerly, and Hardy gave Rough and his two cubs an affectionate lick before padding toward Mighty and Valor. Fearless lay glaring at his sister's new mate.

Mighty was a fine lion, he supposed: he'd just hit his prime, and he was powerfully built, with broad shoulders, a glowing coat, and a luxuriant golden mane. *Of course Valor likes him; they'll make strong, healthy cubs together.* Fearless sniffed with disdain. *But that doesn't mean he can prance about like he leads Fearlesspride.*

Gracious had turned away from him, and she bounded toward the others. "Keen, are you coming? What about you, Fearless?" She gazed back, her eyes bright and hopeful. "It'll be fun!"

Fearless gave an emphatic yawn. "I've got my own hunting plans," he growled.

Valor nuzzled Mighty's ear—Fearless suppressed another disgusted shudder—then padded casually over to her brother. Her expression was amiable as she leaned down, but her voice came out in a low snarl.

"What's the matter with you? We can all learn something from an experienced lion like Mighty."

"I don't need to *learn* anything from anyone," Fearless growled back. "This is my pride, not his!"

Rising, he stalked off, but stifled an irritated growl as he saw Keen sauntering toward him. He wanted to be *alone.*

"You should go with Mighty," Fearless snapped.

Keen looked surprised—and a little hurt—but he slouched reluctantly toward the gathering hunters. Fearless could hear Valor's paws again, trotting briskly after him.

His sister slowed and matched his stride, giving him a sidelong glare. "Stop sulking, you ridiculous lion."

"I'm not sulking!" he snarled.

"How long have I known you? I know what your sulks are like. *Epic.*"

Black fury choked him. "I don't see why everyone's padding along with Mighty all the time! We don't even know anything about him. We don't know where he came from, what he's really like, if we can trust him—"

"What?" Valor halted, baring her fangs. "Mighty is noble, he's strong, and he's done nothing but treat you with respect! He hasn't tried to challenge you, even though you're younger than him and you've barely got any mane!"

"'Hasn't challenged me'?" snarled Fearless. "What's that supposed to mean?"

"It's not *supposed* to mean *anything*." She laid her ears back, exasperated. "It's a fact!"

He couldn't argue, which was infuriating. "Well, why did you deceive me, Valor? Why did you go sneaking around with Mighty and lying about where you were?"

"Why?" Valor looked him up and down, disdainfully. "Because I *knew* you'd react like this. You're so defensive and prickly and—and paranoid!" She turned and raised a paw to set off back to her mate, but threw a last growl over her shoulder. "And I certainly don't need protection from *you*, little brother."

Fearless's gut churned with fury. Valor had stalked off without even giving him time to come up with a retort. Hackles bristling, he marched off in the opposite direction.

"Fearless, wait!" Keen trotted after him.

"No, go with Mighty like all the others. I'm fine on my own!"

"I want to come with *you*," insisted Keen. "Mighty's got plenty on his team. You don't."

"His team?" Startled, Fearless felt the pitch of his rage

quaver. He swallowed hard. "Keen, am I losing the pride?"

"Of course you aren't," Keen told him firmly. "You're decisive, you lead the hunts well, you think of new ideas. . . ." He hesitated for a moment, then shrugged. "They get a bit unnerved when you talk about the Great Spirit, that's all."

"That's their problem," growled Fearless. "Lions are so *arrogant*, always thinking they're the rulers of Bravelands and they don't need anyone's help."

"I agree with you," soothed Keen. "Lions have always strutted around like we own the place. I suppose it's how we are."

"Well, it's time we all realized there are greater powers than us at play," grunted Fearless. It was unsettling that Keen was undermining his bad mood. "But I don't expect you to understand the Great Spirit."

Keen twitched his tail, looking offended. "Why wouldn't I? Aren't I as clever as you?"

"That's not what I meant—"

"It doesn't matter anyway." Keen shook himself haughtily. "As you've said yourself, there's no Great Parent around to talk to about it."

"Look, I'm sorry I said that." Fearless came to a halt, remorseful. "Keen, there might not be a Great Parent—but there's someone who I think can help."

"Oh yes?" Keen flicked an ear forward.

"Come on. We're going to see a friend of mine." Fearless set off at an energetic trot. "He always gives good advice."

* * *

Odd, thought Fearless with a ripple of unease; he would have expected sentries to have been posted at the boundaries of Tall Trees. Yet not a single brown tail flicked among the trees, and there was no chitter of alarm calls from the branches above him.

Slowing his pace, he picked his way through the trees, pushing undergrowth and creepers aside. Behind him he could hear Keen's uncertain pawsteps and his nervous breathing.

"Is that *blood*?" murmured Keen.

Halting, Fearless raised his head and flared his nostrils. Keen was right: there was a hot, stony tang drifting from the depths of the forest.

"Oh no," he growled, and began to trot faster through the scrub.

He hadn't gone far when he caught sight of snapped branches; below them lay a baboon, its limbs sprawled at unnatural angles. Its jaws were drawn back in a death-grimace. Just beyond it, another lay facedown; his heart pounding, Fearless pawed it over onto its back. It wasn't a baboon he recognized. But when he bounded ahead to the next corpse, slumped against a fig trunk, he drew in a shocked breath; this was Leaf, a Brightforest baboon.

"What happened?" asked Keen, gaping at the carcasses.

"I don't know." Fearless sprang over a fallen log and ran on past more bodies. The smell of death seemed to be everywhere now, permeating all of Tall Trees, and it was growing stronger. At last, Fearless burst into the Crown Stone clearing.

With screeching and hoots of alarm, baboons scattered before him, leaping for the trees. A big female swung around, hunching her shoulders and baring her fangs defensively, but as her eyes met the lion's, she visibly relaxed.

"It's all right, everyone!" she called. "It's only Fearless."

"Hello, Mango," he greeted her. He twitched his tail in agitation. "Something's wrong, what is it?"

But before Mango could reply, Berry Highleaf bounded toward them. "Fearless!" she cried, as some of the fleeing baboons began to make their way down from the trees. Her eyes looked strained, and her paws shook a little as she stroked his shoulder. "It's good to see you, old friend."

More of the older baboons clustered around him now, stroking his legs and neck and chittering in subdued greeting. "Moss. Lily," he growled affectionately. "Nut! It's good to see all of you, too. But the bodies back there—something terrible has happened, that's clear."

"We'll explain. Who's this?" Nut angled a wary look behind Fearless.

"This is Keen Fearlesspride. He's my friend." Fearless nodded at the young lion, whose eyes were wide with nervous awe.

"If he's your friend, he's welcome," said Berry. Her shoulders drooped. "I'm sorry we can't be more hospitable. You're right, it is a very bad time for us, Fearless. Nut, there are more wounded who need to be taken to the Goodleaves—"

"I'm on it. See you later, Fearless." The scar-faced baboon nodded and loped away.

Fearless stared after him. Whatever had gone on, it was

serious enough that Nut hadn't even tried to make any snide or clever remarks. Fearless's heart chilled.

A smaller baboon pushed through the others; Fearless noticed he was wincing with every step. "Mud." He nuzzled him gently. "Tell me what happened?"

"We were attacked," Mud told him, his eyes tormented. "Oh, I wish you'd been here yesterday, Fearless." As another baboon squeezed past him to take a look at the lions, Mud flinched again.

Craning around to peer at his little friend's back, Fearless gave a grunt of shock. Mud's hide was covered in vicious scratches and cuts.

"This is terrible," growled Fearless. "Mud, I'm sorry. I wish I'd been here, too. Is Thorn all right?"

The silence that greeted his question was heavy enough to send a claw of fear into his gut. Berry and Mud exchanged a miserable look.

"I . . ." began Berry, and gulped. She put her paws over her mouth and stared at the grass, blinking. Once again, she tried to speak and failed. A small whimper came from her throat.

Mud's whole body was shaking, and his jaws opened and closed several times in distress. "Thorn is . . . Fearless, we think—we think he's dead."

"No!" Fearless froze, his heart clenching painfully. "No, Mud, *how?*"

"We don't know," whimpered the small baboon. "We haven't found his body yet. Probably scavengers took it before we'd started the search." He gave a strangled cry of grief. "It was chaotic. We should have looked for Thorn sooner, but the battle—"

"It's not your fault, Mud." Fearless nuzzled the top of the little baboon's head. "Oh, I'm so sorry. *Thorn.*"

He could only stand in silence, letting Mud hug his leg as he comforted him. Fearless wasn't sure he could move at all. His rib cage felt as if it was squeezing his heart to pulp. *He was my friend since I was a cub. I've known him my whole life. We'd just survived the Great Battle, found each other again—*

"I should have been here." His roar was desolate. He squeezed his eyes shut, clenching his jaws. "Mud, Berry. Is there anything I can do for the troop? For either of you? I want to help."

Drawing away from him, Mud gazed up into Fearless's face. The small baboon's eyes were huge, dark, and despairing.

"It's too late, Fearless. There's nothing any of us can do for anyone." Mud sank to the ground, his face in his paws. "The Great Spirit has abandoned us all."

CHAPTER 10

There was something ominous about the sky, a yellow stain of dullness that made it heavy and threatening. Dust from the dry savannah hung in the air; Sky was raising more of it as she trudged across the grassland. A little behind her, the two cheetah cubs plodded wearily; she could make out their movements when she glanced back, but they were hard to see, almost lost in the cloudy haze.

As Sky turned to face forward again, her foot dragged against a big stone, sending it rolling and bumping across the ground. A sand-colored snake darted from the empty hollow in a panic, skittering for cover. *If I'd been faster, I could have stamped on that*, she thought. It would have made a meal for Nimble and Lively. But Sky wasn't fast, and she wasn't a hunter. She wouldn't know how to go after it now.

"Keep going, you two," she called back to the cubs, trying

to be cheerful. "You're doing so well."

The poor little cats looked exhausted, their tails and fluffy heads drooping. They'd long ago lost interest in chasing pebbles. The three of them had been trekking across Bravelands for days, and although Sky had found beetles and grubs for them, lodged in the branches she tore down for herself, she knew the cubs must be terribly hungry. They couldn't eat leaves or branches or even the softer shoots of grass; they needed flesh, and they needed it soon.

If it hadn't been for the occasional scuffed and windblown footprint in the dry earth, Sky knew she might have given up hope of finding Rock. But whenever she felt like doing just that, she would come across another huge print that could only be his, or she would catch an elusive scent of his dark, leafy musk. Breathing it in, she would feel hope surge within her, and on she would plod, the two cubs limping along at her heels.

His tracks were still going in the direction they were traveling, and that was a cheering piece of luck after so many misfortunes. If it diverged, Sky decided, she would give up Rock's trail for now; the important thing was to find the little cheetahs' aunts. But for now, the coincidence of her two purposes was a happy one.

"Do you remember antelope, Lively?" Behind her, Nimble's voice was weak.

"Oh yes," said Lively, faint and longing. "It was juicy."

"And big," said Nimble. "There was always too much."

"Mother used to catch those gazelles too, you know? The

ones whose tails never stopped moving. They were funny to watch."

"We used to lie in the grass and watch them and you couldn't see their tails, they were spinning so fast." Nimble gave a throaty giggle. "They were so quick too. Mother didn't always catch them."

"And we never would." Lively was suddenly forlorn. "I miss Mother so much."

Sky's heart constricted as the two cubs fell silent again. The poor little things. *I had to bring them with me; there was nothing else I could have done.* Left with their dead mother, they would certainly have starved, or been hunted and killed themselves. With her they had a chance.

The horizon ahead wobbled and shimmered in the heat, and it was hard to make out distinct shapes, but Sky was sure there was something there in the middle distance: a great, dark, humped shape. Was it Rock? Her heart thumping with renewed hope, she flapped her ears forward and picked up her pace.

But the shape lay so still, she realized with dread as she drew closer. And it was surrounded by feasting hyenas, a seething mass of brown-and-black bodies that squabbled and tore and growled. *Oh,* she thought, *please don't let that be Rock. . . .*

Breaking into a trot, she raised her trunk and let out a bellow, startling the hyenas. They froze for a moment, then scattered. As they bolted away from the corpse, she stamped her feet in a thunder of warning; the last hopeful stragglers twisted and raced away, vanishing over a low hill.

With trepidation she strode toward the remains, but a dizzying wave of relief swept over her as she saw that her fears were groundless. It was a huge bull buffalo, its eye sockets wide and empty. Sprawled on its side, its stiff limbs jutted out oddly. Strips of hide and flesh had been ripped from its flank, and its splayed legs had been gnawed, but that was down to the hyenas: the wounds looked fresh, and not fatal. No, the wound that had killed it was the great raw gash in its rib cage, clotted with dried blood. The buffalo's chest had been torn open along the breastbone.

The wound. It's just like Rush's. Instinctively, Sky flinched back.

The cubs were bounding after her, their eyes wide, but at the corner of her vision Sky was aware of much larger, creeping shadows. The hyenas were recovering their nerve and prowling closer.

"Those look delicious," growled one of them.

"Mmmm. Cubs," agreed another. "Little ones."

"Mouthfuls, but such tender flesh."

Hurriedly, Sky beckoned the cubs under the protection of her shadow, pulling them close with her trunk. "Stay away!" she commanded the hyenas.

"They'd be nicer than that buffalo corpse," murmured another. "It tasted funny."

"Even the vultures wouldn't touch it," yowled a big female, shaking her head and smacking her jaws as if to dislodge the taste. "Little cat-cubs would be better."

"I said stay away!" trumpeted Sky, flapping her ears in warning.

Yet they stalked cautiously closer, their eyes bright with hunger. Sky turned, jerking her tusks to drive back a pair that were sneaking up from behind.

"That buffalo does smell funny," chirped Nimble from between her legs. "I don't think we can eat it anyway."

"Nimble's right," agreed Lively. "I don't think it's good, Sky."

Sky was inclined to think the same. There was something wrong and sinister about this death, just as Rush's fatal wound had made her skin prickle. Nodding to the cubs, Sky brushed their fluffy heads with her trunk-tip, then raised it once more in angry challenge to the hyenas. "We won't touch your carrion. Just get away from us. Leave these cubs alone!"

But as she swung her head to threaten one group, another four charged in from her flank. Their jaws hung wide, tongues lolling with anticipation, drool flying from their fangs. Urgently, Sky thrust out her trunk toward the twisting, panicking cubs. "Quick. Up here!"

Nimble leaped, digging his tiny claws into her skin as he scrambled up; Lively was right behind him. Their scratches were no worse than a prickly twig, and Sky let the two cubs run right up her trunk and over her face till they were crouched on top of her head, peering out between her ears. Turning once again to the hyenas at her flank, Sky lifted a foot and stamped it down, hard enough to make the ground tremble.

"Get back!"

Thwarted, the hyenas prowled in a circle, glowering at her. "Not fair," snarled a big male who seemed to be their leader.

"Too bad," harrumphed Sky, her heartbeat slowing at last. "Go back to your rot-flesh. You're not getting these cubs."

Grumbling, the hyenas drew back. Sky could hear their muttered insults—"Great lumbering brute" being one of the kinder ones—but she ignored them all and trudged away, letting the pack slink back sulkily to the dead buffalo.

When they were out of earshot and the cubs had shuffled to a more secure perch between her shoulders, she murmured gently to them, "Stay there, you two. We have to press on, and you'll be safer on my back."

"Sky!" squeaked Lively, and Sky felt the cub's tiny body stiffen with excitement. "Look!"

Her steps faltering, Sky cocked her ears and peered ahead. Sand was blown into a layer of dust, and heat distorted the far hills, but something large was definitely visible in the distance: a dark, swaying shape. That was no dead buffalo.

She swallowed hard. "Hold tight, cubs," she rasped as she broke into a trot.

She couldn't let her hopes rise again, only to be dashed in the arid dust. *It might not be him. It's too much to hope for—*

But that tall form was so distinctive, and as she drew closer, so was his unusually dark hide, even though it was stained and mottled with yellow sand. Sky lifted her trunk and blared, then called his name desperately through her dry throat.

"Rock!"

And as the elephant hesitated and turned, she saw his long, creamy tusks, and their recognizable, slightly uneven curve.

"Rock!"

"Sky?" His astonished cry drifted to her across the desolate landscape.

Sky broke into a canter, and Rock ran toward her. They met in a swirling cloud of sand, entwining their trunks, butting their heads gently together. Sky let herself lean into his strong body, feeling the warmth of his skin and the thud of his excited heartbeat.

"Rock! We've found you at last!"

"Sky," he rumbled, caressing her shoulder with his trunk. "I thought I heard you cry out. I couldn't believe it."

"Is this him?" squeaked a voice from Sky's back. "Is this the elephant you were looking for, Sky?"

Startled, Rock stepped back, peering at the two cubs who were clambering up onto Sky's head once again. "Who are—"

"These are Rush's cubs," said Sky softly, curling her trunk up to stroke them. "Do you remember our cheetah friend, Rock?"

"Of course I do." His green eyes grew troubled. "So, Rush—?"

"Rush has gone to run among the stars," murmured Sky. She lowered her voice still further, so that the excited cubs would not hear her soft-pitched rumble. "She was killed, Rock. But no flesh-eater devoured her. Her chest was torn—"

He swung his trunk in agitation. "Another one? Sky, I came across a jackal with the same death-wound. She wasn't eaten either. Except—" He glanced anxiously at the cubs.

"The heart," whispered Sky.

"Yes." Rock's murmur was so deep, it was like a distant rumble of falling boulders.

On Sky's head, she could feel the cubs bouncing and rolling, reenergized by the appearance of this strange and mighty friend of Sky. *They aren't even listening*, Sky realized. *Thank the Great Spirit.*

"Who is making these dreadful kills, Rock?" she murmured. "It isn't natural."

"It certainly breaks the Code," he rumbled quietly. "And to mutilate the bodies like that? What creature would do such a thing?"

"A creature living in a land without a Great Parent," she whispered sadly. "Something isn't right, Rock. It disturbs me."

"Things have been wrong in Bravelands since we lost Great Mother," he said grimly.

Sky twitched her trunk in silent agreement. On her head, the cubs had quieted once again. "Where are you heading, Rock?" she asked, in a more normal voice.

"Nowhere in particular." He nuzzled her brow with his trunk-tip. "I don't especially want to rejoin my brothers, not yet. I'd rather keep company with you, Sky Strider."

Her heart soared. It was what she had hoped for, and more. "You'll stay with us?"

"I'll follow you, wherever you go," he said. "These cubs look a heavy responsibility, for such little things."

"I won't keep them with me forever," said Sky, feeling an

odd sadness. "I'm going to find a guardian for them—one more suitable than me."

"Then I'll help you." Rock watched Nimble and Lively with amusement as they scrambled and hopped down Sky's trunk. Bouncing onto the ground, they capered around his enormous feet, unafraid, and he stayed very still for a moment. Then, tentatively, he swatted gently at them with his trunk, and they batted him back, flopping onto the ground, rolling and dodging.

"They're sweet," he chuckled.

"They are," agreed Sky warmly. "You look less tired, cubs. Shall we go on?"

"Let's!" they chorused, with enthusiastic squeals.

"Then climb back onto me, Lively. Nimble, perhaps you can ride on Rock? We'll move faster that way." Sky glanced questioningly at Rock, and he nodded swiftly.

As they trudged on toward the horizon, Sky felt her heart lighten with every step. Rock was a strong, reassuring presence, it was true, but it wasn't just safety she felt: it was happiness, and a deep and calm contentment.

The Great Spirit might have left them, she thought. Bravelands might be without its eternal protector and heart.

But perhaps those of us who live here can still find happiness.

CHAPTER 11

The Great Spirit was wasting its time, thought Thorn; worse, it was wasting all its power and benevolence. What was it doing, nestling uselessly inside a baboon who *didn't even want it?* Anxious and angry, he limped on across the savannah, dragging branches aside, scrambling exhaustedly up rocky slopes, and sliding clumsily down again.

His fur was clogged with sand and dried mud, and his paws were scuffed and raw from the hard stone of the mountain. *Those wretched vultures might at least have flown me down.* His leg was able to bear weight, but a constant, throbbing ache pulsed through the limb, and whenever he paused to rest it stiffened, making it even sorer to walk on again.

None of that mattered as much as his fear for his troop. If the vultures had had any way of discovering how the battle against Tendril had ended, they hadn't made an effort to find out. And if they *had* heard, they certainly hadn't let him know. Now Thorn struggled home across jagged stone and hard-packed earth without even knowing if his friends would be alive to greet him.

Maybe he should have done as the vultures had asked. *If I'd drunk from that stinking pool, they'd have flown me home.*

Instead, the stuck-up, self-important, petulant feather-flappers had left him to find his own way. Even from high on the mountain's slopes, Tall Trees had been beyond the reach of Thorn's vision; now, in the barren foothills, it seemed to Thorn that he'd never see it again. The Bravelands savannah stretched in a pale, dry expanse to a faraway horizon blurred by heat haze. The only trees in sight were spiky lone acacias, their tops flattened by sun and wind. What wouldn't he give right now for the verdant, humid greenness of a proper forest?

I hate vultures.

"Murderer! Savage!"

The high trilling shrieks shocked him to a frozen standstill.

"*Killer!* We hate you!"

Whoever it was, they weren't talking to Thorn. The chittering and jabbering came from just beyond the next rocky slope; the creatures sounded too small to be really dangerous, and Thorn's curiosity was piqued. In a limping lope he climbed up and peered over the ridge. His eyes widened.

A mob of some twenty meerkats were clustered around a hollow, tall and skinny, balanced on their ridiculous stiff tails. They were all sharp little noses and even sharper teeth, and their big black eyes glittered with fury. Peering harder,

Thorn could see the object of their anger; they were harrying some poor creature on the ground, a huddled shape of patchy brown fur. The meerkats reared upright on their hind legs, then dashed in to scratch and bite before scuttling back to let the next rank have their go. The smaller and more timid ones darted between the others to chitter and snap at the cowering animal. A chorus of piping filled the air: "Killer! Killer! Rotten brute!"

Thorn peeled back his upper lip and sniffed the air. The creature on the ground was a lot bigger than the meerkats, but it wasn't fighting back, and given their numbers and the sheer violent rage on their little faces, Thorn didn't blame it. It seemed concerned only with curling into as small a ball as possible, to protect its face and belly. Taking a careful pace forward and narrowing his eyes, Thorn at last made out what it was.

A baboon!

It was a stranger of course, not one of his own troop, but instinctive protectiveness seized him. Bounding over the ridge, Thorn plowed in among the meerkat clan, swiping left and right, sending them tumbling and fleeing. Baring his teeth, he snarled at the ones who hesitated, until they too squealed and bolted.

"Another! Another killer!" they shrieked and babbled. "Brute, nasty brute!"

At last Thorn stood alone beside the huddled baboon, a circle of wary meerkats staring at him. He turned a slow circle, glowering.

"*What* is going on here?"

"This!" squeaked the biggest meerkat and the likely leader, pointing at the huddled baboon. "*This* is going on!"

"Stay out of it!" A smaller meerkat bounded forward, emboldened, though at the last moment it ducked and half hid behind its leader.

"A murderer!"

"Nasty!"

"Mean!"

"Not acceptable!"

"KILLER BABOON!" A dramatic, high-pitched wail rose above the rest, and every meerkat turned to gape at the screamer. It was a ridiculously tiny meerkat. Realizing suddenly that his friends were staring, he shuffled backward, looking embarrassed.

"*Nasty mean baboon?*" echoed Thorn, turning back in perplexity to the leader. "That's just an insult. It doesn't explain *anything.*"

The big meerkat only shrugged, but his whole mob started squealing again.

"That thing attacked us!"

"Attack one, you attack us all!"

"Killer killer killer!"

Thorn clenched his jaw, sympathetic but exasperated. If the meerkats would just calm down and explain properly, he might be able to help, but they were wound up to a hysterical pitch of rage. And their big leader simply stood there, looking self-righteous, letting his mob do all the shrieking.

"Let me try to understand," sighed Thorn patiently. "I take it this baboon killed one of your mob?"

The big meerkat still didn't utter a word. He gave a single, emphatic nod, and the whole clan erupted once again.

"*Yes!*" they chorused. "Well said, Skip!"

"You tell him, boss!"

"We're right behind you!"

At Thorn's feet, the bundle of scabby fur stirred. A baboon's eyes appeared, peering out cautiously between his paws.

"Not me," he rasped. "Not me, no indeed. Spider is innocent."

"And who's Spider?" demanded Thorn, bewildered.

"*Me.* I'm Spider and I didn't do it."

Thorn stared down at him. This Spider was an odd-looking creature. His matted fur was patched with bare spots, his fingers scabbed and mottled with strange, pale-pink scars. His huge eyes peered up into Thorn's, pleading but somehow pessimistic.

"I really didn't," he added.

"It *was* you!" Skip the meerkat leader reared up tall and pointed a miniature claw in accusation. "You've been stalking us!"

"Stalking us!" echoed the chorus behind him.

"Prowling around our burrows!"

"Prowling!"

"Maybe I *have.*" The scabby-looking baboon lurched to his paws, suddenly indignant. "But what's wrong with watching, eh? I was just *looking.*"

"Looking!" accused the mob, scandalized. *"Looking!"*

"There you are." Skip nodded firmly to Thorn, as if Spider's confession clinched it.

"See here, you tiny rat-monkey-things," said Spider, sounding offended. "I'm not a Codeless killer."

Thorn rubbed his head hard with a paw. "I don't understand any of this," he muttered. "Who was killed?"

"We'll show you," declared Skip. "Then you'll see." He sniffed and muttered, *"Rat-monkey-things,* eh? We're going to kill him right back."

Rather wishing he'd never got involved, Thorn followed the big meerkat anyway, around a slope that was pockmarked with burrows and down into a shallow rocky dip. Spider followed him, and behind the mangy baboon came the whole clan of meerkats, bobbing and bounding and squeaking.

"There," said Skip, flinging out a paw with an air of satisfaction.

Cautiously, Thorn padded down to the limp form at the bottom of the hollow. The dead meerkat lay on its back, paws splayed, staring up at the sky with an expression that was more startled than terrified. In the sky above the corpse, pied crows flapped and swooped, waiting.

Thorn crouched and gently touched the little creature's chest. It was ripped down the breastbone, its rib cage cavity exposed, the blood clotting and drying in the sun.

"But nobody has eaten it," he muttered, half to himself.

"No, Bad Baboon wasn't hungry," declared Skip. "You see now? Broke the Code!"

"Of course he doesn't see!" exploded Spider. "He doesn't see because it isn't true and it makes no sense, *rat-monkey*."

"Why you—" Skip drew himself up, raising his tiny claws.

"Calm down, will you?" Thorn glared at them both, exasperated. "Skip, just wait and think. Does Spider look as if he eats well?" He spread his paws questioningly, then gestured at Spider's jutting ribs. "No. Come on, Skip. If he'd killed your friend, he'd have eaten him."

"Too right," muttered Spider.

He wasn't helping, Thorn thought, as he took a deep, patient breath. "I really think you've got the wrong culprit," he told the meerkat gently. "Your friend was quite small, Skip. Any flesh-eater could have done this to him. A—a bird; one of those crows, even. Or a jackal, or a hyena—" He stopped. That reminded him. The meerkat's wound looked a bit like what had been done to the hyena back at Tall Trees. "Any creature, really. It's not Spider's fault he was around at the wrong time."

"*Well*." Skip drew himself up to his full height, looking furious and offended. "*Well*. I suppose you might be *right*."

"Might be right." The disappointed murmur rippled around the mob.

"What's more," added Spider, "I don't even *like* meerkat. Give me a good crunchy locust. Locusts are better than meerkats in every way."

"*Meerkats* are better than *locusts*!" cried Skip, enraged. He hunched his back, coiling his muscles to attack, and behind him his mob crouched to pounce.

"All right," said Thorn hastily, flapping his paws. He didn't know Spider, but he certainly couldn't believe the scrawny baboon would kill a juicy meerkat and leave it uneaten in the sun. "I'll tell you what, Skip." Thorn dipped his head respectfully. "I shall take this Spider back to my troop at Tall Trees, and together we will get to the bottom of this. If we judge that he's guilty, we'll give him baboon justice. Will that satisfy you?"

Skip hesitated, narrowing his eyes, while Spider eyed him with misgiving. When the meerkat finally gave a jerky, slightly pompous nod, the baboon's breath rushed out in relief.

"Well, aren't I glad you came along, stranger." Spider patted Thorn's shoulder. "That would have been a *really* humiliating way to die."

"My name's Thorn. And Skip—don't worry. Our new Starleaf has great abilities, and he'll be able to tell straight away if Spider has broken the Code." He hoped the lie didn't show in his face. *Mud might not be the Starleaf. Mud might even be dead.*

"Baboon justice? Good, good. That sounds good." Skip was nodding vigorously, and Thorn had the feeling he was secretly relieved to have the job taken out of his paws. The big meerkat turned and strutted away, tail high, and his mob fell in behind him, jabbering their approval of their leader.

"Justice, yes, good! Good!"

"Skip wins again! Noble Skip! Hurray!"

"Come on, Spider," muttered Thorn. "Let's get you out of here." But at that moment, one of the last meerkats turned back, glaring.

"Hey, *weirdo*. You forgot your thing."

With her tiny paws, she scooted an object to the sand

at their paws; it rolled and clunked against a stone. Spider snatched it up, but not before Thorn had made out what it was: a polished, translucent lump of white rock.

Spider hurried away ahead of Thorn, clutching the stone to his chest. "Spider really didn't kill Skitter, you know," he said plaintively. "I didn't."

"I believe you." Thorn smiled wryly at Spider's hastily retreating rump. "Honestly, you don't have to convince me."

The baboon half turned his head and muttered, "Spider was only trying to be his friend."

"All right," sighed Thorn. "Wait, what?"

"He'd have made a nice friend," said Spider, nodding as Thorn caught up and walked at his side. "A little scared at first, but I soon put him at his ease and he hardly tried to run away at all. See, Spider can even speak like a meerkat." He peeled back his muzzle and erupted into a chattering babble of nonsense. "Killer! Ooh, cozy burrow! Bugs, bugs, bugs!"

"Why couldn't you just make friends with other baboons?" asked Thorn, amused. Spider *did* sound just like a meerkat. "It would be easier, you know."

"Why would I do that?" Spider shrugged.

"Because, uh . . . you're a baboon?"

"I suppose I am. But Spider likes meerkats. I would never kill a meerkat. It's like I said, I prefer locusts."

Spider was making Thorn's head spin, so he shook it hard. "Where's your troop?" he asked kindly.

"Spider doesn't have a troop. I'm on my own. I *like* it that way."

"Except you were trying to make friends with a meerkat." Thorn hesitated. "Are you *sure* you didn't kill him? Maybe by accident?"

Spider shook his head vigorously. "No, no, no. Spider wasn't anywhere near Skitter. Oh, here's another of my friends, and I wouldn't kill him either. Hello there, Choot-Choot."

An oxpecker flapped down, landed on the baboon's scabby neck, and began to peck busily for parasites. It kept one wary, white-rimmed eye on Thorn as it hunted, but it seemed quite at home on Spider's hide, and the baboon whistled and trilled to it. He wasn't speaking Skytongue; Thorn was all too aware of *that*. Spider was just mimicking the bird's calls, and doing it unnervingly well.

"Spider hasn't met another baboon in a *long* time," Spider said at last, when he seemed to tire of his meaningless conversation with the oxpecker. "Glad to meet you, Thorn, I'm sure."

"But where were you born?" asked Thorn, bewildered. "You must have had a troop once."

"Spider doesn't remember." He shrugged.

"So who named you?" Thorn pressed him.

"Spider chose Spider all by himself. Because he had a spider-friend. Used to spin webs over my fingers at night. Mm-hm. I liked her."

Thorn shot a sidelong glance at his new companion. That meerkat hadn't been far wrong when she called him *weirdo*. "The afternoon's getting late, Spider. The sun will start going down soon, and I can't see much shelter apart from that place." He pointed at a clump of trees ahead. "We should make camp there before dusk starts to fall."

"That would be fine, Thorn-friend."

At least, he thought, meeting and rescuing Spider had made the time pass faster; Thorn had barely registered the trek over the last stretch of dry grassland, and it was good to see proper green woodland once more. "Maybe there's water among the trees."

"Mm-hm. Water might be good."

Yet as they crept into the shadowy and moist undergrowth and followed the trickling sounds of a spring, Spider didn't seem remotely excited. Light shimmered on a rippling green pool, and Thorn fell on it and drank greedily, but Spider hung back, playing idly with his stone.

Thorn rubbed the wet fur around his mouth. "What *is* that thing?"

"Spider will show you." For the first time, the baboon's eyes lit up with enthusiasm.

He scrabbled in the undergrowth with his paws, gathering dead leaves into a pile, picking out the freshest ones, and tossing them away. Experimentally patting the ones that remained, listening to them crunch and crackle, he nodded with satisfaction.

"Look, Thorn-friend." Spider peered up into the branches. It was a small copse, and the canopy wasn't thick; strong beams of slanting sunlight pierced the branches and dappled the forest floor. Fastidiously, Spider lifted his stone and lined it up with one brilliant ray, adjusting it until it sparkled so intensely, Thorn had to shield his eyes.

"Now, you see?" Spider angled the stone a little more. The late sunlight streamed through it, focused to a single, dazzling beam on the pile of dry leaves.

"I don't see anything," complained Thorn. "It's pretty enough, but it's giving me a headache."

"Thorn must wait," scolded Spider.

Thorn sighed. Spider was absolutely motionless now, and he didn't look likely to stir anytime soon. Thorn slumped back against a pine trunk and wriggled to make himself comfortable, his eyelids drooping.

"There!"

"What?" Thorn started, wide awake. He felt his jaw slacken. Spider still stood there, the stone held steady in its focused ray of light, but he was grinning. Wisps of dense mist were rising from the leaves. In the silence, Thorn heard a faint, whispering crackle.

"Spider." Every muscle in his body tensed. This thing, this mist, this noise: Thorn wasn't familiar with it, but it was *bad*. He knew it in his bones. "What's that?"

"Smoke," said Spider. "It's a kind of fog, like you see on the mountaintops in the morning. Spider thinks it's pretty."

"Yes, but can you stop now?"

"No, no, it gets better. Spider promises!"

Despite his uneasiness, Thorn was fascinated. He leaned closer to the leaves, edging his paws forward. He drew back his upper lip and sniffed. "It looks a bit . . . dangerous . . ."

"No, not dangerous. Keep looking." Spider stared at the leaves with eagerness.

The *pop* was so sudden, Thorn tumbled back. Something bright bloomed in the smoke, a dancing leaf of pure orange light. As he stared, terrified, the leaf grew faster than any plant he'd ever seen, rising and blossoming into a blade of hot yellow.

"Stop!" he cried.

"Pretty!" shouted Spider.

A hot breeze gusted through the glade, and the dead leaves glowed violent orange; the living one sparked and grew, and yet more leaves of light erupted around it. They danced in the smoldering smoke, spreading and swelling.

"That is a beautiful and special plant," declared Spider proudly. "It lives in dead things. Also sometimes living things."

"Kill it." Thorn leaped to his paws, feeling his fur rise and prickle as if his whole hide was trying to jump off him. *"Kill it!"*

Spider gave him a puzzled look. Then he shrugged, crouched, and cupped his forepaws around the shining light-leaves.

They sputtered, flickered, and finally died. As tendrils of smoke curled around Spider's fingers, he gently drew them away and raised his palms to Thorn: the hairless flesh was reddened and swollen and beginning to blister. His heart thundering, Thorn sucked in a horrified breath.

But Spider's face was filled with innocent excitement, and he smiled.

"Fire!"

CHAPTER 12

"*I want to tell you about* Thorn Highleaf," rumbled Fearless, sadly. "But I hardly know where to start. He was my friend for so long, Keen."

"I wish I could pretend to understand." Keen gazed at Fearless, his golden eyes soft. "But I do know how important my friends are to me, so I can guess."

"He used to ride on my back when I was patrolling Tall Trees," Fearless went on, barely listening. "And when he hunted, he'd try to bring back as much flesh as he could and save it for me. And he tried to teach me how to climb trees, and he didn't even laugh when I fell out of them. And he was so kind, always covering for our friend Mud, because Mud was weaker. And . . ."

"Fearless," said Keen, clearing his throat, "it's getting late. Don't you think we should be getting back to the pride?"

Fearless, about to tell him a long story about Thorn and a wayward jackal, paused and eyed his friend. Keen looked a little uncomfortable and out of place, lying here among the scrub and tree trunks as baboons settled in the branches overhead for the night.

Fearless swallowed. Of course Keen wouldn't understand; he hadn't known any of these baboons. He probably wondered why Fearless was making such a fuss. "I . . . can't, Keen, not yet. I have one more thing to do before I go back."

"With the baboons?" Keen's voice sounded strained. "They're all going to sleep, Fearless."

"No, it's not that. I agreed to meet Ruthless before sunset. I left a signal."

Keen nodded. "All right. I'll come too."

Fearless hesitated, licking his jaws. "You don't have to come."

"Fearless, I just want to help. I know you're unhappy, because of Thorn. Let me come with you. I won't interfere." The young lion nudged Fearless gently with his head. "I'm learning a lot about you today, my friend. And I want to help you as much as Thorn always did."

Fearless gave a fond rumble in his throat. *Keen does understand, as much as he can.* "All right. Thanks, Keen, I appreciate it."

The plains were shadowed by the onset of night, a blue twilight settling across grass and sky and turning every feature of the landscape to gray silhouette. A glowing line of orange and pink lay on the western horizon, but it was fading fast as the two lions padded toward the distant kopje. The rocks rose black against the emerging stars, looking far more forbidding than they did in daylight, and for a moment Fearless felt a qualm of uncertainty. What if Ruthless wasn't there? The cub had already told Fearless it was growing much harder to sneak away from Titanpride.

But as he and Keen sprang up onto the lower rocks and climbed higher, Fearless caught sight of the young lion. He was no more than a dark shape, standing very still just outside the cavern entrance.

"Ruthless," growled Fearless softly. He loped eagerly up onto the small, bone-strewn plateau.

The cub didn't immediately rush to meet him; he stared at Keen and Fearless, trembling where he stood.

As Fearless took a hesitant pace forward, he realized why and gasped in shock. He stopped.

This was wrong, very wrong. The cub's fur was torn at the shoulder and at the rump; in the moonlight Fearless could see dark blood dribbling from the wounds. Ruthless's foreleg was bleeding badly, and as he tried to take a pace toward Fearless, he lurched and stumbled.

"Fearless!" he grunted, his voice scratchy with panic. "They're here! Run!"

Instantly dark shapes bounded from the den mouth, surrounding Ruthless. Four huge, fully grown lions paced forward, their savage teeth gleaming, their eyes glowing with hate.

Fearless froze, staring from Ruthless to his captors in disbelief and horror. Behind him, he heard Keen give a high, frightened snarl.

One of the adult males stalked forward, shaking his mane. A few lion-lengths from Fearless he halted, slaver dripping from his exposed fangs. "Fearless Treasonpride," he growled. "Well, well."

"Resolute," roared Fearless, recognizing Titan's burly lieutenant. "Let Ruthless go!"

"Oh, I don't think so," growled Resolute. "We know what this brat has been up to, sneaking off to meet with a traitor. That makes him a betrayer of Titanpride, too. He'll pay the price. Just as you will."

"Let him go, or Great Spirit help me, I'll—"

"You'll what?" Resolute's snarl was silky and menacing. He lifted a forepaw and placed it forward, the claws popping out of their sheaths. "Come, then, cub. If you want your friend, come and take him."

"Fearless, no." Keen's warning growl was right at his ear. "That would be suicide. They want you to attack."

Breathing hard, Fearless stared at Resolute and his three huge comrades. He and Keen were so much smaller . . . and Ruthless was badly hurt . . . but if Fearless made a sudden spring, feinted, and lunged at Resolute's leg, he might—

"Fearless!" cried Ruthless, his voice trembling but determined. "Get away from here!"

"Shut up, you." Resolute turned and lashed a paw across the cub's face.

Ruthless shook himself violently and gave an angry snarl. "Go! I'll take my punishment."

"Indeed." Resolute reared up on his hind legs and slammed

his forepaws against Ruthless's shoulder, nearly knocking him to the ground. "I'm looking forward to that, brat."

Ruthless staggered and yowled in fear and rage. "Don't give them what they want, Fearless. Go!"

Fearless shuddered with helpless fury. All he wanted was to leap at Resolute and tear that sadistic smirk from his muzzle, but he couldn't. He couldn't help his friend, or punish his brutal captors. *I'm not grown enough. They'd kill me.*

"I'll see you later, Fearless Treasonpride," called Resolute, turning away and shoving Ruthless into a lurching walk. "You can be sure of it."

The other three Titanpride lions followed Resolute and Ruthless, jumping away down the rocks of the kopje, their tails flicking contemptuously as they vanished. Fearless gave a strangled roar of frustration, then bounded to the edge of the drop and looked down.

He could make them out below, four massive males with rippling manes. Between them Ruthless was a far smaller figure, hemmed in by their powerful bodies as he limped toward his fate. Fearless stood motionless and watched them pad away, far across the plain, until their shadows were swallowed in the darkness.

"I was a coward," he roared. "I should have stopped them."

A little distance away, Rough raised her head, gazing at him with mild surprise and flicking her ears. Realizing there were no enemies in sight, she sank down again into the grass with her cubs.

"Fearless," murmured Keen. "Keep your voice down. And don't torment yourself about this. Ruthless knew the risks."

Fearless glowered at the ground, his head on his forepaws. "I could have rescued him," he snarled. "I could at least have tried."

"No, Fearless, you couldn't." Keen licked his ear. "You'd have met your death. You're the bravest lion I know, but that would just have been stupid."

"So I'm a *clever* coward."

"You're not a coward," said Keen patiently. "There was nothing you could have done."

"Fine. But there was Thorn, too. I could at least have done something for Thorn." Fearless felt a stab of guilt and grief in his chest. "I might not be able to fight grown lions, but I could have taken on a bunch of baboons."

"You didn't know," insisted Keen softly. "How could you have defended Thorn when you didn't know the battle was happening? You've got to stop blaming yourself for things that aren't your fault."

"But what if they—" Fearless stopped, turning his head at the sound of approaching pawsteps.

Mighty's powerful shape loomed out of the darkness, Valor at his flank. Behind them walked the rest of the pride, their movements slow and content, their tails flicking idly. Even from where he lay, Fearless could make out the roundness of their bellies.

"That was a good hunt." Hardy slumped down onto the grass beside Rough and dumped a rack of rib-flesh beside her.

"I don't think I could eat for a moon."

"The size of that eland!" exclaimed Tough. "Honestly, I wouldn't be surprised to see Mighty bring down a bull elephant."

Fearless opened his mouth to snap something derogatory, but Mighty beat him to it. "Oh, don't go on about it," he rumbled modestly. "It's just what lions do, isn't it? It wasn't a big deal."

He stalked closer, and for a horrible moment Fearless thought the bigger lion was going to lunge for him, tear out his throat, and take over the pride on the spot. But the tang of warm blood filled his nostrils as Mighty dropped a chunk of eland-flesh at his nose.

The big lion dipped his head respectfully. "For our pride leader," he said.

Valor gazed admiringly at her mate. Tough, Hardy, and Gracious growled among themselves, their tone approving. Keen flicked his ears forward, looking impressed.

Fearless glared at the meat. Was Mighty mocking him? No, probably not. He was too *good* for that.

Capable. Self-effacing. Modest. Respectful.

Great Spirit, I hate him.

"Is something wrong, Fearless?" Gracious asked anxiously.

"Nothing's wrong," he snapped. "Why would it be wrong? Everything's quiet here. No trouble. We've been just *fine* on our own."

"All right." Gracious backed away, looking nervous.

Fearless ignored them all, even Keen, until he heard them

settle to a contented, full-bellied sleep. Hardy's deep rumbling snores mingled with Rough's lighter ones; Mighty grunted drowsily and rolled even closer to Valor. Rounded, well-fed flanks rose and fell in the moonlight. But Fearless's own head buzzed with wakefulness and irritation.

And guilt, he realized despondently.

He'd failed Ruthless. And he had to find a way to put it right.

CHAPTER 13

Dawn was rising behind Tall Trees as Thorn limped homeward with Spider at his side. A pale yellow glow outlined the treetops, vanquishing the last stars one by one, and from the familiar canopy he could hear the vibrant sunrise song of the birds. A single thrush sang a fluid melody, and was joined in a cresting wave by the trilling and piping of bulbuls and orioles.

"Morning, morning, it's morning . . ."

"The sun is rising, wake up! Sing, sing, sing . . ."

A dove began to coo rhythmically. "Another be-a-utiful day, be-a-utiful . . ."

Thorn wished they'd be quiet. It still shocked him that he could understand their lyrical Skytongue words, and they made him even more uneasy. His heart felt like a stone in his chest.

I don't know yet if there's anyone left in Tall Trees to greet me. Thorn's steps slowed, reluctant with dread, as he stared at the forest.

"I hope they're all right," he muttered to himself. "Oh please, Great Spirit, let them all be safe."

"Well, well, you'll find out soon enough," mumbled Spider, his gaze roving across the grass and the trees. Suddenly, a spark of greed lit his eyes. "Oh, is that a mango tree I can see?"

Thorn shot him a glance, hurt. "I'm more worried about my friends right now."

"Spider knows." The mangy baboon shrugged. "I'm sure you're worried. But Spider also knows that having close friends is more of a nuisance than anything. See how anxious you are? See how stressful it is?"

"You must have cared about somebody in the past," said Thorn, exasperated. "What about your mother? You must have been close to her."

"Spider doesn't remember." He shrugged again. "I might have been. Spider doesn't know."

Thorn set his teeth. It was beginning to grate on his nerves, that habit Spider had of talking about himself as another baboon. "Well, Spider needs to understand that other baboons have feelings—*ahhh!*"

The vision came on him like a thundering cloudburst, swamping all his senses and blotting out the world around him. *He was straddling Stump Middleleaf, gripping him by the throat as he pounded the big baboon's head against the ground.*

Fury washed over Thorn, lending him new urgent strength. Leaning close to Stump's terrified face, Thorn tore at his muzzle with his teeth, drawing blood that splashed into his own eyes. Over and over again he slammed his fists into Stump's chest and head. He couldn't stop. He might want to, but he couldn't; a force far bigger than himself had control of his body and his mind and his temper. Only distantly could he hear the helpless baboon's feeble screams. Those cries didn't matter, and they didn't make Thorn feel any pity. Stump had to die. Stump had to suffer. STUMP HAD TO DIE—

"Thorn-friend! Thorn!" Strong, lanky arms were shaking him, breaking the vision into fragments that blew away on the breeze. "What is it? Spider wants to *know*."

"Wh-what . . ." Dazed, Thorn sat up. His paws were trembling and his head stung as if a thousand bees were loose inside his skull. The hot pain was almost unbearable. Crying out, he clutched his forehead.

"Hmph. That was funny. What happened?" Spider stepped back, tilting his head.

"I . . . don't know." Shaking himself, Thorn staggered to his feet. "Listen, Spider, why don't you, ah . . ." *Ow. This headache, it's the worst yet.* "Why don't you wait here for a while. Stay in those bushes there. I'll go, uh . . . into Tall Trees. See who I can find." In a miserable mutter he added, "If anyone's left."

"All right." Contentedly, Spider crouched in the scrub and began to play with his stone.

Drawing aside a thick veil of creepers, Thorn edged into the forest. He realized he was holding his breath, and as he exhaled shakily, he felt his heart begin to pound almost as painfully as his head.

It was so quiet in here. The birds still chorused, but they seemed very far above Thorn's head, and their song was muffled by the ringing in his ears. *Oh, Berry*, he thought. *Oh, Mud. Please be alive.*

The leaf litter felt soft and damp beneath his paws. It would have been bliss to be back, after the barren bleakness of the mountain and the plains, if not for the gnawing fear in his heart. Thorn gripped a fallen log and clambered over it, his paws slipping on wet moss. The forest smelled richly of damp earth and fungus and rotten wood, but beneath it all there was still a baboon-tang.

That couldn't give him too much hope, Thorn knew. After all, the familiar scent was overlaid with the unmistakable reek of death.

Clenching his jaws, Thorn picked up his pace and bounded across a small glade. The scent was stronger here, powerful enough to pull him forward almost against his will. *What if they're dead?* A snake darted away as he shoved aside branches. Taking a deep breath, he stumbled forward into the Crown Stone clearing.

Baboons. They perched on branches, crouched on rocks, nestled babies against their chests. Every one of them snapped their heads around as he emerged from the undergrowth, and for a moment there was stunned silence. Then a screeching hoot of joy split the air.

"Thorn!"

Berry bounded down from a fig branch and flew into his arms. Right behind her came Mud, with Nut at his heels. As they embraced him, squealing with joy, Thorn could hardly breathe. His blood pounded in his veins, hot with relief and delight.

"Berry, Mud! You're all right!" His voice was muffled by Mud's shoulder. "Nut! Moss, Lily—you're alive!"

He was surrounded by furred bodies, rocked back so that he almost fell, but he didn't care. The baboons who couldn't reach him through the melee were bouncing up and down, hooting, and pounding the earth with their fists.

"The battle. You fought Tendril off, Berry? You won?" he gasped, breathless.

"Yes!" Berry hugged him again.

"But Thorn, we thought—we thought you were dead," gasped Nut. "We couldn't find you!"

"I knew Thorn wasn't dead," shouted Mud joyfully. He danced on the spot, clasping his paws. "I never lost hope, I *knew* you'd be back. The stones told me!"

Thorn glanced at him, startled. "The stones? You're getting the hang of them?"

"But where have you been, Thorn?" pleaded Berry, still gripping his shoulders tightly. "What happened? Why were you gone so long?"

He took a deep breath. He didn't know if they were going to believe this, but he'd been practicing his excuse for long enough inside his head. *I can at least sound convincing.*

"I must have been knocked out when I fell from a tree," he began. "I was fighting Tendril and some of her Highleaves—in one of the other clearings. She'd drawn me away, you see, lured me into an ambush. I lost my footing and hit the ground hard, and when I woke up I was lying alone. I was covered in broken branches and leaves." Thorn gazed around at his troop, trying not to blink too rapidly.

"I can't believe it," breathed Nut. "I thought we'd looked everywhere. Honestly, Thorn, we searched high and low—mostly low—and we couldn't find a hair of you."

Thorn forced a wry laugh. "I'm as surprised as you are. I think—maybe something dragged me away. Some rot-eater who thought I was dead? Then they realized I wasn't, and I could still bite and scratch, and maybe they got scared. It's all a blur. But whoever it was, they'd hauled me a long way by then. I didn't know where I was. I had to find my way home. And I couldn't even think straight."

Creeper Highleaf prowled forward through the crush, an expression of suspicion on his battered face. He looked worse than ever, thought Thorn: one of his eyes was missing, and the empty socket looked raw and accusing. "It's very convenient," he muttered darkly. "You missed most of the battle, Thorn."

"That doesn't matter, Creeper." Berry's eyes narrowed as she turned back to Thorn. "But you've been gone for so long. It's been days. How did you get so lost?"

She wants to believe me, but she doesn't, Thorn realized with a sinking heart. *Not entirely.* "I have no idea, Berry. I had a bad crack on the head. I didn't know where I was when I woke up."

"I thought you were *dead*," she cried, sounding almost angry. "I was devastated!"

"I know. I'm—I'm so sorry, Berry," he whispered. He jerked his head up abruptly, remembering his alarming vision at the edge of the woods. "But Stump! How is Stump?"

"Stump?" Berry exchanged a confused look with Mud. "He's fine, Thorn. Why do you ask? He's on sentry duty right now."

"And it looks like he's asleep," muttered Nut with a roll of his eyes. "He didn't even notice Thorn arriving."

"Quite," said Berry dryly. "Somebody should have a word with Stump later."

Viper Highleaf gave a hoot from the back of the crowd and slapped her palms against the ground. "I know this is exciting," she called, "and I'm sure we're all very pleased to see Thorn, but we should get on with the election. It's important."

"Election?" Thorn glanced quizzically at Mud. "That's why you're all gathered in the Crown Stone clearing?"

His friend lowered his eyes. "I'm sorry, Thorn," he murmured. "You've missed your chance to stand for Crownleaf. The vote's already in progress."

"That doesn't matter." Thorn squeezed Mud's arm as the other baboons drifted back, gossiping excitedly, to their places in the glade. "I'm just so delighted to see you all safe and well. But who's standing?"

"Berry and Mango Highleaf," Mud told him.

"Berry?" Thorn blinked in surprise and turned to her. "I never thought you were interested in being Crownleaf."

She drew herself up a little, looking offended. "You may never have *thought* so, Thorn," she said, "but you never actually *asked.* And someone had to step up once you were gone."

"Oh, don't be angry, Berry." He embraced her hastily. "I think it's a wonderful idea. You'd make an amazing leader."

"Well, I admit I'd never thought of myself that way," she said, sounding mollified, "but when the opportunity came, I thought: Why not? And—I'd like to do something good for the troop. My father caused so much damage. . . . This seems like a way to begin to fix that."

"I understand," said Thorn softly, hugging her close.

Together the three friends followed the other baboons into the center of the clearing; the votes were already being counted out in the flat space in front of the Crown Stone. Very carefully and slowly, Moss and Viper were checking two neat piles of pebbles. It was the way the baboons had chosen their leaders for countless generations, and the very sight was reassuring in its staid formality: each baboon given a pebble, each baboon placing it in the voting pile for the candidate they liked best. Mango and Berry loped forward to resume their places at their respective piles, and Thorn leaned forward eagerly to peer over Lily's shoulder.

"It's no good," declared Viper, rising onto her hind paws with an expression of weary disappointment. "That's the third recount, and it's still tied."

Mud pushed forward, his eyes shining. "Thorn hasn't voted yet."

"But he wasn't here—" began Mango Highleaf, starting up from her seat on a rock.

"He's here now," Mud told her firmly. "And Thorn's still

part of this troop, isn't he?"

There were hollers and whoops of approval, and Thorn padded into the center of the clearing, feeling awkward. Every eye in the troop was fixed on him, and he couldn't help worrying that they could see right through his skin to his secrets. *No, that's silly.* And it didn't matter that he'd missed his chance to be Crownleaf, did it? Berry was a much better candidate than he was. Besides, it was his own fault for prevaricating for so long. Thorn shook off a last twinge of regret and picked a pebble from the scattering of uncast votes that remained.

Mango was still grumbling. "He's *obviously* going to vote for Berry, isn't he?" She slumped back against her rock.

Thorn shot her an apologetic look. Yes. Of course he was. With a tiny shrug, he placed his pebble ceremoniously on the heap assigned to Berry.

Every baboon knew there was no need for a further recount. The clearing erupted in whoops of celebration as Viper padded to Berry and placed a paw on her shoulder.

"I declare that from this day on, Berry Highleaf shall be known as Berry Crownleaf of Brightforest Troop!"

Hooting cheers rang out, and baboons pummeled the ground as a rather stunned Berry climbed up onto the Crown Stone. She swallowed hard as she gazed around at her new charges, and Thorn felt his heart swell with fierce pride.

"I . . ." Berry cleared her throat and tried again, waving a paw to calm the enthusiastic baboons. "I thank you, all of you, for trusting me with the leadership of the troop. That includes those who did not vote for me—because, as is our tradition, I shall rule for the benefit of all."

Approving whoops chorused again, and fists pounded the ground.

"Thank you, Mango Highleaf, for a fair contest." Berry nodded to her rival and gulped. "I have only one announcement to make for now, but I think it's an important one."

An attentive silence fell. Baboons glanced at one another, quizzical.

"I propose to rename this troop," declared Berry, her voice growing stronger and clearer. "We have come through terrible struggles, and a dark time for Bravelands, and I hope we can put it behind us and look forward to a bright future. This is a new beginning for us, and I think we should mark that in a very special way." She paused, meeting each baboon's eyes, and let her gaze rest fondly on Thorn. "From this day, Brightforest Troop shall be known as *Dawntrees*."

Thorn was first to shout his approval, but the clamor of cheers rose swiftly around him. Branches shook as baboons jumped up and down with delight. Nut beat his chest and hollered. Mud was dancing again, his eyes bright with happiness.

Thorn watched as Berry slipped down from the Crown Stone and was instantly surrounded by baboons congratulating her and wishing her luck. The last vestiges of disappointment inside him dissolved. Berry looked as if she had been born for this position: she was every bit the Crownleaf of this troop. Thorn's heart felt warm and huge inside him. *I'm so happy for her. She deserves this, so much.*

"Well done, and well spoken," he told her softly as she

squeezed through the crowd to his side. "Berry, I'm so glad you're Crownleaf. You're going to be a wonderful leader."

She smiled up at him. "I hope so, Thorn. We've been through so much, all of us. Our troop deserves a better future."

He hugged her. *Spoken like a true, inspiring leader,* he thought.

The baboons were darting off now, returning with gifts for their new leader: a spiky melon, a pawful of beetles, a cluster of ripe figs. Happy and proud, they all laid their offerings before her, and Berry looked overcome with affection and gratitude.

"Thank you. Thank you, Lily. Oh, Grit, what a beautiful mango. I'm so thrilled to—"

But before she could finish, there was commotion and crashing of foliage, and two baboons staggered out into the clearing, a hefty body carried between them. Berry gave a cry of shock as the troop rushed to gather around.

"Stump!"

The big baboon was unconscious, bleeding from a multitude of bites and scratches, and his flesh was swelling around bruises and cracked bones. Thorn stared at his limp form in utter horror. "What happened?" Berry demanded of the two sentries who had brought him back.

"We found him like this," said Root, grim-faced. "We don't know."

Stump stirred as they laid him gently down on the soft moss. He muttered something inaudible. As Berry leaned down to listen, Thorn felt a prickling in his hide.

He glanced nervously over his shoulder. Several of the troop were staring at him, and some were muttering among themselves. Viper, murmuring to Creeper, gestured at Thorn, and Creeper nodded.

The realization hit him like a punch from an angry monkey. *They think I had something to do with this.* Because Thorn had asked after Stump. *You fool, Thorn Highleaf!* How could the troop have known about his vision—and how could he possibly tell them? All they knew was that Stump wasn't a particular friend of his, and Thorn had been suddenly asking after him with frantic concern. Even Mud was eyeing him in bewilderment.

"Stump, can you speak?" Berry asked the wounded baboon urgently. "Tell us. Try to stay awake."

"It was . . ." he mumbled, and licked blood from his jaws. "Tendril. Some of her thugs. Couldn't fight 'em, Berry. Sorry . . ."

Thorn sagged, breathing again. Stump had exonerated him. He was in the clear.

But Viper and Creeper were still gazing at him darkly, and his heart sank. *They still suspect me.* The pair looked almost disappointed, as if they'd *wanted* Thorn to be shown up as some kind of traitor. Perhaps they still thought he'd had *something* to do with the attack on Stump. . . .

That wretched vision! Why had he blurted out his concern for Stump? *Stupid, Thorn!* He had to be very careful now. Viper and Creeper were the last baboons he wanted to know his secret.

"I'm sorry," mumbled Stump again. "Wish I'd spotted 'em quicker, Berry. . . ."

"Don't worry about that, Stump. And don't apologize." Berry's face was hard as she patted Stump's shoulder. "Just get better, my friend. We need you. Goodleaves! Take Stump to your glade and tend to him."

Berry leaped back onto the Crown Stone and rose onto her hind paws. She gave a commanding screech, and every baboon spun to face her.

"The battle with Tendril's troop is over," she announced grimly. "But the war is not yet won. That much is clear. Dawntrees: we will have to fight another day."

The troop yelled and whooped angrily, chittering their fangs. Only Berry's mother, Pear, looked nervous and uncertain, edging forward to speak to her daughter. Spotting her, Berry raised a paw for silence.

The old Goodleaf coughed. "Berry. Please. Will you allow me to go to Leopard Forest and speak with Tendril? She may listen to the words of an elder, one she has known all her life. I can calm this conflict, I know it."

"That may be so, Mother," said Berry, with gentle sternness. "But I will not risk your safety. So I do not give my permission."

It was the kind of tone no baboon would dare challenge. *Berry's already a leader,* Thorn thought with pride.

Pear Goodleaf nodded. "All right, Berry. Tendril's actions make me sad, but I accept your decision." She backed respectfully away from her daughter.

Things were developing so fast, thought Thorn. Berry had been their leader for only a heartbeat, yet already she had a crisis to face, with the troop plunged back into war and danger and doubt. He swallowed hard, and as he turned away, he caught sight of Viper once more.

She and Creeper were still muttering together, and they cast sidelong suspicious glances at Thorn. Oh, why had he ever hinted at his last vision, however obliquely?

The vultures on the mountain had told him he could have control of his strange dreams, that he could use them for the good of Bravelands. *Accept your responsibility, Thorn Greatfather. Accept your power!*

The visions did not feel like power, not right now.

So far, all they had done was get him into trouble.

CHAPTER 14

Fearless knew it with a fierce certainty: he could not leave Ruthless to the brutal fate of his father's paws. He might be Titan's son, but he was also Fearless's friend—and if Fearless didn't save him, who would?

The shade beneath the acacias was quiet, the pride sleepy in the afternoon heat, but Fearless couldn't relax. His gut tightened as he imagined how Titan might already be punishing his firstborn cub. Titan had no tolerance for any lion who did not give him full and unquestioning loyalty; how much worse might it be for his own offspring? *Mother and Father have only got time for Menace now. . . .* That blood-bond would not save Ruthless: it would only make Titan's wrath worse.

Fearless could not rest, could not sleep. The sun was too hot. Leaping to his paws, he shook his head to dislodge the flies.

"I can't just lie here," he growled to his pride. "I have to help Ruthless Titanpride. Come on—we've got to get him away from his father."

"What?" Valor blinked at him, then shot a bewildered look at Mighty. The other lions stirred and half rose, looking perplexed.

"He needs our help," said Fearless curtly. "You're just going to have to take my word for it. I saw him earlier and he's in trouble with his brute of a father, and I haven't got time to explain."

"You can't just spring this on us," rumbled Tough, twitching her ears.

"It's a pride leader decision," said Fearless haughtily. "I'm telling you, the cub's in trouble. *Bad* trouble. I'll explain after we rescue him."

Valor stared at him in disbelieving silence.

Hardy flicked his ears and gently pushed away the tiny cub that was clambering on his shoulder. "That's crazy," he growled. "Why would you do such a thing? Titanpride isn't even threatening us right now. We have no reason to go into their territory."

Valor and Mighty both sat up, silently facing Fearless. Gracious exchanged an apprehensive glance with Tough.

Keen sat up on his haunches, his expression anxious. Quietly he murmured in Fearless's ear: "I told you, Fearless. There was nothing you could have done for Ruthless."

"Not at that moment, maybe. But I can help him *now*."

Fearless lashed his tail in frustration. Maybe he *did* have to explain, at least briefly.

He raised his voice so that the whole pride could hear him. "Ruthless is a friend to Fearlesspride. He is *my* friend. He's been risking his life to bring me information about his father's movements, and now Titan has found out. Ruthless has risked everything. *For us.*"

The startled pride stared at one another, making growling sounds of surprise and confusion. Valor simply gaped at her brother. She looked as if she'd been run over by a charging hippo.

Fearless cleared his throat, feeling his blood run hot beneath his hide. "*That's* why we have to save Ruthless. We owe it to him. Fearlesspride takes care of its own!"

"He isn't our own," grumbled Hardy, but with less confidence.

"I don't know," mused Mighty, rising to his paws. He stared thoughtfully at Fearless. "Maybe this isn't such a bad idea, Hardy. Fearless *is* our pride leader, and we should do as he asks—but also, it might be useful to see for ourselves how Titanpride is faring. What they're up to. After all, if what Fearless says is true, and now Ruthless is in mortal danger, we won't be getting that information from him anymore."

Recovering from her astonishment, Valor rose to stand at her mate's flank. "I agree," she said.

Of course you do, thought Fearless irritably. *You agree with every word he says.*

"I guess Mighty has a point." Keen shrugged. "But we'll have to be careful."

"Of course we'll be careful," snapped Fearless. It rankled that the pride was coming around to the idea because of something Mighty said. Not that it mattered, he reminded himself sternly. *What matters is helping Ruthless.*

"If we want any chance of success," suggested Mighty, "we should go when Titanpride least expects us."

Reluctantly, Fearless nodded and glanced at the midday sky. "And that means now."

One by one, the pride padded after Fearless as he set off from the camp. The sun was so high, the file of lions cast barely a shadow; its heat beat down relentlessly on the parched savannah. Far away, a blurred, shifting line of gold was visible: it was a herd of gazelles, drifting idly eastward as they grazed, but there was no time for hunting. Heads low and eyes firmly ahead, the lions strode toward Titanpride territory.

Fearless felt a powerful, urgent determination, but he couldn't help a flutter of unease as they came in sight of the Misty Ravine. No mist hung over it right now—the fierce sun had burned it away—but the ragged slope of rocks that marked the ravine's edge was instantly recognizable. The fur on Fearless's neck rose, and his blood pumped faster.

"We should slow down," growled Mighty behind him. "We have to be stealthy about this."

Fearless snapped his head around in irritation. "We're downwind."

"Not that there's much wind to speak of," pointed out

Mighty. "And besides, it can change in an instant."

He was right. Much against his will, Fearless slowed his pawsteps and lowered his shoulders to take advantage of the grass's cover. They were almost within roaring distance of Titanpride now; he could see the outlines of dozing lions, shimmering in the distant heat.

Paw by paw, Fearless crept closer, his pride silent behind him. The lions of Titanpride sprawled in the patchy shadow of some scattered thorn trees. Titan himself lay sleeping against Artful; the mean-faced lioness was on her flank, suckling a small cub. *That must be Menace.* Fearless halted, his muscles quivering.

In the heart of the Titanpride camp, flies buzzed above the torn remains of a zebra, blackening in the heat. *So they're hunting well.*

A movement caught Fearless's eye; an adolescent, maneless cub was creeping toward the zebra carcass. Fearless recognized Ruthless at once, despite his terrible condition. His golden hide was matted, scored with claw marks, and a wound had been torn across his jaw. One ear had been tattered by savage fangs. Fearless drew in a breath of rage.

Titan sprang suddenly to his paws. "You, Ruthless! Misbegotten cub of my blood! Stop!" In the calm quietness of the midday, his bellowing roar resounded across the grassland. "Traitors do not eat!"

Ruthless froze, trembling as he glanced back at his father.

"They're starving him!" whispered Keen in horror. Fearless gave a sharp, angry nod.

"We'll have to rename him." The amused snarl came from Resolute, who had lifted his head to sneer at the cub. "He's getting pathetic. I suggest *Useless*."

Barking laughter rippled around the other lions of Titanpride as Ruthless slunk back to his place in the blazing sun; he hadn't been allotted any shade, Fearless realized with angry pity.

"Those Titanpride brutes," growled Valor under her breath. "Maybe this isn't such a good idea, Fearless. We could be getting into something we can't handle."

"We can't abandon him," muttered Fearless. "*Especially* not now. Look at him! We'd be leaving him to his death, that's obvious."

Mighty padded forward to his flank. "On reflection, Fearless, I think Valor's right. This is Titanpride business, and we have no real right to interfere. Challenging them would be an unnecessary risk to all of us."

Fearless turned on him. "Like the unnecessary risks Ruthless took for *us*?" he hissed.

There was silence for a moment. At last Mighty nodded, reluctantly.

"All right." He lowered his eyes. "This is Fearlesspride, and you're its leader. I'll go along with whatever you decide."

"Good," grunted Fearless. "Besides, I have a plan. Mighty, Hardy—both of you go far over there, upwind." He nodded into the distance. "Once you're in place, roar, really loudly. The sound of two invading male lions will draw Titan's attention, for sure. Gracious, Valor, and Tough—you're the fastest, so you create another distraction on the other side. Any Titanpride lions who aren't busy chasing Mighty and Hardy—they'll come after you." He nodded at the grassland. "With two separate distractions keeping them busy, Keen and I will dash in and get Ruthless."

"That plan sounds complicated," whispered Gracious nervously.

"And a little unpredictable," added Mighty, narrowing his eyes.

"It's something I once saw cheetahs do," said Fearless irritably. "It worked perfectly well for them. They ran rings around Titan. Distraction and speed, those are the elements."

"Cheetahs," said Keen slowly, "are a lot faster than us." His anxious eyes met Hardy's, and the stocky cub licked his blunt jaws uncertainly. Both of them looked at Mighty.

Not at me, Fearless thought with a surge of rage. *At Mighty, rot him!*

But the big lion was nodding. "It might just work, Fearless," he said. "It's a good plan."

Fearless shook himself. Pride discipline could wait. "Right. Let's get going. Keen, you come with me."

The two of them slunk through the grass as the others set off briskly, following Fearless's directions.

"Perhaps Mighty isn't so bad," murmured Keen, glancing after the big lion. "He makes a lot of sense, and when you make a final decision, he's pretty submissive to you."

Fearless said nothing. Keen's opinion of Mighty didn't matter, he decided: all his attention had to be focused on Ruthless now. Prowling closer to the camp, his paw pads placed sound-lessly with each step, he sank his belly as low as he could. His heart thrashed so hard in his rib cage, he could only hope it wasn't audible.

From far across the plain came a bellowing roar, joined at once by another. *Mighty and Hardy, just as planned. Perfect timing.* The heads of every Titanpride lion jerked up, and their black-maned leader sprang once again to his feet.

"Strange lions!" snarled Titan. "Resolute! Take the others and investigate!"

As Resolute and three younger males bounded off, Fear-less risked lifting his head to check that Valor, Gracious, and Tough were in position. He spotted them straight away, golden streaks already racing across the grassland.

With a bellow of fury, Titan spun around.

"It's an attack! The rest of you, come with me! Kill the intruders!"

His breath in his throat, Fearless watched the remaining lions and lionesses leap into the chase. He could only hope that Gracious, Tough, and Valor were fast enough to outrun the enraged pride. But their work was done: just Artful, Men-ace, and Ruthless remained in the flattened grass beneath the trees.

"Go!" he growled to Keen. The two of them rose and bounded into the heart of Titanpride's camp. Dust flew up as Fearless's paws pounded the scrubby grass.

"You!" Artful sprang to her feet, protecting little Menace between her paws.

Fearless ignored her. "Ruthless. You're coming with us."

Ruthless was on his paws too, staring at Fearless and Keen in disbelief. *"Fearless?"* He took a hesitant step toward them.

"Don't you touch my cub." Artful curled back her muzzle to display vicious yellow fangs.

"We're not going to," snarled Fearless, swinging his head to glare at her. "Not the one you care about, anyway. Come on, Ruthless—there's no time to lose."

"Don't you dare move, Ruthless!" Artful snapped.

Ruthless gave her a sad, sidelong look and took a pace away from her. "I'm sorry, Mother."

Glaring at her son, the lioness gave a snarl of fury. Then she spun back to Fearless. "You'll pay for this, Gallantbrat." She hunched her shoulders as Menace stared at them from beneath her forepaws. "When Titan finds out what you've done, he'll kill you all."

"Let him try." Fearless gave Ruthless a swift nuzzle as the young lion limped to his side. "Let's go, Ruthless. We'll keep you safe."

"Of course you will. Until Titan destroys your pathetic pride," snarled Artful. "I warn you, Ruthless. Walk away from here, and there's no coming back."

Ruthless swiveled his wounded head to face his mother. There was deep sorrow in his eyes. "I won't be coming back."

Fearless nudged him gently. Together they turned, and he and Keen flanked Ruthless, leading him in a lurching run from the pride of his parents.

* * *

"I don't know how to thank you," Ruthless murmured as he limped into the Fearlesspride camp. "I would have died there."

"It was the least we could do," growled Fearless, nuzzling his neck. "I'm just sorry I didn't come for you sooner." Raising his head, he nodded approvingly to his waiting pride. "Well done, all of you. That went perfectly."

Mighty and Valor stood side by side as always, dipping their heads in greeting; Hardy, Rough, and Tough stood a little apart, with Rough's cubs squirming at their paws. Gracious lay with her back to them, her head resting on her forepaws.

Keen bounced forward. "Titan was livid, Hardy! Were you close enough? Did you *see* his face?"

Hardy did not laugh. His eyes were dark and angry. "Have *you* seen *Gracious's*?"

Fearless sucked in a breath, and Keen's whiskers drooped. They stared in horror as Gracious rose with a wince. As she turned toward them, Ruthless gave a guilty, whimpering growl.

Four claw marks were scored across the beautiful lioness's face, from cheek to jaw. A flap of skin hung loose beneath her eye. Her muzzle was stained and clotted with blood. Fearless made a strangled sound in his throat.

"Gracious . . ."

"Titan caught her," said Hardy curtly. "She's lucky to be alive."

"Hardy. Really. It's all right." Gracious's words were distorted, and it was clear that speaking caused her pain. "I knew what I was getting into, and it was worth it. I'm glad you're safe, Ruthless."

Fearless could feel a hard stare; it made his fur prickle. Sure enough, when he turned, Valor was glowering at him.

"Was it worth it, Fearless?" she demanded. "Was it really?"

"Yes," he croaked. "We owed it to Ruthless."

"The cub's your friend," sniffed Valor curtly, "but he doesn't look much of a hunter."

Ruthless cleared his throat. "I'll do my best, I promise," he murmured, shame-faced. "I owe you all my life. But I'm sorry this happened to you, Gracious. I'm sorry my father is such a vicious brute."

Fearless swallowed hard. The looks he was getting from Valor, Hardy, and Rough felt as if they were biting into his heart. Mighty simply looked disappointed, and a little sad. Poor Gracious, ironically, looked guilty and awkward. Only Keen glanced at Fearless with any sympathy.

"You're not responsible for your father, Ruthless," Fearless muttered. "And I know you'll make a fine member of this pride when your wounds heal."

Ruthless was safe, and free of Titanpride.

But it seemed that in saving him, Fearless had thrown away his pride's respect.

CHAPTER 15

The valley that lay before Sky was a treat for her tired eyes after the arid desolation of the plains. It sloped gently down in undulating steps to a broad, green bowl that was dotted with flowering trees. Cool shadows striped the lush grass; though the ground wasn't wet, the damp shade had protected the valley from the worst glare of the sun. Sky stretched up her trunk to snap a young branch bursting with leaf buds.

"This is beautiful," she murmured.

"It feels good to be off the plains," agreed Rock, chewing on a mouthful of green leaves. "This was worth the long journey, just for the shade and the browsing."

As he shambled forward, a ground squirrel's tail fluffed up in alarm, and it skittered into a burrow. Far across the valley floor, Sky could make out a small herd of gazelles, and closer by there were other, different antelopes: white-spotted bushbuck and shy little duikers browsed beneath the trees, their tails flicking at flies. The grass-eaters seemed so peaceful and contented. Rock was right—this was a beautiful place to rest. But perhaps she had come to the wrong place entirely? It seemed a refuge from the very predators Sky sought.

Then she spotted them: a coalition of three male cheetahs, hunched on a cluster of rocks, observing the gazelles at a distance. As one of the cats turned his head, whiskers twitching, she recognized the pattern of the black tear marks on his face.

"Fleet!" Her heart in her throat, Sky ambled toward him, keeping her movements easy and unthreatening.

The big cheetah tensed, ears pricking and tail bristling, but as his eyes found Sky's he seemed to relax. He gave her a small nod.

"Sky Strider. I remember you. Great Mother's granddaughter." He glanced at Rock, then back at Sky. "I am sorry for Bravelands' loss. Your grandmother was a fine leader."

"Thank you, Fleet," murmured Sky.

The cheetah was staring at the ground between her feet. "What in the name of the Great Spirit—"

He put an elegant paw forward and hunched down to sniff tentatively at the two cubs. They stopped capering and gazed up at him, wide-eyed. "Young cheetahs?" he rumbled in bewilderment.

Sky nodded. "Nimble and Lively have been traveling with us. They are the cubs of Rush."

"Rush of the Gray River? I know her."

Sky lowered her eyes. "Rush was killed," she told Fleet as

the other cheetahs approached to peer at the cubs. "They need someone to look after them. They're too young to be on their own."

Fleet took a startled pace back. "I am sorry to hear about Rush," he purred. "But we can't look after them."

"No indeed," said another of the cheetahs, his eyes wide with surprise. "We males don't raise cubs. We don't know how."

"I understand that," said Sky, stirring the dust with one foot and letting Nimble and Lively pat playfully at her toes. "But Rush had littermates, didn't she? I heard her talk about them. They're female, I think?"

"Both of them." Fleet nodded. "Sleek is with her own cubs right now. I haven't seen Breeze in some time, but they may be together. You'll find them farther down this valley. Follow the streambed that's almost dry. Beyond a rockfall beside a copse of thorn trees—you can't miss the spot. That's the beginning of Sleek's territory."

"Thank you, Fleet. Good hunting to you." Sky dipped her head to the cheetahs, and she and Rock walked on toward the streambed, the cubs trotting between them.

From the edge of her vision she could see that Fleet and his coalition were staring after them, and she caught his mutter: "The strangest things are happening in Bravelands these days. . . ."

The cheetah had explained it perfectly; the tumble of fallen rocks was distinctive, and a grove of thorn trees grew nearby, their roots clinging to the dry bank. Sky cocked her ears as they strode on, and she let her gaze rove across the sloping ground, alert for any sign of Sleek and her cubs.

"This cheetah may be far from her cubs, and hunting," warned Rock. "We may have to wait for her to return, perhaps for days."

"I know . . . but look over there!" Sky halted, smiling, then broke into a slow trot. "There, Rock!"

The mother cheetah lay in the shade of a small hillock, five tiny cubs competing to nurse at her belly. At the elephant's approach, she sprang nimbly to her paws, dislodging her infants, and her muzzle wrinkled in warning.

"Sleek?" Sky slowed and stopped, twitching her trunk nervously. *I mustn't alarm her!* "You are Sleek, sister of Rush of the Gray River?"

Warily, Sleek nodded. "I am. What is it to you?"

Sky lowered her head respectfully, and beside her Rock did the same. "I am Sky Strider, and this is my friend Rock. We've been searching for you and Breeze, because—" Hesitating, she glanced down at the cubs, who had just caught up and were staring at Sleek, jaws parted in awe. "Because Rush died, Sleek. She has left these cubs, and they need protection."

Sleek watched the cubs for a long moment, silent. Her thick black tail-tip twitched. Her own cubs, far smaller than Nimble and Lively, squirmed and mewled.

"I am sorry," the cheetah said at last, her voice even. "I have five cubs of my own, and it's all I can do to protect them." She flicked her tail, and Sky followed the gesture. The cubs were mewing pitifully for their mother, thin little things with half-open eyes.

"I can't afford to take on more," added Sleek. "Not even my own sister's cubs."

"Truly, Sleek?" The rejection was so sudden, so uncompromising, Sky felt shocked frustration rise in her throat. "Can't you try? They're so small."

"No. It isn't possible. I'm sorry, Sky Strider."

Sky clenched her jaws, her heart fluttering in distress. But as the uncomfortable silence stretched, she could reluctantly accept the cheetah's reasoning. *She may not even manage to keep her own cubs alive.*

"What about Breeze?" Sky suggested, making her tone bright and positive once more. "Do you know where we can find her?"

"Breeze?" Sleek flicked an ear forward. "Breeze is dead. It seems I have lost both my sisters."

"Oh." Sky felt a lurch of despair. "I'm sorry, Sleek."

"Was Breeze sick?" asked Rock gently.

"Anything but." Sitting down, Sleek hunched her shoulders. "She was the quickest, strongest cheetah I knew. That's what was so strange."

Sky frowned. *Quick and strong.* Breeze sounded a lot like Rush, yet both sisters had fallen to an unforeseen killer. And Sleek had called her death *strange.* . . .

Sleek sighed deeply, interrupting Sky's thoughts. "My sister was in a bizarre state of mind, though. Lately, anyway. Imagining terrors, seeing creatures that weren't there. She may have panicked, fled straight into real hunters. Still, whatever killed her must have been fast and powerful."

Fast. Powerful. And cruel enough to take a living heart? Sky shuddered.

"Whatever it was, it didn't eat her." Sleek twitched her whiskers in resignation. "Odd. But odd things are happening these days."

Sky felt a tremor of foreboding. It was as if Sleek was echoing her own ominous thoughts. "May Breeze hunt well in the stars," said Rock solemnly.

Sleek lowered her head. "Thank you. But you'll understand, I can't take Rush's cubs myself. I'm afraid they'll have to fend for themselves."

There was no more Sky could do. "They're so little . . ." she murmured, mostly to herself. "So vulnerable."

"Sky, don't worry." Rock butted her gently. "Perhaps we can find another cheetah, or . . ."

Sky straightened, lifting her head in determination. "Or they can simply stay with us."

"That sounds like a reasonable solution." Sleek nodded, lying down again next to her cubs.

"Sky, are you sure about this?" Rock looked startled.

"Yes. I'm sure. I won't abandon them now. And we've done all right so far, haven't we?"

"But the cubs . . . surely they need to be with other cheetahs." Rock stroked Lively's fluffy head with the tip of his trunk.

Lively and her brother were looking from Rock to Sky in

trepidation. Nimble swallowed hard.

"We can't hunt, little ones, so we can't teach you," Sky told them gently, "but you'll learn as you grow, I'm sure of it. You have your mother's strength, and her cleverness. Deep inside, you know what to do. I have faith in you—and in the Great Spirit who will guide you."

Nimble's little chest swelled. "Do you really think so?"

Sky smiled. "I really do. And until then, I'll protect you. We'll find food somehow. If you cubs are happy to stay?"

"I like traveling with you," said Lively shyly.

"Me too!" Nimble pranced up and batted Sky's trunk. "Grubs don't taste too bad anyway. We like being with you, Sky. And Rock."

"We're having fun," agreed his sister, adding nervously, "if you don't walk too fast?"

"You can stay with us for as long as you need to." Sky curled her trunk around both the little cheetahs. She glanced up at Rock. "We'll manage, I know it."

"I believe you," he assured her, tilting his ears forward. "But the sun's going down, Sky. We should find shelter before nightfall."

She nodded. "Good-bye, Sleek. I wish you good fortune."

"And the same to you," purred the mother cheetah as her cubs latched on to nurse again. "I believe we all need it. The times are strange and dangerous, Sky Strider."

Sleek was right, thought Sky, as she watched the stars twinkle into life above her. An unseen stream trickled and gurgled in the darkness of the undergrowth. Nimble and Lively were nestled in a hollow stump nearby, concealed by foliage; she could hear their tiny purring snores, and Sky was glad they could sleep so soundly. They must truly trust her and Rock, she realized with a little skip of her heart. Rock had scent-marked the trees and stones around their sleeping-place, a thorough warning to any predators that a bull elephant was near; with luck that would deter any flesh-eaters from venturing near the vulnerable cubs.

There would be peace for a few night hours—or there would be, if only Sky knew what the Great Spirit planned for her now. Nothing seemed to be straightforward anymore, she thought. After the Great Battle with Stinger and his forces, she had thought life would be simpler; instead it seemed more complicated than ever.

But it was she who had killed Stinger. And if the Great Spirit *was* still watching over Bravelands—and she had to believe it was—perhaps caring for these orphaned cubs would redeem her in its all-seeing eyes. *Great Mother,* she thought yet again, *how I wish you were still here. I would dearly love to talk to you, just one more time.*

Though if the new Great Parent would only show themselves, Sky thought, at least life could *begin* to get back to normal. . . .

Rock loomed from the darkness beside her. "Sky," he murmured. "Are you all right?"

"I'm fine," she reassured him. There was nothing he could do about her worries, so there was no point burdening him.

But as she curled her trunk around his, his touch, usually so solid and reassuring, was strangely hesitant and nervous.

Sky stepped back, studying him. "What is it, Rock?"

He took a breath. "I . . . I want to say something to you, Sky. But it's . . . difficult for me."

She gazed into his eyes. "Whatever it is," she said softly, "don't worry. We're safe, at least for tonight. And whatever you want to tell me—that's safe with me forever."

His head drooped slightly. "I don't know how to begin. . . ."

Sky's heart tightened with apprehension. *Perhaps he doesn't want to be with me anymore. . . . Perhaps the cubs are too much responsibility for him after all. . . .*

But she was strong, Sky reminded herself. She had fought in the Great Battle for Bravelands. She had lost Great Mother, and lived. She had carried the Great Spirit in her own heart, searching for its new host. Whatever Rock had to tell her, however sad, she could bear it. She gave him a calm nod.

"Just begin," she said softly. "Tell me, Rock."

She felt his hide tremble against hers, and when he spoke his voice was hoarse. "You—you have changed my life, Sky. You've been an inspiration to me. You're so brave—ever since I first saw you, the day you fought to defend Moon, I have admired you more than any elephant I've met."

"That's . . . that's kind of you, Rock," she stammered, taken aback. His compliments made her feel suddenly awkward. Was he saying such things to let her down gently, to ease the moment of his leaving? "I only did what I had to."

"That's just it." His green gaze was intense and bright.

"You've done all that you had to, Sky—and you've done it with a courageous heart, without ever losing your sweet kindness and your sense of justice and—and fairness, and ... I ... I find myself drawn to you and I ... I'm expressing this so badly, Sky, I'm *sorry*—"

Gently, Sky touched her trunk to his brow, and he lifted his dark green eyes to stare into hers. "What is it, Rock? What's wrong? Tell me."

"Not wrong, Sky, never wrong, but—I'm bad at saying such things. That's all." Rock drew a deep, steadying breath and straightened. His gaze met hers.

"Will—will you be my life-mate, Sky?"

She gasped. Her heart tripped and thudded in her chest, and she took an involuntary step back. "Rock. Oh, Rock. I didn't expect—" Her voice dried in her throat as his words sank in. "We're both so young still. . . ."

Rock and I. Life-mates . . .

Could he possibly mean what he was saying? Of all things, she had truly not expected this. Yet however hard she tried to still her racing blood and think calmly, she could not deny the flood of excitement rushing through her. There was a deep, golden warmth in her chest; it took her long, shocked moments to recognize pure happiness. It suffused her whole body.

But I have to be sensible! Both of us do. . . .

"Rock," she said hoarsely. "Think about what you're saying."

"I have," he murmured, pressing his forehead to hers. "I've

thought about it over and over, Sky."

She paused, gathering herself, summoning all her inner strength. *But* why *am I arguing, why am I protesting?*

Because she had to, she knew. There was more at stake than her own happiness.

"Why, Rock? Why would you want to be with me?" Her voice rasped with the effort of denying him. "Life would not be easy as my mate, you know that. I'm not like other elephants. I don't stay with the herd; I defy the matriarchs—and at the most vital moments of my family's journey. I've carried the Great Spirit inside me, and I know it will need me again—and I will have to be there for it. I have to do as it wishes, always." She lowered her eyelashes and swallowed hard. "And, Rock—more serious than all that: I've broken the Code. I've *killed.*"

For a moment that seemed to stretch forever, Rock was silent and still. Then, with his trembling trunk, he touched her cheek.

"You think I don't know all that, Sky?" he whispered. "It's what makes you special. All the things that make you different, Sky Strider—they are why I love you."

"Rock." Overwhelmed, she leaned into his head, closing her eyes. How could she resist him?

Or rather, why would she? She didn't even want to. She made one last, strenuous effort. "But what I said is true. We're so young, both of us. . . ."

"I know." He gave a deep, shaky sigh. "But we can still

promise ourselves to each other. Sky, I've known for a long time that I want to be with you. I just didn't know how to ask. I'm sorry if—if this upsets you. If I've been clumsy. If I've said the wrong—"

"No." She shook her head. "No, Rock. I'm not upset, nothing like it. I'm glad." She pressed her head to his, reveling in its hard strength. "All right. Yes. If this is crazy, so be it. Yes, Rock. I want to be your life-mate."

"Oh, Sky." He sounded choked. "Then we should take our vow together."

"We should do it now," she whispered. "The night's so beautiful."

With a nod, he hooked his trunk over her neck. "Come with me. I know the place."

Sky followed him, their feet splashing into the cool water of the stream that was hidden by overgrown foliage. Her heart thudded in her chest as they followed the water's course, until it broadened into a deep, still pool. Palms and fig trees clustered thickly around its banks, but above the elephants was the open sky; stars glittered above them and on the surface of the pool at their feet. As Rock waded into the water and Sky followed him, their ripples shattered the reflections into sparkling streaks.

Rock stood very still as Sky faced him. "This pool," he murmured. "It's sacred. I've heard about this valley before, and this part of it especially. My brothers have come here with their life-mates for the same purpose."

"It's perfect," she said softly, letting her eyes flicker around the starlit glade. "It's so beautiful. What better place to make such a promise?"

"There's just one thing." Rock cleared his throat. "I don't know the true ceremony, Sky. I don't really know what to do."

His admission should have dampened her joy, but instead, a sudden warm certainty stirred inside her.

"Yes, you do," she whispered. "I think deep down we both do. The ritual will come from our hearts. The Great Spirit will guide us."

Quivering, Rock stretched out his trunk, and Sky extended hers to touch it. They coiled their trunks together, nestling their heads close. No visions swamped her, no fearful images sparked in her head to distract her from the moment. The last of her doubts and fears dissolved in the quiet darkness of the glade. All around, Sky heard the piping of tree frogs, the gentle whirr of crickets and cicadas. From far in the trees, a night bird gave a haunting cry. She could hear Rock's breathing, too, deep and tremulous like her own.

As if at a secret inner signal, they stepped back from each other at the same time. Gazing into Rock's dark green eyes, Sky dipped her trunk to the water, then lifted it and sprayed his neck and back. As she closed her eyes, she heard him touch the water too, and then she felt the cool splash of water on her own hide.

Sky blinked her eyes open and saw that Rock was gazing into them. She couldn't look away. Around them, the stars seemed to have fluttered down from the sky to glow golden around them; then Sky realized they were fireflies, dancing above their reflections in the shimmering water. Over and over again the two elephants splashed each other gently, until at last they stood quite still, their trunks linked once more. A long sigh escaped Rock, and he closed his eyes.

Their trunks slipped apart, slow and reluctant, and Sky raised hers skyward. Drawing a deep breath, she trumpeted her joy to the stars, and Rock joined her, their calls harmonizing and echoing until they faded into the night.

Silence fell around them, undisturbed by anything but the hum of fireflies.

"Did we do it right?" she whispered, warmth and happiness filling her heart.

"Oh yes, Sky." Rock pressed his trunk to hers once again. "I think we've done everything exactly as we're meant to."

CHAPTER 16

"Oh, stars, where is he now?" Exasperated, Thorn stared around the grassland, then parted the scrubby bushes with his paws and peered through them. "Spider! *Spider!* Where are you?"

There was nothing in the undergrowth but a few scattered scorpion husks and discarded tails. The eccentric baboon was nowhere in sight, and no reply came to Thorn's calls. Thorn tutted and growled, then dusted his paws together and turned away. Maybe the oddball baboon had wandered off somewhere else. Maybe he was having incomprehensible chats with egrets and beetles and snakes. Maybe he'd find a meerkat to befriend, and *maybe* this time he wouldn't end up accused of its murder. Thorn had enough worries without hunting Spider across Bravelands; Spider would be *fine*. He bounded back to Tall Trees.

All the same, lingering guilt hung over him. He was so

distracted, he almost yelped when Claw Deeproot sauntered out of the bushes right in front of him. Claw's snaggletoothed face brightened, and he grinned in greeting.

Thorn skidded to a halt, slipping on moss. "Hello, Claw. Are you looking for me?"

"Yes! I am! I've got something for you, Thorn." Claw Deeproot smiled and gave a rather obsequious little nod as he handed Thorn a fat fig. "I thought you might be hungry."

"Thanks, Claw." Absently Thorn took it from him, his claws digging into its soft flesh. In fact he wasn't particularly hungry, but it was a kind gesture, he thought. He brought the fig to his jaws and sank in his fangs.

Stench and rot flooded his mouth, and he gagged, spitting furiously. Claw jumped back, eyes wide.

Thorn stared at the bitten fig. It was rotten, the flesh blackening with mold, and a maggot writhed between the seeds. "Claw! What is this?"

Claw put his paws to his mouth; Thorn had the sneaking suspicion he was hiding a grin. "I—I don't know, Thorn! Honestly, I had no idea."

"Don't worry." Thorn gritted his fangs and rubbed the flesh inside his lip. "It was an accident, wasn't it?"

Claw scurried away. As Thorn spat again and snatched a handful of leaves from the nearest bush to try to take the taste away, he thought he heard a muffled chuckling.

"Traitor," he heard as the bushes rustled, and at least two sets of paws scampered away.

He clenched his jaws, anger kindling in his gut. So the

rotten fig hadn't been an accident.

On the surface, at least, everything had seemed normal for the last few days; Berry and Mud were as friendly to him as ever, of course, and most of the troop chatted and laughed and complained with him as they always had. Thorn knew, though, that something wasn't right. The mutters, the swiftly silenced conversations. The averted eyes. The baboons who turned quickly away when he looked at them.

They know I'm not telling the truth. A shiver of guilt rippled across his hide.

Besides, *traitor* wasn't the only word he'd caught mumbled as he passed. He'd heard *coward*, too.

How could they think that of him, after all that had happened with Stinger and the Great Herd? *Easily*, he thought miserably. His story *wasn't* believable in the slightest. If some other baboon had vanished in the middle of a battle and trailed home days later with some lame excuse about rot-eaters and a knock on the head, Thorn wouldn't have believed it for a moment.

His secrets felt like sodden mud, clinging to his fur, filling his whole body from throat to gut, weighing him down so that even his paws felt too heavy to lift. And he was so tired of keeping them: the secret of his trip with the vultures to the mountain, the secret of Spider.

Worst of all, there was the awful secret of the Great Spirit that lived inside him. For how much longer could he keep it all to himself?

Hauling himself to his paws, Thorn slouched off in search

of Mud. At least his oldest friend was always there for him, always ready to listen, and these days Thorn knew where he could find him—in the stinkwood clearing to the west side of Tall Trees, studying his stones.

Sure enough, Mud was crouched on the grass in the dappled sunlight, a reddish-brown pebble clutched in his paw. The other stones lay scattered around him where they'd fallen; Mud frowned at the red stone as if he expected it to form a mouth and talk to him.

"You're wrong," Thorn heard him mutter as he tapped the stone with a claw. "This can't be true, you stupid thing. Is it me? I'm reading you all wrong, aren't I?"

"Mud," Thorn hailed him. "What are they saying?"

Mud leaped to his feet and spun around, his eyes goggling. "Thorn! Sorry, I didn't hear you coming." Hurriedly he crouched and scooped all the stones into his paws, clutching them against his chest and blinking in embarrassment.

Thorn smiled. "What are they saying now? Are we all going to be eaten by hyenas tomorrow?"

"No, no, no." Mud made a quiet groaning noise. "No, nothing like that, nothing." He backed off, but his eyes were riveted on Thorn in a kind of embarrassed dread.

Thorn's blood chilled a little. *Oh stars. Surely he didn't see something about me. . . .* "No, really, Mud, what did you see? Is it bad?"

"No, no," said Mud again. He shook his head violently, almost dropping one of the stones. But he was still gaping at Thorn. "No. No, no, no."

"Well." Thorn paused and tilted his head. Whatever Mud

had seen, he wasn't telling. Forcing himself to sound bright, he said, "What about becoming the Starleaf, Mud? Have you spoken to Berry? Have you pressed your case?"

"I . . . I haven't had time," Mud stammered, seeming to gather himself. "Everything's been so, uh, busy."

"But you've obviously been practicing so much," Thorn pressed him. "You must know the stones so well by now. It would be a shame to waste all this experience by not even *asking.*"

Mud hesitated and stared sadly down at the stones. "I don't think anyone will take me seriously," he murmured.

"Of course they will!" said Thorn heartily. "I'll tell you what, Mud. I'll speak to Berry if you like."

"Would you?" Mud's muzzle twisted uncertainly. "Thank you, Thorn. I just feel so . . . so awkward. Like I'm shoving myself forward, and I . . . I don't like that. I don't want to make a fool of myself."

"I will speak to her." Thorn was firm. "And it'll be worth it, I promise. Berry will listen."

"If you say so," said Mud feebly.

He wasn't as excited as Thorn had thought he might be, but it didn't matter. Mud would cheer up soon enough when Berry made him Starleaf. *And it gives me a reason to talk to Berry,* Thorn thought, clenching his jaws as he padded away.

It was time to put a stop to all the secrets gnawing inside him. Why was he so afraid of telling Berry, after all? He'd start by pleading Mud's case, and then—then he would explain the truth to her, about the vultures and the mountain, and all that nonsense about him being Great Father. It might be a wild story, but that was just the point: it was too crazy to be a lie. It didn't sound any more stupid than the story he'd invented, he thought wryly.

In fact, why not tell the whole troop? The vultures thinking he was Great Father was *clearly* too ridiculous to be true. The troop would agree. They'd have a laugh about it, and Nut would tease him relentlessly for a while, but it would all be worth it. He wouldn't be carrying around this lump of guilt in his belly anymore.

Thorn picked up his pace, filled with a new eagerness. Nothing could be worse than the sidelong glances and the muttered suspicions. The sooner he got this over with, the better—

"Viper!" He came to a halt, smiling at the gruff-faced baboon who squatted at the entrance to Berry's favorite shady glade. Viper had become so protective of the new Crownleaf, carrying messages for her, bringing her food, and conveying her instructions. Thorn felt a twinge of irritation.

No. No, it was *good.* Berry deserved all the help she could get, now that she had responsibility for the whole troop.

"What do you want, Thorn?" Viper sat back on her haunches and glared at him. "The Crownleaf's very busy right now."

"I just need to talk to her," said Thorn, a little taken aback. "I'm Berry's mate, in case you've forgotten."

"Well, she's got a lot to do and she hasn't got time for— hey!" Viper staggered in shock as Thorn pushed past.

Berry's gentle laughter rippled through the trees; she didn't *sound* busy. Frowning, Thorn padded on into the glade, ignoring Viper's indignant protestations.

Berry Crownleaf sat in the center of the dark-leafed glade, surrounded by an awestruck circle of young baboons. Something skittered on the ground at her paws; narrowing her eyes, Berry stabbed down a length of forked twig, pinning the creature in place. Deftly, she snapped off its curled tail. The small baboons looked enthralled and delighted, clapping their paws as Berry smiled and lifted the tailless creature, and as she bit into it, they erupted in *oohs* and *aahs*.

A scorpion. She was teaching the youngsters how to catch them, just as Stinger used to do. For a moment—just a fleeting instant—she was her father's image: focused and smiling and charismatic, and—

Thorn shook off the chill that rippled through his fur. Berry glanced up and she was his mate again, warm and loving and easygoing. He grinned and raised his paw in a greeting.

As Viper chittered angrily behind him, Thorn padded into the circle to Berry's side. She smiled up at him. "They're learning fast, Thorn! Oh, Viper, don't worry, I don't mind *Thorn* interrupting me. Here, you youngsters. Share this scorpion, and I'll find you another."

"Berry," murmured Thorn, as Viper padded sulkily away. "I need to talk to you."

"I'd love to talk with you, too, Thorn," she said warmly. "We get so little time together now. What was it you wanted to say?"

"It's delicate, but it's important. There's something I need to tell you—"

"Frond, wait, use the two prongs on the end of the stick! Don't try to pierce the scorpion, that's too difficult—here, I'll show you again. You mustn't try with a live one till you get this right!" Half glancing at Thorn, Berry smiled. "Sorry, Thorn, what were you saying? It's so all-consuming, being Crownleaf. I never realized there was so much to do!"

"I understand, Berry." He stroked her shoulder.

"Come and help me with these young ones, and we can talk while we teach. Oh, what is it *now*, Viper?"

"Berry Crownleaf." Viper dipped her head respectfully. "You asked me to remind you when the marula trees were coming into season. And they are. We should send out a party to gather the nuts."

Thorn sighed inwardly. This clearly wasn't a good time. "If you like, I'll go and organize a foraging party," he told Berry.

Before Berry could answer, Viper had rolled her eyes and curled her muzzle. "Oh, you're *much* too important for such a basic mission, Thorn Highleaf." She paused, and a mean light sparked in her brown eyes. "Besides, we wouldn't want you getting lost again."

Thorn drew an angry breath, but Berry seemed oblivious. "Viper's right, Thorn—you *are* too important, and there's so much I need you to do here. Viper, get some Lowleaves and Deeproots together, will you? They can handle this."

"Of course, Crownleaf." Viper gave Thorn a smirk as she stalked away.

He seized his chance. "Whatever you need me to do, I'll do it," he told Berry. "But can we talk first? It's about what happened to me—"

"Oh, it must have been *awful*. Waking up, wounded, not knowing what had happened . . . Yes, Creeper?"

Thorn clenched his paws and breathed deeply as Creeper loped up and bowed. "The Crown Guard is ready for inspection at the Crown Stone, Berry."

Thorn stiffened. *Crown Guard? What?*

"Oh! Already? Very well, Creeper." Berry touched Thorn's arm and gave him a soft smile. He returned it, firmly quashing his unease. Why should Berry's Crown Guard be anything like the Strongbranches her father had appointed to terrorize the troop? Besides, a Crownleaf was perfectly entitled to organize the troop's defenses in her own way.

"I'm so sorry, Thorn," she murmured. "I did ask Creeper to fetch me. Perhaps we can speak later?"

"Or I could come with you now," said Thorn with strained patience.

She smiled at him warmly. "That would be perfect."

Thorn followed Berry as she strutted after Creeper toward the Crown Stone clearing. "Berry, what's the Crown Guard?" he asked. "That's new."

"It is!" Her eyes sparkled with enthusiasm. "I want a rank of baboons who will be our first line of defense in any attack. Dawntrees must be better prepared if there's another assault like Tendril's, don't you agree?" Without waiting for Thorn's answer, she went on fiercely: "I won't see the most vulnerable hurt anymore. Every baboon will have the Crown Guard's protection. The Guard are the best fighters, the toughest and most experienced baboons in the whole of Dawntrees Troop. Oh—the name was Viper's idea! What do you think?"

Thorn shuddered. "I, uh . . ."

"I'm so glad you approve. I knew you would, Thorn! Tendril and her gang are still in the vicinity, you know." Berry frowned. "I'm putting a new rule in place, just while the danger is out there. Baboons have to stay in groups of at least three when they go outside the forest. Don't you think that's safer? And it's only for a little while, as I say. Only until we deal with Tendril—ah!"

Berry halted, her face rapturous with approval. Lined up before the Crown Stone was her new Crown Guard: fifteen or so baboons—big, sturdily built individuals, Thorn noticed, and drawn from every rank. Highleaves and Deeproots; Middleleaves and Lowleaves; every one of them was gazing at Berry with a solemn, fierce loyalty. She bounded onto the Crown Stone.

Watching from the edge of the glade, Thorn was speechless. How had all this been organized without him realizing? Clearly it was common knowledge in the troop, yet Berry had said nothing to him. *Why would she keep it from me?* he thought, unable to repress a pang of hurt. But the answer was obvious.

Because she knew I wouldn't approve.

Rising onto her hind legs, Berry clasped her paws and let her gaze drift across the ranks.

"I thank you, my friends and comrades," she murmured,

her voice breaking slightly. "I thank you all for agreeing to be part of my Crown Guard. You have willingly lent me your strength, to protect the vulnerable among us."

Blinking, Thorn stared at her. Berry looked so strong, so noble and so gentle. He should feel proud. He *was* proud. He admired her, he loved her. . . .

So why are spiders crawling along my spine?

"You, my Crown Guard—you will be my delegates, my representatives, when I can't be there. You will act as my own paw." Berry smiled again. Her gaze swept toward Thorn, but she didn't quite meet his eye. "In times of war and trouble, you will be our defenders. You will be the strong and sturdy branches that protect the great central trunk of our troop."

Creeper stepped respectfully forward. "I have personally selected each of these baboons, Berry Crownleaf. They're strong, and they demonstrated their bravery in the battle against Tendril and her horde. They want to swear their oath to you now."

"Oh." Berry raised her paws, eyes widening. "Creeper, I don't need an oath to know these baboons are strong and loyal in the defense of Dawntrees."

"With your permission, Berry, they *want* to do this." Creeper bowed his head, then lifted his remaining eye to hers. It was dark and steady. "All of us feel it's right that we proudly display our allegiance to you."

Berry hesitated. Then, at last, she gave a nod. "Very well, Creeper. I thank you—all of you. I understand what this means to you. The oath is not for me—but for Dawntrees itself."

Creeper rose up on his hind paws, and in a single movement, the Crown Guard followed his example. Creeper thumped his chest with his right paw, and as he spoke, the baboons behind him joined in, clear and confident.

"Berry Crownleaf, solemnly elected leader and guide: We vow our allegiance to you. We fight for you and for Dawntrees. We fight for the security of the troop. We follow you, we shed our blood for you, and if called upon we will die for you. This we swear, by the mothers who bore us and the trees that sheltered us. May Dawntrees prosper!"

Staring at them, and at Berry, emotion surged in Thorn's chest. This was *wrong*. Deep in his gut, he was certain of that. This—this creation of an elite force answerable only to the Crownleaf—it was something Stinger would have done. No— it was something Stinger *had* done, disastrously for the majority of his cowed and terrified troop. Of course Dawntrees must be defended; Thorn knew that as well as any baboon. But this wasn't the way, this was *dangerous*.

Berry's words echoed in his head: *You will be the strong and sturdy branches that protect the troop. . . .* It was right there, from her own mouth—the spirit of Stinger's Strongbranches. What if the Crown Guard was just as cruel? What if Berry had changed, now she had tasted power? What if she took after her malevolent father after all? What if—

"Stop it!" Thorn hissed to himself. His claws were dug into his palms and he was shaking. He knew Berry. She was his

mate, and he loved her. Why was he thinking this way? What made him doubt her like this? He hated it—and suddenly he knew what was responsible.

Great Spirit! he snarled inwardly. *I never asked for you! If this is how you make me feel, then get out!*

Berry jumped lightly down from the Crown Stone. The Crown Guard surrounded her, bowing their heads and declaring their support as she smiled at them. Thorn's gut felt cold and tight, but he ignored that and pushed his way toward her.

"Berry, you did so well," he told her warmly. "That was a moving ceremony."

"It was, wasn't it?" She rubbed her brow as the Crown Guard dispersed, their faces solemn and proud. "Completely unexpected, but such a good way for my Crown Guard to establish their camaraderie, their spirit." Her eyes shone with emotion. "I'm so proud of them."

"I know. And you should be." He was convincing himself, he knew it. "You deserve all the loyalty baboons can give. And you have mine, too, always. You know that." He hesitated. *Now.* Now was the moment to tell her everything: about the vultures, about the mountain, about the Great Spirit. He wanted to silence that awful, doubting voice in his head once and for all. What truly mattered—the *only* thing that mattered—was him, and Berry, and their love for each other.

"Berry." He gazed into her eyes. "Can we find somewhere to be alone?"

"Of course, Thorn," she said softly. "You wanted to talk to

me, didn't you? Come on, let's—" She glanced over her shoulder. "Twig?"

The thin baboon dipped his head. "With respect, Berry Crownleaf, the Highleaf committee is waiting for you."

Thorn clenched his jaws so hard, they hurt. If he punched Twig in the muzzle, right here and now, he was sure the Great Spirit would forgive him *that*.

"Oh, Twig, I almost forgot! I'll come now." Berry turned apologetically to Thorn. "It's about reestablishing the Three Feats. I'm so sorry, Thorn."

"Of course," he gritted, forcing a smile. "Life has to get back to normal. And we'll have plenty of time to be together later." Remembering his other promise, he seized his chance. "Only . . . speaking of getting back to normal, it's time the troop had a Starleaf again. Mud is very keen."

"Mud?" Her brow shot up. "I didn't know he was even interested!"

Then you haven't been paying much attention, thought Thorn dryly. "He really is, Berry. And he's been practicing hard. I think he'll be really good."

"Well," she said doubtfully, "I suppose if he's enthusiastic, we could let him do it. His mother was the previous Starleaf, after all." Her muzzle wrinkled. "If you really think he's capable, Thorn, I don't have any obj—"

"There is one thing, Crownleaf," interrupted Viper, who had sidled up to Berry's side. "Every potential Starleaf must pass the Moonstone Rite."

Berry slapped her forehead. "Of course."

"Mud is well aware of the Moonstone Rite," growled Thorn tetchily. "And he's more than willing to go through the test, Viper. In fact, it's a full moon tonight, so it would be the perfect moment."

"Oh, you're right," exclaimed Berry, looking relieved. She gave a rather impatient glance into the forest, where the committee was waiting. "Well, that's perfect. It's all solved! Thank you, Viper." She started to bound into the trees, then turned back, the stump of her tail quivering. "Thorn, by the way—have you seen my mother? She hasn't returned from her scavenging trip."

He shook his head. "I'll keep an eye out. I'll see you, Berry, after—"

But she was already gone, her haunches vanishing into the shadows between the mahogany trees. Thorn sighed in frustration.

"Hmph," muttered Creeper into the uneasy silence. "Don't look so mad, Thorn. Berry's our Crownleaf, now. She's too busy to fuss over *Middleleaves*."

The barb took Thorn's breath away. For a moment he could only stare at Creeper.

The big baboon shrugged. "Well, you never officially became a Highleaf. It was only that barbarian Tendril who gave you that honor, while you lived with Crookedtree—and that was by default, right? *She* didn't know any better."

"I'm a Highleaf," barked Thorn angrily. "This troop conferred my status after the Great Battle, or had you forgotten?"

Creeper hunched his shoulders, indifferent. "Yes, sure. Because you were so used to being a Highleaf, after being treated like one by Crookedtree. Actually, it wouldn't be surprising if you still felt something for that troop." He paused for devastating effect. "Loyalty?"

Thorn gave a snarl of fury. "I've got no love for Crookedtree, and you know it," he spat. "I'm a Dawntrees baboon to my bones. And I'm Berry's mate, and I'll never stop protecting and defending her."

"Don't worry about *that*." Creeper set off into the trees and threw his last words dismissively over his shoulder. "The Crown Guard can protect Berry. That's none of your concern anymore."

CHAPTER 17

The moon hung huge and silver over the forest, its glow casting shadows across the path Thorn and Nut took toward the Crown Stone glade. The night was hot, the song of the insects muted.

"I'm sure Mud will pass the test," said Nut quietly. "Don't worry too much, Thorn."

"Oh, I'm not worried," Thorn told him, distractedly snatching up a grub and popping it into his mouth. "I've got confidence in Mud. I know he can do this." He wished he could tell his heart; it seemed to be thumping far too hard.

"It'll be good for the troop to have a new Starleaf," Nut went on, and hesitated for a moment. "It makes for a bit of balance. . . ."

Thorn shot him a sideways glance. "What do you mean?"

"I mean, uh . . ." Nut scratched at his muzzle, then shook his head. "I just mean that there'll be another voice. You know, guiding the troop. Advising us. Rather than it just being—you know. The Crownleaf."

"Huh?" Thorn stared at him in surprise.

"I reckon it's a good thing," mumbled Nut, "when the Starleaf is a bit of an irritant. Sort of a bug that bites the Crownleaf, keeping them on their toes. If the Crownleaf gets annoyed with a mouthy Starleaf, it's always a good thing. Remember how angry Stinger used to get with Mud's mother? Because she sometimes contradicted him. Being inconvenient—being a nuisance to the Crownleaf—that's a good thing. I reckon," he finished lamely.

"I think you're right—a Starleaf is a good thing for any troop," said Thorn. "But Berry's our Crownleaf now! She won't need one in the same way Stinger did. She won't *need* to be contradicted or inconvenienced. Because she's nothing like Stinger." He could hear the volume of his own voice rising. *Why am I shouting?*

"Well, of course she isn't." Nut looked as if he was about to say more, but instead he closed his muzzle firmly.

"Come on, Nut," Thorn coaxed him. "You can't leave it there. What are you trying to say?"

Nut took a deep breath, then puffed it out in resignation. "You want the truth, Thorn? I didn't really want to vote for Berry."

"*What?*" Thorn halted, startled.

"I just felt like I had to," said Nut, giving him an apologetic look. "Because she's your mate, and we're all friends. All that. But really . . . I kind of thought a break with the past would be better."

Too taken aback to reply, Thorn caught his breath. *Other baboons are thinking like this?*

Everything felt so wrong and confusing: half of him was resentful on Berry's behalf, and half was relieved he wasn't the only one with doubts.

But I love her! I should be supporting her with all my heart! Opening his jaws to remonstrate with Nut, Thorn felt his forepaw land on a familiar patch of soft moss, and he glanced up, startled. It was too late; they'd arrived in the Crown Stone clearing, where the Moonstone Rite would take place.

Thorn took his place in the crowd of waiting baboons. They were packed thickly in the trees and in front of the bushes, and in the empty space before the Crown Stone; on the Stone itself sat Berry, her brown eyes anxious. Now and again she would glance down at the Crown Guard who surrounded her; she would mutter an inaudible instruction, or bite her lip, or scratch at her shoulder. Her eyes wandered constantly to the fringes of the glade, as if she was looking for someone. She looked so very fidgety and ill at ease, thought Thorn, frowning.

The troop had assembled in ranks according to their status, and the Highleaves were in the front row; Thorn made his way there, gently easing his way through the crowd, muttering apologies as he bumped into shoulders and stood on paws. As he moved to the front and Berry caught sight of him, her face brightened.

"Thorn!" she called urgently, and beckoned him closer to the foot of the Crown Stone. "Have you seen my mother yet?"

Thorn shook his head. "I haven't, Berry. I'm sorry."

She chewed her lip again and sat back, her brow furrowing.

So that was why Berry looked so anxious. It wasn't unusual for baboons to wander off on their own errands, but Thorn too was starting to worry about Pear Goodleaf. Now that he came to think of it, he hadn't seen her for a long time.

If he could just summon one of his visions—deliberately this time . . .

On the mountain he had entered the mind of a rat, an eagle, and an elephant, so why not Pear's? Drawing back into the bustling horde of baboons, all exchanging their own gossip, it wasn't difficult to stay silent and close his eyes.

Creasing his face, Thorn concentrated hard. *Pear. Where are you?* He thought of her kind, wise face, the eyes darkened by years of sorrow at losing her daughter, the dimpled notch at the side of her mouth formed by all those sad half-smiles. Thorn frowned and squeezed his eyes tighter, thinking himself into the old baboon's head.

But there was nothing, only blackness. Snapping his eyes open, Thorn gave a soft *tut* of frustration. He didn't even have a headache. *So much for my vaunted powers, Windrider, you old fraud!*

The chattering baboons were gradually falling silent around him, and Thorn forgot about Pear to concentrate on his friend. Mud was creeping hesitantly into the cleared space before the Crown Stone, his stones clutched tightly in his paws. Even from where he stood in the crush of baboons,

Thorn could see that the little baboon was trembling with nerves.

Come on, Mud. I know you can do this!

Berry rose to her paws, her eyes roving across the troop. "We welcome Mud Lowleaf, candidate for the new Starleaf of Dawntrees Troop! Some of you have not witnessed this rite before"—her eyes softened—"and I freely admit this includes me!"

A ripple of laughter went around the troop, and many baboons nodded.

"But our elder troop members have advised me, and they have instructed Mud about what is required of him tonight. With his eyes covered so he cannot see, Mud must scatter his divining stones on the ground. Still blind, he must then choose his Moonstone from the others. In this way, he will prove that he has the abilities demanded of a Starleaf. I wish you good fortune, Mud Lowleaf!"

"So do I," declared Thorn, edging forward. His eyes met Mud's, and he tried to convey all the reassurance and faith he could in a glance. "I know you can do this, Mud!"

Mud gave him a nervous smile, but before he could reply, Viper stepped forward, bearing the ancient, bleached-white skull of a gazelle. Only its long, backswept horns were dark, patterned with rings all the way to their sharp tips, and its blank eye sockets were stuffed with red leaves. Standing behind Mud, Viper raised the skull high, then lowered it over his head.

It looked ridiculous, Thorn couldn't help thinking. The

skull was enormous on Mud's small body, and it slipped sideways so the horns jutted up askew. Yet at the same time there was something sinister about it, as if Mud was some unnatural creature of night, and his misplaced eyes were aflame with Spider's fire-leaves.

As Mud took a step forward, he swayed a little beneath the weight of the massive horns, but steadied himself. The skull glowed eerily in the white glare of moonlight. A hush fell over the troop as Mud lifted his paws and flung the stones in an arc across the ground.

Thorn held his breath. Mud was standing very still, the skull turning slowly first one way, then the other.

There were mutters behind Thorn, so quiet that he didn't recognize the voices.

"He can't do it, can he?"

"Ha, I knew it. He's deluded."

"Right? He's no Starleaf."

Thorn gritted his teeth and clenched his paws. *Come on, Mud. Prove them wrong.*

Mud walked hesitantly forward; then he stopped, crouched, and reached out. The Moonstone glowed bright among the other stones, a beetle-length from his claw-tips. Mud stretched his paw farther, and it hovered over the white pebble like a confident hawk.

Yes! I knew he could do it. I knew it! Thorn could hardly breathe.

Then, abruptly, the heavy skull swung in the other direction. Without even hesitating, Mud seized a cloudy green stone and raised it above his head.

Guffaws and gasps rang out around the clearing. A voice shouted from the Deeproot ranks: "He blew it!"

Viper padded forward. Mud stood absolutely still as she lifted the gazelle skull from his head; his paw was still raised high, clutching the green pebble. He glanced at it, then back at the troop, and his face was oddly impassive.

"That's a shame." Berry sounded distracted rather than disappointed. "Dawntrees, I'm afraid we are still without a Starleaf."

Mud shrugged, his eyes locked on Thorn's. He ignored the teasing taunts from the rest of the baboons. "I thought I had the power," he said flatly, "but I obviously don't."

Thorn could only stare at his friend. Mud's eyes, usually so bright and open, seemed opaque; Thorn had no idea what was going on in his friend's head. Mud had wanted this so badly; why did he now look simply resigned? Misery, Thorn would have expected, but not this dull acceptance.

Mud's hiding something, he thought.

"A pity, but Dawntrees Troop doesn't need a Starleaf." Creeper picked at his teeth. "With the Great Spirit absent from Bravelands, it's time we started thinking differently. Prophecies, star-readings—what do they matter if there's no guiding Spirit?" He indicated the Crown Guard with a paw. "What we need is a strong leader, certainty, rules to live by." Turning his head, he looked meaningfully at Berry.

Thorn shot a glance at Nut. Nut gave him a wry, knowing nod. Clearly he remembered as well as Thorn did what they'd talked about on the way to the clearing. Thorn swallowed hard.

To his surprise, though, Berry rose onto her hind paws and looked severely at Creeper. "Every troop needs a Starleaf, Creeper. It's not right to be without one. We will have another candidate by the next full moon, I'm sure of that."

She jumped down and padded away from the Crown Stone, escorted by her Crown Guard; the rest of the troop began to drift away, chattering and gossiping. Thorn searched through the press of bodies until he found Mud, small and insignificant now without his absurd skull head.

"Mud? What happened? What was that all about?"

"What was it about?" Mud furrowed his brow and peered up at Thorn. "I don't know what you mean."

"Yes, you *do*! You were so sure of yourself, Mud. *I* was sure of you! You nearly had the Moonstone, you were about to lift it! But you changed your mind. And you *knew* you'd chosen the green one, the wrong one. You knew before you picked it up." Thorn took his friend's shoulders and shook him gently. "And I saw your face after you picked the wrong stone. You didn't look sorry. Something happened, Mud. You can't lie to me—it's *me*, your best friend, remember?"

Mud's taut muscles went suddenly slack in Thorn's grip, and the little baboon went limp. His head hung forward in shame. "All right. I couldn't do it!"

"Yes, you—"

"I don't mean I wasn't capable, Thorn." Mud shook his head vehemently. "I mean, I couldn't *do* it. I couldn't take on the Starleaf's mantle. It wasn't right."

Thorn's jaw slackened. "But *why*? Mud, I don't understand—"

Mud nodded. "I know. Come with me, Thorn, and I'll show you."

The glade was almost empty now, and the forest was already quieting as baboons nested for the night. There was no one to disturb the two friends as Mud led Thorn to a nearby clearing, darker and overgrown and spotted only faintly with moonlight. Mud halted and took a breath, then cast his stones onto the mossy ground.

They jolted and rolled and came to rest in a pattern that meant nothing to Thorn: two pebbles off to the right and three to the left, with the Moonstone at a point above them both. Resting against the pure white stone, and covering it slightly, lay a black pebble of obsidian.

Shaking his head, Mud pointed to each stone in turn. "*That* is the problem, Thorn. That's what I don't understand. They always fall in the same pattern. *Always.*"

"You know I can't read these, Mud."

"No, but take my word for it, Thorn: the stones always tell me the same thing. And it isn't right."

Thorn frowned. "What do you mean?"

Mud took a deep breath, his eyes bright and serious. "The stones say we're following the wrong leader."

"What?" Thorn blinked in shock. "That doesn't make—"

"Sense. I know. But it's what they say, every time I cast them. We're walking along a bad path, setting ourselves against the Great Spirit." Sitting back on his haunches, Mud gazed sadly up at Thorn. "Now, you tell me, my friend. How could I deliver that message to Berry Crownleaf?"

Thorn opened and closed his jaws, lost for words. He wanted to argue with Mud, tell him he *must* be wrong. That the stones were faulty, that he'd misunderstood the rules, that the interpretation had been skewed by—bad weather, broken branches, a moon that wasn't as full as they thought—oh, he *didn't know.*

All he could hear in his head were Nut's words earlier tonight: *I didn't really want to vote for Berry.*

Mud cleared his throat. "You know who should be our leader, Thorn. And it isn't Berry."

Thorn stared at him, a hot coil of dread in his gut. "But she was elected! Fairly, by the whole troop!"

"Because you weren't here," mumbled Mud, staring down at the pattern of the pebbles. "You saved Brightforest Troop, Thorn, and you saved the whole of Bravelands. It was clear as day who should be our Crownleaf, and everyone understood without having to say it. But the way things have turned out since then? It isn't right, and the stones are telling us so. They know it. *You* know it. Be honest!"

"But Mud, I . . ."

Mud's head jerked up, and he stared into Thorn's eyes. His own were suddenly fierce and frighteningly certain. "You haven't been yourself since you disappeared in the battle, Thorn. I don't believe that stupid story, about banging your head! Something happened to you, didn't it? Tell me!"

Thorn felt as if his whole self was being turned inside out, as if he was raw and exposed down to his very bones.

"Mud. Mud, I . . . I hardly know where to start." Thorn's

throat felt dry and tight. "There's so much I haven't told you. So much I want to tell you. I—"

Angry hoots and screeches of alarm erupted from deeper in the forest, so loud Thorn almost jumped out of his skin. He growled with furious frustration, yet somehow he wasn't surprised; he was beginning to believe the truth was not meant to be told. Was the Great Spirit thwarting his attempts to come clean?

Without another word he turned and bounded from the clearing, leaving a bewildered Mud behind. The commotion was coming from the Crown Stone clearing; other baboons were running toward it. Some were waking, blinking in shock, scrambling down from their nests in the trees.

"What is it? What's—" Breaking through the undergrowth into the clearing, Thorn stopped short.

The Crown Guard stood around a captive baboon, their faces fierce and remorseless, their fists punched into the ground, their muscles tensed for any attempt at escape. "We've caught a Crookedtree spy!" shouted Root.

Thorn stared in disbelief at their cowering captive. He knew that scabby fur, and he recognized the pink scars on the palms that were outstretched in injured innocence. Most of all he knew those wide, fey, moon-dazed eyes.

Spider!

CHAPTER 18

Lying on the hard, dry ground next to Keen, Fearless could feel his fur prickling. It was the same sensation he'd been aware of for days; his head felt fuzzy from nights of disturbed sleep. It wasn't a warning of immediate danger, he knew; there had been no scent or sight of Titanpride since they'd rescued Ruthless.

No: his unease was down to nothing but the mood of poisonous animosity that hung over his own pride. It buzzed in the air around the young lions like the maddening, ever-present flies. Lions would snap at their pride-mates for no obvious reason, and when an argument really took root, Fearless often thought it would end in bloody bites and scratches, or worse.

He and Keen had taken to relaxing some distance from the rest of the pride and hunting as a pair. He felt desperately sorry for Gracious, and would have taken her with them if only to make her feel better, but her wound was not healing as it should, and she no longer took part in hunts at all. Her face remained swollen, and Fearless did not like the way those claw marks smelled. At night he could hear hyenas barking nearby, as if they sensed the presence of a lamed victim, and vultures had taken to landing in the pride's shade trees. Several flapped down there now, stretching their huge black wings as they clutched branches. One by one the birds settled, hunching to observe the lions below with beady black eyes.

The vultures were supposed to be sacred to the Great Spirit, Fearless knew. But as much as he'd respected the Spirit since his life with the baboons of Brightforest, he still knew his lion heritage. And lions had always seen the vultures for what they were: harbingers of death, and eaters of corpses.

Rising to his paws, he turned to the vultures and let out a deep, resonant roar. The biggest of them swiveled its bald head and eyed him; unhurried, it took off into the sky once again. Its companions followed its lead, their black wings beating lazily.

"I don't like those things," Fearless muttered to Keen as he lay back down. "At least, not here, and not right now."

Keen yawned, showing his long fangs. "I know what you mean. We don't want them hanging around Gracious. She's going to get better soon, and she can chase them off herself."

"I hope so."

"The good news is, Ruthless looks a lot better." Keen turned as the cub came bounding toward them. "Food will do that for a lion."

"Food, and not being bullied by your own pride," Fearless grunted. "Hello, Ruthless."

The cub bent his head to nuzzle Fearless's jaw. "Your pride is wonderful, Fearless. So much better than Titanpride! It's a good place to live."

So he was still oblivious to the tensions, thought Fearless with an inner sigh. "What have you been up to today, Ruthless?"

"Mighty's been showing me the best trees for honing my claws," said Ruthless proudly. "He knows a lot, doesn't he?"

Fearless gave a noncommittal grunt and turned to peer at Mighty and Valor. Their heads were close together as they murmured to each other, and a shiver of resentment raised Fearless's fur. Were they talking about him again? It was clear that Ruthless was smitten with Mighty now, just like the rest of the pride; a pity they didn't see him as Fearless did. Mighty and his own sister lay with the others, at the heart of the pride, as if it were *theirs*.

Resentment surged inside Fearless. Why shouldn't he claim his place there too? He didn't want to look as if he was sulking, especially since he *wasn't*. He belonged with Fearlesspride more than Mighty did. Getting to his paws, Fearless nudged Keen's head.

"I'm going to join the others," he growled.

As he padded toward them, Mighty and Valor stopped talking and pricked their ears, watching him. Had they been gossiping about him? Feeling a twinge of suspicion in his gut, Fearless walked on, ignoring the stares of the rest of the pride.

"Don't let me interrupt," he said a little sharply. "Carry on. What were you two talking about?"

Mighty and Valor exchanged a glance. "We might as well tell you," said Valor. "We were just wondering if the pride should move on. Go somewhere safer, where Titanpride can't reach us."

Fearless bristled. "You two were discussing a decision like *that*? Without consulting your pride leader?"

"Yes," said Valor calmly.

It was so enraging, Fearless could not even think of an appropriate retort. "Titanpride can reach us *anywhere*," he snarled at last. "Don't you understand anything?"

"Of course I do," said Valor patiently. "But—"

"More to the point, we don't *want* to be far away from them!" Fearless lashed his tail angrily. "If I'm to get my vengeance on Titan, I have to be in claw-reach of him, don't I?"

Valor took a breath, as if she were holding on to her patience by a hair. "It would only be for a short while, Swiftbrother. Just until Gracious recovers, and we're back at our full strength."

"You need every single lion in the pride to confront Titan? Even the wounded ones?" snapped Fearless, tossing his head. "Are you *afraid*?"

"Of Titanpride? Yes. It would be stupid *not* to be. Are you calling me a *coward*?" Valor drew back her muzzle to expose her fangs, and her eyes narrowed to golden slits. "Because that, *little brother*, is a different accusation altogether."

"Hey, hey." Keen padded hesitantly between them. "Let's not fight among—"

"Valor and Mighty are right," interrupted Hardy, padding over from his place beside Rough and the cubs. "It would be wise to move on. We might find better hunting grounds, too. There's not much growing here for the grass-eater herds."

"I do know a good place," put in Mighty, twitching his ears as he looked from one lion to the other. "It's not more than two days' walk from here. Plenty of prey, good defensive positions—"

"That's enough!" With a roar, Fearless slapped his paw onto the ground, raising a cloud of dust. "This is *my* pride, not yours!"

Keen licked his jaws nervously. "Mighty's only trying to help. . . ."

"Are you sure? It sounds to me as if he's challenging me for the pride!" Fearless knew he was going too far, but he couldn't stop himself. Rage seethed inside him like a river in spate.

"You're still such a *cub*, Fearless," sneered Valor, her fangs bared as she rose. "You and your vanity. Are you sure you've grown up at all? We know Fearlesspride is yours! The clue is in the *name*. Nobody's out to get you, you paranoid fool!"

"Then why are you trying to thwart me?" he roared. "Titan killed our father!"

"*Our* father?" Valor took an aggressive pace forward, snarling. "Don't you mean mine? Gallant could have beaten Titan in a fair fight, we both know that. But you? You're still a cub, and you don't even have his—" She stopped.

There was a horrible moment of silence, as heavy and ominous as a brewing storm on the savannah.

"Blood!" snapped Fearless bitterly. "That's what you were going to say, Valor: I don't have Gallant's blood! And you're right—as if it matters! Because I have Loyal's!"

"Of course it doesn't matter! You had a brave, strong father, but he isn't here now to—"

"He's not here, no, because he was killed by Titan too! Are you taunting me about *who my father was?*"

"That is not what I said! I just meant that somebody has to protect you, if only from yourself! And Loyal isn't here any-more—"

"You *are* taunting me! And I don't need protection!" His snarling jaws were almost touching Valor's; he could feel her slaver on his face, and her hot angry breath, and he knew the reverse must be true.

But both their heads were abruptly butted apart as another lion sprang between them. Valor yelped in shock, stumbling; Mighty's passing shoulder cracked against Fearless's jaw, and he fell back, dazed.

"Calm down, both of you!" the big lion growled.

"Stay out of it, Mighty," snarled Fearless, shaking his reel-ing head. There were hairs from the lion's mane in his mouth, and he spat them out. "I'm in charge of this pride, and I'll say what I like to its members."

"Might be better if Mighty *was* in charge." It was Rough's voice; she had come to stand beside Hardy, and they were both listening intently to the squabble. Fearless froze.

He should be really, furiously angry now, he knew. But a Fearlesspride lion had spoken the unthinkable. The shock of it washed through him like a cold stream of water, draining his muscles of all their strength. He felt like a helpless, foolish cub again, crouching in shame as the grown lions stared at him with disapproval.

It was too much. Gathering himself, he peeled back his muzzle and let out another agonized roar. "If that's what Mighty wants—if that's what you all want—he can challenge me right here, right now!"

The silence that fell was as taut and tense as the muscles of his thrust-out chest. The whole savannah seemed to grow quiet and expectant; even the birds had stopped chirruping.

Then, to Fearless's utter horror, the lions burst into laughter around him.

Not all of them, he realized: Keen stood in appalled silence, and Ruthless gazed at the scene in stupefied horror. But the rest laughed. They were *still* laughing.

"A challenge?" barked Hardy, his eyes watering.

"Mighty would eat most of you for breakfast and save the legs for supper!" That was Rough, barely able to contain her hilarity.

"Seriously, Fearless, don't be silly." Valor tried and failed to repress a hiccuping chuckle.

Mighty glanced at him and licked his jaws, his dark golden eyes apologetic. The remorseful pity in his face hurt Fearless worse than all the mockery of the others.

"Stop it, all of you," rumbled Mighty. "Truly, Fearless, I don't want to take your pride. Believe me! All I want to do is look after my—" He turned to Valor, hesitant.

"Your cubs," she finished quietly, and took a pace to stand at Mighty's side. She gazed at Fearless, her eyes softening. "I'm pregnant, Swiftbrother."

Fearless opened his jaws, then shut them again with a snap. Valor had cubs in her belly? His sister was going to be mother to Mighty's offspring?

He cleared his throat and shook his head. "That's why you've been so secretive," he rasped at last. "That's why you've been all over each other, muttering together. First you kept your new mate from me, Valor. And now here's another secret you didn't tell me." Something hot rose in his throat, and he gulped.

"I'm sorry, Fearless." Valor twitched her tail. "But how am I supposed to tell you anything when this is how you react?"

Slowly, Fearless took a pace back, then another. Realization sank through him, chilling his blood and making him feel sick. *I can't lead now. My pride isn't mine anymore. We can't go on.*

His voice was hoarse. "Mighty isn't going anywhere, is he?"

"No," said Valor softly. "Of course he isn't. Fearless, don't say something you'll regret—"

"He has to stay to care for his cubs," Fearless went on, as if she hadn't spoken. "And that means the tension in this pride is never going to get better."

"Fearless, *you're* causing the tension," murmured Valor. "Not Mighty. Can't you see that?"

"You know the worst thing? I can see why you all admire him." Fearless circled, staring for a long moment at each member of his pride. "Who wouldn't? Mighty doesn't even *have* to make a formal challenge. He's the leader of this pride just by *being here.*"

Wordless, they all stared at him. Hardy looked slightly contemptuous; Rough and Tough rolled their eyes at each other, but they looked awkward and embarrassed. Keen wore an expression of tormented sympathy.

"I can't stay," said Fearless suddenly. "I can't stand it. I'm sorry."

"Fearless, you can't leave!" exclaimed Rough. "Look, we're sorry you feel this way—"

"That's not the point," he growled. "It's not a matter of feelings. I simply can't stay where I'm not wanted, where I'm not even necessary. I'm leaving the pride."

Valor growled in exasperation. "No one wants you to leave, Fearless! Can't you just stay with the pride and prove your worth, like lions do?"

He shook his head rapidly. "Maybe I'm not all lion after all; maybe I stayed too long with the baboons. But I'm sorry, Valor. I can't stay. Not in Mightypride."

Mighty simply stared at Fearless as the siblings argued back and forth. His dark eyes were mystified. Fearless couldn't bear his gentle condescension.

"Good-bye," he said curtly. "I'm sorry, all of you. I'll leave now."

"I'm coming with you," exclaimed Keen, bounding to his side.

"And so am I." Ruthless padded forward, looking bewildered but determined. "I don't really know what's happening, and I'm sorry if I caused it. But I'm loyal to Fearless, and I'm going with him."

"Oh, this is ridiculous," muttered Valor. "But we can't stop you, can we?"

"No," said Fearless. "This is the only way for me now." He tilted up his head, clenching his jaw, then nodded jerkily to each member of his pride.

If he didn't walk away right now, he knew, the humiliation would be even worse. Turning, Fearless stalked away across the dry grassland, his muscles so tense that only the tip of his tail twitched to betray his turmoil. He hadn't even managed to choke out his thanks to Keen and Ruthless, but he could hear them anyway, padding after him, their pawsteps soft on the dusty earth.

He didn't look back. He couldn't. He could not bear to watch his pride grow distant, shrinking until they were lost in the haze of heat that simmered over Bravelands. *His pride.* It wasn't even that anymore.

All his efforts, all his struggles and disappointments and joys: they had all been for nothing in the end. Fearlesspride was finished.

CHAPTER 19

Dawn was spilling over the horizon ahead as Sky and Rock emerged from the forest where they had made their promise. On Sky's shoulders, she felt Nimble shiver, then shake out his furry mantle. The night's chill was already warming to the rays of the sun, and its sparkling light gilded the grass of the savannah; birds chorused in the trees, greeting the morning with a swelling harmony of chirruping, liquid trilling and coos.

The glow of the sunrise was echoed by a deep warmth of contentment in Sky's heart. She had no doubts, no moments of asking herself what she had done; the commitment to Rock was the right thing, she was absolutely certain of it. This simple, profound happiness was a wonderful contrast to all the doubts and fears and losses of the last few seasons; it was something she knew she could hold on to in her heart forever.

They walked on in an easy silence, needing no words; apart

from the birdsong the savannah was peaceful. So when the ground began to tremble beneath her feet, Sky gave a start.

She halted, frowning slightly. "Do you feel that, Rock?"

He didn't reply. His head came up a little more, and his ears twitched forward.

The vibrations were becoming a low, grumbling thunder. Sky tensed: it could only be elephants. Could it be her own family? But the Striders had headed in the opposite direction entirely; what would they be doing this far west? And these elephants were *running*—she could feel the ground shake harder with every moment.

Rock's ears flapped in anxiety. "I think that's a herd of bull elephants."

"That probably isn't good—" began Sky, but he interrupted quickly.

"We should avoid them," he growled. "Bulls can be unpredictable. Let's—"

But it was too late. The herd appeared over the next ridge, thundering diagonally across their path. Their great gray legs were almost obscured by a massive rising cloud of yellow dust, but their tusks glinted in the morning light, long and sweeping and curved. They were *huge*, Sky realized with a tremor in her belly; some of them were far bigger even than Rock. On Sky's back, she felt Nimble shiver with fear; his sister cowered as low as she could between Rock's shoulder blades.

A small watering hole shimmered some distance to their right; that was clearly where the bulls were heading, and they took no notice of Sky and Rock, to her shuddering relief. But

Sky couldn't help staring as they milled and splashed at the pool's edges, spraying their parched skin, pouring trunkfuls of water down their throats, rolling their vast bodies until the watering hole was churned to red mud.

"Come on," rumbled Rock in a low voice. "We should leave."

"Yes," agreed Sky with feeling. "Follow me."

But as she shambled into a brisk walk, aiming her path to give the bulls a wide berth, a bellowing trumpet resounded through the still air.

Sky froze, one foot raised. She took a breath and cocked one ear back.

"Sky, what?" said Rock urgently.

She swiveled her head toward the bulls. "I know that voice! But it can't be—"

The call rang out again, more insistent this time. It sounded eager, questioning. "*Sky?*"

"*Boulder?*" she breathed.

It had been so long since she had heard his voice, but surely she recognized it. Even if her ears weren't certain, the rest of her body seemed to be: a thrill of recognition and gladness rippled through her blood.

"Nimble," she murmured excitedly, lowering her trunk. "Hop down, little one. I need to go see a rather big elephant! Stay in that clump of thornbush, I'll come back very soon."

Surprised, the little cheetah scrambled down, and his sister shuffled backward down Rock's trunk to join him. They both huddled under the bush and watched Sky with curiosity.

"What are you up to, Sky?" Rock looked apprehensive, his

green eyes widening. "Sky, don't—"

"It's Boulder. My *brother*!" Without another word, Sky turned back and trotted toward the bull herd. One of them had broken away; he was cantering toward her, his ears tilted forward with joy.

"Sky!" he hollered. "Is that really you?"

"Boulder!" Sky picked up her feet, feeling lighter and suddenly far less tired. Her brother looked so well—and stars, he'd *grown*. She could tell even at a distance. He'd already been big when she knew him, but as he cantered toward her she could see that his chest was broader, his shoulders massive, and his tusks far longer than she'd remembered: long, near straight, and as pale white as drought-dust.

There was a single, sudden blare of anger from the bull herd. Taken aback, Sky jerked up her head. Behind Boulder, the other bulls were turning from the watering hole, raising their trunks in challenge as they glared past her. Her heart stuttered in frightened perplexity. Then, suddenly, the bulls were charging in Boulder's wake, like a mob of gigantic starlings following a leader. In moments the bigger elephants were overtaking Sky's brother, leaving him half obscured by billowing dust. One bull raised his trunk and gave another trumpet of fury, and more joined in.

The closer they came, the more intimidating they looked. The mood had changed distinctly, and now the air smelled powerfully of male aggression.

Rock had taken a step back, his tusks raised defensively,

but it was too late. The bulls were circling them now, shaking their heads and flapping their vast ears, and Sky could hardly see for the grit in her eyes. She flinched from their bellowing voices.

"Traitor! How dare you return!"

"Get out of here, exile!"

"Rock! You *murderer!*"

Rock? What were they talking about? Sky spun around in shock.

One of the big bulls lowered his broad head and charged forward, taking three or four steps before halting and raking the ground with his huge foot. Rock flinched and swung around defensively as another bull did the same.

"Rock? Rock, what's happening?" Sky twisted toward him, bewildered.

He opened his mouth, then closed it again. His eyes were wide and frightened; it was such an unusual expression on his brave face, Sky felt her heart skip.

"Rock!" she demanded, desperate to get through to him.

"Sky, I . . ." His voice dried again, even though the racket of bellowing was fading. He gazed at her, pleading, but at that moment Boulder shoved through the press of gray bodies and stood before Sky, his eyes hard.

"Sky!" he rumbled. "What are you doing with this elephant?"

"His name is *Rock!*" Sky glared at Boulder; this was not how she had pictured their reunion. "He is my life-mate, brother!"

"He's *what?*"

But Boulder's exclamation was drowned out by the angry trumpeting of his herd-mates.

"No! That outcast?"

"He's with your sister, Boulder? That cannot be!"

"He threatens your honor, Boulder, and ours!"

As their cries died away, Boulder swung his trunk, gazing at Sky with a look of profound sadness and regret. "Oh, Sky. You've made a terrible mistake."

"What?" Sky sidled closer to Rock, glaring defiantly at her brother. She had faced down the matriarchs of her herd, had left them and set out on her own to be with Rock—and now this? "I don't know what you mean, Boulder. And really, it's none of your business!"

"It is, Sky, for one simple reason." Boulder nodded at Rock, an expression of disgust twisting his lip. "Rock is exiled from our herd. We drove him out for breaking the Code. Tell her, Rock! *Tell my sister the truth.*"

"I . . ." Rock's gaze darted to right and left, as if desperately seeking an escape.

"Rock, what's this nonsense about?" Sky touched his shoulder with her trunk. "Why would they say such things? It's a mistake. Explain to them how wrong they are!"

Boulder's stare was unwavering. "Go on, Rock. Tell her why you were exiled. Tell her about River Marcher. Tell my sister that you're a *murderer!*"

Sky gave a gasp of angry shock. *River?* Sky remembered meeting her many seasons ago, when they'd joined the Marcher herd on migration; she'd been older than Sky, a lightly built elephant with warm brown eyes. They'd all been sad to learn that River had died.

"River's death was an accident. The Marchers told us she fell into a ravine," Sky snapped at Boulder. "What can that possibly have to do with Rock?"

"It was no accident," retorted Boulder. Despite his fury, Sky heard his voice crack. "Ask Rock!"

Sky turned to her life-mate, bewildered. He had swung his head to face her, but didn't seem able to meet her gaze. "I can explain, Sky. I . . ."

"Since you're having trouble, Rock, I'll do it for you." Boulder's hard voice trembled. "I wanted River for my life-mate; Rock was my rival. Nothing wrong with that. You must know, Sky, that when a female cannot choose, it is the custom of bulls to fight in honorable combat for our mates. And River loved us both."

Again Sky heard his voice break a little, but Boulder kept his implacable stare on Rock's drooping head.

"Yes," she whispered. "I've heard such stories."

"So fight we did, in the presence of River," growled Boulder. "But perhaps Rock knew he was losing. Because he turned and shoved River over a ravine to her death."

Sky's heart lurched with a shock of pain. She looked from Rock to Boulder, and back again. She wanted to speak, but she could not find her voice.

She remembered her vision now—the one she'd seen when she first touched Rock, when the Great Spirit was still within her and had allowed her to read the living. She had seen Rock, running away from other elephants, running desperately, fleeing for his life.

Now she knew what the vision had meant. Because as she stared desperately at him, hoping against hope that he would deny everything, Rock simply lowered his gaze and studied the ground at his feet.

"No," she whispered.

"Yes," said Boulder curtly. "Rock couldn't have River, so he sent her tumbling to her death. Now do you see? Rock can never be your life-mate."

Sky stood trembling, stunned.

Boulder touched her lightly with his trunk, then spun to face Rock. "Go, outcast," he said harshly. "You cannot be with my sister. You don't deserve her."

Rock seemed to rally for a moment, taking a pace toward Sky, his eyes pleading. "Sky, please let me explain."

"There's nothing more to explain," thundered Boulder. "Go!"

"Boulder, please." Sky set her jaw firmly. "Please let me have a moment with Rock."

"I don't think—"

"I am perfectly capable of making my own decisions, Boulder." Her voice was rough with emotion. "Let me speak to Rock now. *In private.*"

Boulder drew himself up to protest, then shook his head. "Very well." He gave Rock a savage look as he withdrew a little distance with the other bulls.

Sky could feel their protective stares as she walked close to Rock; restlessly, the bulls milled and stamped, and now and again one would take a pace in her direction before halting. She ignored them.

"Rock," she murmured, her voice cracking. "Did you really kill her?"

Lifting her head, she tried to meet his eyes, but he still wouldn't look at her. He brushed his trunk-tip against the dry earth, over and over again, swaying.

"It's true," he said hoarsely. "I'm sorry. But Sky, your herd was right: it was an *accident*. I was—I had the Rage. I didn't see her. I didn't even know I'd touched her until . . . until it was too late."

"The Rage?" Sky's heart chilled. She'd heard of the terrible madness that could seize bull elephants, but it had never occurred to her that might include Rock.

"I can't even explain how it feels," mumbled Rock. "The sheer overwhelming force . . . The Rage is a terrible thing, Sky."

"But *you*, Rock? *You* wouldn't fly into some wild, uncontrollable fury. You're not like that. I *won't* believe it!"

"You don't understand," he moaned. "It's not *me*. It's not something I want, Sky, it just *happens*. When I fought Boulder, all I could think of was fighting and kicking and stabbing and gouging. . . . I lost control of myself. *I'm sorry*."

She stared at him. Her mouth was dry. "I don't know you at all, do I?"

Rock reached for her with his trunk. "Yes, you do, please—"

"Rock." She took a step back. Her heart twisted and wrenched inside her, like a branch torn by a hungry elephant. "Rock, I need time to think. I need to be on my own for a while."

"Oh, Sky." His voice rose in frantic remorse. "I swear by the Great Spirit I would never hurt you!" He reached for her again. "Please, let me stay with you. I can protect you—"

"That's enough." Boulder appeared, shoving his great body between them. He glared menacingly at Rock. "Get away from my sister, you thug."

Rock tried to shoulder his way past the gathering bulls. "Sky, please—"

"I said *go*." Swiveling, Boulder lashed his tusks at Rock, who started back.

The other bulls advanced, swinging their tusks in threat and flapping their huge ears. All Rock could do was back away, then turn at last and stumble across the plain, the blaring of the herd driving him farther and farther from Sky. Boulder remained at Sky's side, overseeing this second exile with an expression of stern fury.

Sky watched Rock go, numb. Her heart was breaking somewhere inside her; she knew it, but somehow, for now, she couldn't feel it.

The patter of tiny paws was audible in the awful silence, and Sky glanced down, still frozen with shock and grief. The two little cheetah cubs had at last grown bored and emerged from their hiding place, and now they bounded between Boulder's legs, unintimidated and curious.

"Sky?" mewled Lively. "Sky, where is Rock going?"

"He's got to go away, little one." Sky's voice rasped against her throat; it felt as if it didn't belong to her, as if another elephant was speaking through her mouth.

"Why?" demanded Nimble. He took a couple of bounding paces, staring after Rock in dismay. "Why is he going?"

"Because he can't be with us anymore," said Sky in that same, strange, flat voice. *I will feel this soon, I know that. But right now I feel nothing.*

"But we liked him!" cried Lively. "Why does he have to go? Doesn't he like us anymore? Sky! Bring him back!"

"I can't, Lively. He has to leave." And at last the emotion was released, flooding out of her heart and filling her body with an aching, suffocating pain. She whimpered, deep in her throat.

"Don't worry, Sky." Boulder's deep voice was at her ear, and he laid his trunk comfortingly across her shoulders. "I and my brothers will protect you."

She didn't need protection, she thought, but she couldn't speak. She could look after herself.

And I will have to.

Nimble and Lively were keening at her feet, mourning for Rock, calling him hopelessly back in their tiny, high cries. But Sky did not even have the strength to comfort them.

Her future was gone; she had thrown it away last night at the sacred waterfall. *Elephant betrothals are binding for life.*

She would never have a mate. She was bound to Rock now: bound to an elephant who had lied to her and betrayed her.

She had left her family for him; Comet and her aunts had been right all along. She should have trusted them, trusted their ancient, well-honed instincts.

Her life-mate was gone. Sky would never see him again. And she no longer wanted to.

CHAPTER 20

The atmosphere in the Crown Stone glade was dense with hostility. Even the air Thorn breathed seemed sharp with it. There was a bloodlust that crackled from baboon to baboon, infecting them all with a savage, heightened rage. The Crown Stone guards stood in a circle, shoving and flinging the bewildered Spider between them, their faces twisted into snarls.

Thorn had felt this murderous strain in the air once before: when Brightforest Troop exiled Nut for the murder of Grub Crownleaf. Then, too, the bloodthirsty thrill had seemed contagious, each baboon inciting the others to higher and higher pitches of hatred.

And Nut had been innocent. Just as, he was certain, Spider was now.

Thorn sprang forward, pushing Grit aside, grabbing Creeper's shoulders, and pulling the big baboon back. "Don't!" he shouted. "Stop. You'll kill him!"

"So what?" snarled Viper.

Thorn clenched his jaws and growled. "How can we question the wretch if he's dead?"

That seemed to bring Viper up short. She narrowed her eyes and gave a slight nod, and the others calmed down too, grumbling.

Edging around Viper, Thorn bounded to Spider's side and seized him, as roughly as he dared, by the arm. The fey baboon looked more disoriented than ever.

Thorn brought his jaws close to Spider's head. "Pretend you don't know me," he growled quietly. "I'll get you out of this mess." He raised his voice to a ringing hoot of righteous anger. "You'll answer to our Crownleaf, stranger!"

"Where is this intruder?"

Startled, the troop fell back, parting to make way for Berry Crownleaf. The baboons' yells faded, their eyes widening with awe as she stalked through the mob, her brown eyes flashing with anger.

"Bring the enemy to me!"

Creeper and Grit seized Spider's arms, yanking him from Thorn's grip and marching him over to Berry. She stared at him coolly; but Thorn noticed that Spider didn't seem particularly intimidated. He blinked up at her, his expression vague.

"Quiet, Dawntrees Troop!" Berry's commanding voice rang across the glade, and the last mutters and growls died away. She stared at Spider once again. Berry seemed, thought Thorn, a little irritated at his lack of fear.

"What's your name?" she demanded.

Spider chewed his lip. He glanced up at Creeper, and then at Grit, and scowled sulkily. "Spider is Spider."

Berry looked taken aback. Then her jaw set firm. "Spider of what rank? What troop?"

"Spider Spider." His singsong voice was distracted, and he kept glancing up at the trees as if looking for one of his bird-friends. "Spider No-Rank doesn't have a troop."

"Don't be ridiculous," snapped Berry. "Every baboon has a rank and a troop!"

"Oh." Spider looked surprised. He squeezed his eyes half shut as if he was considering the issue for the first time. "All right, then. Spider Prettyleaf from Cloudy Troop. No, Spider Hairyleaf from Puddle Troop. Wait a moment." He tugged an arm free so that he could bite a nail and frown. "Ah! I am Spider Fluffyleaf from . . . Bugsquash Troop. That's it!"

Berry was staring at him as if she couldn't decide if he was insolent or simply mad. *Mad*, thought Thorn. He shut his eyes. *Come on, Berry, he's mad. Mad as a nest of beetles, surely you see that.*

"There are no such troops!" she cried at last.

"No, I made them up." Spider nodded in satisfaction. "I thought you wanted me to have a troop, so I made one." He glanced around the troop, raising his brow as if expecting approval.

"Fool." Berry clenched her teeth. "Then who were your parents?"

Spider tilted his head in thought. "Mother Earth and Father Sky."

"How old are you?"

"Ooh, that is a hard one for Spider. To an ant, say: very old. To an elephant . . . well, young."

Thorn stared at him. Didn't Spider realize the trouble he was in? The troop was on the verge of killing him just to stop his nonsense, Thorn knew.

Then he thought: no, that's the trouble. Spider had no idea how serious this was. He was giving the answers he thought Berry wanted.

"Enough of this," growled Viper. "What do you know about Pear Goodleaf? What have you done with her?"

Spider blinked. "Pear? Mm, pears *are* tasty." A little apprehensively, he glanced at Viper for approval.

"This is a waste of time," spat Creeper. "Berry, he's obviously a spy for Tendril. We should kill him and be done."

"Wait!" exclaimed Thorn, bounding forward a pace. He glowered at Spider. "You—what's your name, Spider? Spider, listen very carefully, because your life depends on your answer. An older baboon, with streaky gold fur, a crease at one corner of her mouth. *Have you seen her?*"

Spider stared for a long, puzzled moment. Then, to Thorn's relief, his eyes brightened.

"Old baboon, my my. I *did* see an old baboon. Very pleasant and polite, she was. Spider and her, we had a nice chat. About birds, it was. Birds and clouds and stars and crocodiles."

Berry gave a shrill gasp. "You saw her?" She lunged to seize Spider's chest fur in her claws. "Where is she? *Where is my mother?*"

Spider looked no more than mildly taken aback, though Berry's trembling jaw almost touched his. "Walking that way." He skittered his fingers in the air, miming a striding baboon, then pointed south. "Long, long way away."

Releasing him, Berry stepped back and dropped to all fours, her stare still fixed on his innocent eyes. "South? Beyond the forest? That makes no sense."

"All Pear's herbs and plants grow out toward the grassland, on the west side," said Grit. "Why would she go south?"

"And she wouldn't need to go so far for her supplies," added Viper. "She can't be foraging."

"Spider, think very carefully about your next answer," gritted Berry through her clenched fangs. "Where is Tendril Crownleaf right now?"

"Tendril, Tendril, Spider knows no Tendril." He shook his head vehemently. "But Spider can show you where the old baboon was. Before she went for a walk. Does that help?"

"I daresay it helps a bit," muttered Berry.

"Enough to keep you alive for now, *maybe*." Creeper picked his teeth sullenly. "Unless you're just buying time to save your scabby hide?"

"I reckon that's exactly what the liar's doing." Viper nodded.

"It's worth checking out, surely!" said Thorn hurriedly. "I can take him and scout out that area. Have him show me where he claims he saw Pear. See if there's anything to this wild story."

Berry nodded distractedly. "Thank you, Thorn. That would be helpful—and brave."

"Hmph," muttered Creeper, shooting Thorn a suspicious one-eyed glare. "I'm not so sure. I think I should go with Thorn. To protect him."

Thorn did not like the sharp edge in his voice, but Berry nodded. "That's a good idea, Creeper. And since baboons should only go out in threes, as I decreed, we need someone else to go with you both. Who—"

"I'll go!" yelped Nut, loping to Thorn's flank.

Thorn grinned gratefully at him. At least he would have one ally at his side.

"Very well," said Berry. "Now, waste no more time. Go, Thorn! Please find my mother."

Spider was quite enthusiastic as he bounded along, pointing out landmarks and sniffing around tracks. "This rhino trail— yes, yes. I saw her walk this way. Toward that lone fever tree, see? Only one way to go after that. Too many rocks for poor paws the other way. See . . ."

Grimly Thorn loped after him, only too aware of Creeper at his heels. He had the sense it wouldn't take much for the big baboon to turn on him and try to kill him, so he was hugely glad of Nut running at his side. *At least it'll be two against one.*

They had been traveling for most of the morning, and the sun was rising fast toward its highest point. The landscape was white and glaring, the horizons to every side shimmering in the heat. Alongside Thorn's niggling distrust of Creeper there was a far worse torment in his gut about Pear. He didn't know what could have taken her so far from Tall Trees, or kept her away so long, but he feared it couldn't be good.

The dappled shade of a dense acacia grove was a relief from the burning heat. Thorn padded into its relative coolness after Spider, who had slowed his pace. With his wounded hands, Spider stirred a pile of sandy soil.

"Baboons have eaten." He licked his lips. "Lucky baboons."

Thorn peered over Spider's shoulder as Nut and Creeper came up to his side. Sure enough, there were fragments of fruit and shreds of soft leaves here, and a few husks of scorpion and beetle. Thorn's muscles tensed into alertness.

"This wasn't Pear," he muttered. "There's no scent of her."

"And look." Spider pointed up. "Nests. Baboons have *slept*, lucky—"

"Never mind that," interrupted Nut. He nodded toward a high sloping outcrop of rock beyond the trees. "What's in that cave?"

The four baboons crept closer to the shadowy hole in the rock. Overhung by jagged boulders, the gash looked as black as a lion's throat against the sunlit sandstone. A thrill of nerves rippled up Thorn's spine.

"We need to be careful," he growled. "The baboons we smelled might be in here, or nearby."

A few lengths from the hole, Creeper flared his nostrils and sniffed carefully. "There have been baboons here," he growled, "but the scent's stale."

"It's our only lead," said Thorn, loping a last few hesitant paces to the cave mouth. Gripping the rock, he leaned forward and peered into the darkness. "This tunnel's deep. We have to check it, make sure Pear's not trapped inside somehow."

He led the way, placing his paws with infinite caution as he crept down into the shadows. It was cooler in here, at least, but that wasn't a comfort; something about the dank atmosphere raised the fur on his neck. He realized his teeth were bared, and that he could taste the stale unpleasant air on the inside of his lips. Thorn tried to relax his muscles, but it was impossible.

There were no forks, no branches in the tunnel. That made the search easier, but it did nothing to ease his nerves. Thorn blinked, letting his eyes adjust. In the gloom he saw that the walls rose sharply from the cavern floor, smooth but ridged with narrow ledges; the ground beneath his paw pads was cool and gritty. There was not a hint of vegetation; this was a dead place, he thought. *A place of death . . .*

A pungent smell permeated the cavern: the droppings of some creature, Thorn guessed. But underlying that was another, more ominous odor that caught the back of his throat, dark and sickly sweet. Instinct made his fur rise and his hide prickle.

Thorn stopped. There was something huddled a little way ahead, there against the rough stone wall. He could see only an outline in the traces of light.

His gut clenching, Thorn padded forward again. He could hear the hard, anxious breathing of the others behind him, but he kept his eyes locked on that odd shape.

And then he saw. As the strength went out of his limbs, he

crouched limply beside the body of Pear Goodleaf.

With a trembling paw, he touched her fur. She was quite dead, quite cold, and her flesh felt stiff.

He shut his eyes as a racking grief seized him. *This will break Berry's heart.* It was very nearly breaking his. Berry had only just found her mother again, after so many years.

Now he knew why his powers had failed him. When he had tried to look through Pear's eyes he had seen nothing— because Pear saw nothing. She felt and heard nothing. She had been dead all along.

"Aw," said Spider, miserably. "Nice old baboon."

At Thorn's shoulder, Creeper was breathing fast and angrily. "Spider did this! Come here, you brute! I'll—"

"Hush!" Thorn sprang to his feet, ignoring Creeper and the cowering Spider. "Listen."

"Pawsteps," murmured Nut.

Many pawsteps, Thorn realized; they were quick and urgent and just beyond the cave mouth. He jerked his head toward the sound, and a sickening suspicion gripped his belly.

"We have to get back out," he barked as he sprang back toward the entrance. "Come on!"

The tunnel felt too long, his paws pounding painfully against the hard gritty ground. Behind him he heard the others racing, their breath panting with fear. But it was fine, it was fine: there was the dazzling light of the cave mouth ahead of them, and escape was a few sprinting paces away.

Squinting, he saw blurred, warped shapes move against

the sun's brilliance. Thorn's heart turned over. He could not make out what those shadows were, but he could hazard a guess. "Hurry, we have to—"

Before he could finish, his voice was drowned out by a rumbling thunder. Skidding to a halt, Thorn watched, appalled, as the glare of the sunlight was blotted out by tumbling, crashing chunks of darkness.

The racket of the rockslide resounded and throbbed, disorienting and sickening, and the cave mouth vanished swiftly beneath falling rubble. A last few cracks and glimmers of light were blotted out as boulders went on tumbling, smashing, rolling. Then the light vanished altogether, and the four baboons were in utter darkness.

For long moments after the echoes faded, Thorn could hear nothing but the distorted, frightened breathing of his companions. A few dislodged pebbles pattered to a stop.

Then: "Rockfall," snarled Creeper. "And not a natural one, I'd bet."

From the other side of the rocks a voice drifted eerily, muffled and warped by stone, but the taunt was clear.

"A trap, and you fell for it. Stupid baboons!"

Trap trap . . . stupid stupid stupid . . . The echoes bounced around them in the darkness. Cold fear flooded Thorn's blood.

"Dawntrees Troop is just as stupid as Brightforest, then," mocked Tendril Crownleaf from behind the rockfall.

Thorn let out a howl of impotent fury. "You let us out of here, Tendril, or so help me—"

"You'll do nothing!" *Nothing nothing nothing.* "You'll die in here." *Die die die . . .*

"What did you do to Pear?" yelled Creeper.

"The spy?" High, chilling laughter seeped from beyond the rocks, echoing through the cavern. "She paid the price. And so will you."

"Pear Goodleaf was no spy!" shouted Thorn. "She wanted to help!"

"Yes, yes, so she claimed. 'Oh, I'm here to make p-peace, I p-promise.'" Tendril mimicked Pear's gentle timidity, and Thorn clenched his fangs in rage. "But she couldn't fool me. I am Tendril Crownleaf!"

Thorn's fury ebbed a little, swamped by a dark and heavy sadness. "Pear Goodleaf was the kindest, most honest baboon I ever knew," he growled clearly. "You've broken the Code, Tendril, and all to kill a baboon who intended nothing but good for you and your troop."

Silence fell, heavy and dark.

"You let us out of here!" roared Creeper suddenly. "Do you hear me, crazy monkey? Let us out!"

"Ha-ha, as if I would," sneered Tendril. "You'll stay here and starve to death as you deserve. Look on the bright side, Dawntrees idiots. At least you won't have to watch your troop being wiped out."

"What?" snarled Thorn as his heart chilled. "What are you plotting, Tendril?"

"I'm not *plotting*, Thorn Highleaf, it's as good as done. We'll hit your troop tonight before dawn, catch them by surprise. And we'll take out all the females with young. All of them, Thorn. Every baby and infant and their mothers! That will put an end to your miserable troop once and for all. It will *destroy you!*"

Thorn sucked in a horrified breath. "Tendril! You can't. No! Tendril! *Listen to me!*"

Creeper and Nut were hollering their outrage too, and the echoes of his own yells and theirs hurt Thorn's ears. But however long they shouted and protested, it was useless. Spider was quiet, thought Thorn distractedly, and perhaps he was smart not to waste his energy; as their desperate voices faded at last, there was only silence. Tendril was gone.

"We have to stop her!" said Nut.

"We can't," growled Creeper. "We're stuck in here! That vicious little—" Hot breath struck Thorn's face suddenly, and he realized Creeper had swung around to him. "This is your fault, you stupid monkey. You led us in here!"

"Back off!" Thorn snapped his jaws wildly in the darkness and lashed out a paw. He felt Creeper flinch back abruptly, and the stink of angry breath was gone from his nostrils. "This isn't the time," he snarled. "We've *got* to get out of here! Look for a way, Creeper. Don't do it for me, do it for the troop!"

He heard a grumbling and cursing as Creeper shuffled cautiously toward the cavern wall, and he exhaled in relief. They couldn't fight among themselves, not *now*.

Turning, Thorn began to feel his way desperately along the stone, searching the rock for any cranny or breath of air.

"There has to be a way out. Tendril might have missed something."

"That cunning brute? I doubt it." Creeper had moved closer to him again, but this time he was scratching and fumbling at the stone. "She outsmarted you. Not difficult," he growled bitterly.

Thorn ignored Creeper. He could hear Nut close by too, and the scraping of his friend's claws as he checked the line where the walls met the rocky floor. From what Thorn could make out, Spider didn't seem to be helping at all—but his great resigned sigh was perfectly audible.

"Going to die," he said dolefully.

Thorn ignored him, even though he had a suspicion Spider was right. He couldn't bring himself to be afraid: not when the troop was in far greater danger. Gritting his teeth, Thorn scraped his paws fiercely against the rock, hunting frantically for cracks, not caring that his palms were already raw.

"There's a crack here," came Nut's eerily resonant voice. "But there's no way we'd get through."

"Up here there's a hollow, and I think it goes farther," said Creeper. He was scrabbling at the back of the cavern; Thorn had noticed earlier that the rock there rose up in a series of narrow ledges. "We could try it, but it might just take us deeper into the cliff." Creeper growled in frustration.

Thorn went still.

Creeper and Nut too fell silent, listening. From somewhere in the cavern came a strange, stirring rustle, like leaves whispering in a breeze. Thorn angled his head; it was hard to make out where the noise was coming from.

Spider hissed and squeaked and piped, and Thorn realized he was working out how to mimic the sounds coming from above.

"Shut up, Spider," muttered Creeper. "I don't like this."

"Me either." Nut shook off a shiver; Thorn heard him.

"Hush." Thorn suddenly tilted his head upward, staring into the blackness. "You too, Spider. Be *quiet*."

"Something's talking," said the eccentric baboon. "Spider hears voices."

He's right. Thorn tensed. The words were an odd, sibilant squeaking, but he could make out the language: a bizarre combination of Skytongue and Grasstongue.

"Hunting, comradesss?"

"Noooo. Ssstill day. Sssometing woke usss. Let me ssstretch wingsssss. . . ."

"Night'ssss taking too long. I hungry for bugsssss. And beeeetles."

"Patienccce, Slitherwing. Ssstretching . . . Ahhh. Go to sleeeep. Night soooon."

"What a sinister racket," complained Creeper, but Thorn touched his shoulder to quiet him.

"I think they're bats," he murmured.

"Ooh," said Spider with interest. "Spider likes bats."

"So this is where they go in the daytime?" Nut sounded reluctantly curious.

"Looks like it," murmured Thorn. "That must be what they are." In fact he knew it—all that talk of wings and bugs—but he wasn't about to admit he could understand what the bats were saying.

"Very interesting," said Nut dryly. "But it doesn't help us."

"No." Thorn's heart slumped again. "They're as trapped as we are now. Poor things."

"Everybody's going to die," said Spider, almost cheerfully.

A rage of helplessness suddenly filled Thorn, and he slammed a paw against the rock. He didn't care that it hurt.

Spider was right again. Tendril Crownleaf was heading for Tall Trees at this very moment, and she and her troop were going to slaughter the innocents of Dawntrees Troop.

And there wasn't a single thing he could do to stop it.

CHAPTER 21

Thorn had no idea how much time had passed in the darkness. There was not even a sliver of light, and though Pear's corpse did not unsettle him, it was sad to think of the poor old baboon lying here in the cold and lonely cave.

But at least Pear was beyond danger now. Thorn's heart turned over as he recalled Tendril's words yet again. *The mothers. The infants.*

He had heard Creeper and Nut slump at last against the wall, frustrated and simmering. Occasionally, Creeper would growl under his breath and slap the ground, but neither of the two spoke. Spider was scrabbling at small stones on the floor, intent as always on something completely unimportant.

Thorn got to his paws and prowled through the darkness, blinking hard. No, it was no good. No light had miraculously seeped into the cavern.

The bats had quieted long ago, but now he heard a faint rustle above him. He craned his head back to peer up.

More rustling, a sleepy squeaking. A flutter and hiss of leathery wings.

"Night'sss heeeeere! Hunt!"

Poor things, thought Thorn. They'd find out soon enough that there would be no hunting tonight, or ever again.

Above him, the ceiling erupted in a whirring chaos. Peering up, Thorn wondered if that was blacker shadows he could see, or if he was only picturing the bats. Nut sprang to his paws. Creeper grunted in surprise. Spider said, "Ooh, they're flying."

Thorn turned, trying to locate the bats by sound alone. To his ears it was nothing but confusion up there, but at last he realized that the bats were coalescing into a flock of sorts. They were gathering, orienting themselves, flapping away in a great mass—

And not toward the cave mouth.

Thorn tensed. He was sure of it now; the bats were flying deeper into the tunnels, and higher; none of them were returning, and he heard no squeals and cries of disappointment.

"Are they getting out?" asked Nut.

Thorn's gut stirred with excitement. "I think they are!"

He closed his eyes. He couldn't let on to his companions, but an idea was forming in his head. *Come on, Windrider. Please be right after all!*

It was hard to focus on a single bat in the spinning cloud

that diminished by the moment. But at last Thorn locked onto one bat-mind and let himself plummet into its consciousness.

And he was flying. His leather wings caught the air, cool and free, and his tiny heart brimmed with excitement. The hunt! The hunt!

The wingtips of his comrades brushed his, but it was no distraction. He was flying forward, the other bodies a reassuring cloud of rushing movement around him. The familiar tunnel was right ahead, and he adjusted his wings and swept through it, feeling the space open out around him. There was dusty darkness all around, but his ears and his head sensed every bump in the wall, every curve of the tunnel. It was easy instinct to find the way through. He smelled night and the forest, dark and green, and suddenly he burst with his comrades into the open, starlit savannah.

The ssstarlit sssavannah . . .

Thorn blinked and gasped, and he was deep in the caverns once more. He was a *baboon* once more. He shook off a lingering yearning for the taste of mosquito and grabbed Nut's arm.

"I think I know how to get out!"

"Oh, come on," drawled Creeper. "How could you suddenly know that?"

"I don't want to get stuck in some little bat tunnel," said Nut warily.

"Better die right here," offered Spider. "More room."

"Look, I can't explain. It was . . . I heard where they went," said Thorn urgently. "Come on, we have to try!"

"Because all your ideas have been so good?" said Creeper sarcastically. "Fine. I suppose we'd better make the attempt."

The cavern felt hollow and quiet with the bats gone, but Thorn was confident. He bounded to the rear wall, felt his way along it, then hoisted himself onto the narrow ledge he'd spotted through the bat's eyes. A faint hint of fresh air drifted to him from the narrow opening ahead.

"Follow me."

They already were. Thorn could hear Nut, Creeper, and Spider behind him as he ducked and wriggled through the gap. Creeper gave a grunt of annoyance, and Nut made an uncertain sound in his throat, but Thorn pressed on, squirming along a tight tunnel. Rough stone scraped his back, but he took a deep breath, wedged his paws against the rock, and shoved himself through. Behind him he heard Creeper's panicked grunts as he tugged and wrestled his way through. The big baboon was much larger than Thorn, of course. *I hope Creeper makes it*, thought Thorn guiltily, *but I'm not sorry he's having to struggle.*

The tunnel broadened, enough for Thorn to speed up into a crouching lope. Behind him, he could hear the slapping pawsteps of his companions, the click of claws, and their panting breath. Thorn didn't look back; he knew he could trust them to follow.

The passage narrowed upward, and for a moment Thorn felt a lurch of despair. *I'm not a bat. I'm a lot bigger!*

But the earth was loose here. Clawing at it, he dislodged soil and small stones until the opening was wide enough to squeeze through. He dusted grit from his fingers and bounded on.

Beneath his paws, the rock was sloping upward even more steeply. Was that faint light he could see ahead?

Yes, I saw it not long ago. Through a bat's eyes.

His heart leaping, Thorn scrambled up the last sloping stretch of tunnel, pebbles and dirt tumbling and rolling
beneath his claws. The patch of blackness ahead of him was
paler than the rest, dusted with stars.

Thorn burst into the open air and sucked in a joyful breath
of freedom.

They bounded the whole way back to Tall Trees, not pausing for breath as they raced across the grassland and through
the groves of starlit acacias. Thorn doubted they would have
stopped for a pride of hungry lions; a desperate urgency drove
at least three of the baboons on. What drove Spider, Thorn
suspected, was something he was never going to work out.

"How am I going to tell Berry about her mother?" panted
Thorn as they ran. He was dreading the terrible moment.

"Leave it for now, if I were you," suggested Creeper grimly.
"It should wait until the immediate threat is over. Dawntrees
needs our Crownleaf to be focused."

It sounded callous, especially coming from Creeper, but
Thorn knew he was right.

The four of them broke into the undergrowth on the
edge of Tall Trees. There was no sign of Tendril or her troop
yet, Thorn realized with a grim sense of relief; the cunning
Crownleaf must be so confident, she was in no hurry. Perhaps
she was waiting until the deeper, darker hours. *Before dawn,*
she'd said, though that could mean anything.

"Dawntrees Troop!" Thorn yelled as he bounded through

the forest. "Dawntrees, wake up! Danger! Danger!"

Baboons were already scuttling down trees and emerging sleepily from bushes. There were cries of surprise and confusion as Thorn led the way, still running, toward the Crown Stone glade.

"What danger? He said *danger*."

"Is that Thorn?"

"Yes, and Creeper."

"And Nut, *and* the weirdo stranger. They're back from reconnaissance."

"What's happening?"

The whole troop seemed to be at Thorn's heels as he burst into the Crown Stone glade; Berry appeared at the same moment, loping into the clearing from the opposite direction. She was flanked by four of her Crown Guards, their faces grim and hard.

"Berry." Now that he had halted, Thorn felt the exhaustion catch up with him, and he panted for breath, his body sagging. "Berry, Tendril Crownleaf is on her way here with her troop. They plan a sneak ambush. They're going to target the young and their mothers."

Berry's eyes opened wide, flashing with shocked fury. "She *what*? How dare she?" Turning to her Crown Guards, she snapped out immediate orders. "Go to the family nests and get them all to a safer place. Make sure they're guarded. Then station yourselves in the nests instead, but don't reveal yourselves until the last moment." She grinned coldly. "If Tendril can send assassins after our most vulnerable, she deserves the most brutal shock we can give her."

"What about Tendril herself?" asked Viper.

"She'll find she's bitten a lion," said Berry savagely. "And you kill a lion at the first bite, or not at all."

Thorn crouched in one of the family nests, every muscle tensed. He could clearly hear Tendril's bloodthirsty mob of baboons as they crashed through the forest foliage. Around him, he knew, the Crown Guards waited in nearby nests, and he found himself longing for the moment of the ambush. His heart hammered in his rib cage, but it wasn't fear. It was fury.

Then, below him, Tendril and her troops emerged at a run from the scrub, their muzzles twisted with battle-fury as they bounded toward the trees. Thorn allowed himself a grin of satisfaction as he coiled his muscles. A baboon was below him, scrambling up the fig's trunk; Thorn heard the quick, eager rake of its claws against the bark. Clearly it couldn't wait to murder Dawntrees infants.

When its scarred face appeared at the edge of the branches, Thorn gave a wild holler. Baring his fangs in a vicious grin, he flung himself down at the startled Crookedtree baboon.

The attacker gave a gasp of shock and tumbled back. Around them, there was a sudden uproar as the Crown Guards sprang out of their own hiding places. But Thorn did not have time to enjoy the commotion and the shocked screeching of the Crookedtree baboons. He focused on his own opponent, bounding down after him and tearing at his face with his claws.

The attacker had never stood a chance. Thorn flung his bleeding body aside and spun around to find another enemy. Across the small clearing beneath the trees stood Tendril, spinning this way and that in confusion as the wreckage of her plan slowly dawned: her eyes wide and white-rimmed, her paws uselessly clenching and unclenching. The look on her face had gone from cold triumph to horror. Flinging back her head, she gave a shriek of impotent fury.

Tendril had thought she'd laid and baited the perfect trap. *But she didn't reckon with our Crownleaf!* This, thought Thorn: *this* was a trap to boast about. His heart swelled with pride in Berry.

Between him and Tendril, an enemy baboon was trying to flee; Thorn sprang onto her back and brought her crashing to the ground. Around him, Dawntrees Troop was falling on the invaders like angry eagles, leaping down from the trees and setting about their enemies with claws and teeth and brutal blows. Nut had a Crookedtree baboon by the shoulders, slamming him over and over against a tree trunk till he collapsed. Mud was screaming with fury as he scratched and bit at a big warrior, and the warrior was reeling backward, stunned. Viper and Mango pummeled a baboon on the ground, screaming insults as each blow landed.

Dawntrees Troop was *angry*, thought Thorn as he pounded his opponent into unconsciousness. And that anger was justified.

A lanky Crookedtree fighter was sneaking up on Viper, his muzzle peeled back to show vicious fangs. And he was gripping a huge rock in one paw. . . .

Thorn flung aside his limp opponent and raced up behind the sneaky attacker. Just as the baboon raised the rock to smash it into Viper's skull, Thorn leaped onto his back, sending him crashing against a tree. Viper spun around in shock.

The enemy baboon stared goggle-eyed at Thorn and went limp. Blood spurted from his chest. He had fallen against a spike of broken branch, and it had pierced him through. With one last angry gurgle, he died.

Thorn staggered back. He felt revolted at what he'd just done, but he knew he'd had no choice. *Only kill to survive.* The Great Spirit seemed to agree; he sensed no protest from wherever it lay within him.

Clearly Viper agreed too. "Thanks, Thorn," she yelled, and he nodded.

When the troop is threatened—none of us are enemies.

A violent scream made him spin around. The battle had spilled into the Crown Stone glade, and in the melee he could make out Berry, fighting savagely on top of the Crown Stone itself. He recognized her opponent instantly: Tendril. And Tendril was so much bigger and stronger than Berry, and the Crown Guards were occupied in their own duels. . . .

Desperate to fight his way to his mate, Thorn slammed aside an attacker, but another Crookedtree baboon snarled and lunged at him. Thorn snapped and scratched at her. *Berry, hold on. I'm coming!*

His fangs bit deep into his opponent's shoulder, filling his mouth with warm blood. She screeched, wriggled away, and bolted, and Thorn spun around to run to Berry.

He was too late. Tendril was crouched over the stunned Crownleaf, her jaws wide to bite into Berry's exposed throat. Thorn opened his jaws to shout in helpless warning, but at that moment, a shadow scuttled up onto the Crown Stone, lanky and quick, like a—

Spider!

Spider bounded onto Tendril's shoulders, then hung on, biting and biting at her skull. Even from where he fought through the crowd, Thorn could see the blood spatter. Tendril reeled back, clawing at her head and her attacker, but she lost her balance and crashed back onto the flat top of the Stone.

As Berry scrambled to her paws, panting, Tendril finally toppled right off the Crown Stone and hit the ground hard. Immediately Crown Guards leaped on her, snarling as they pinned her down. Spider tumbled away from her shoulders and slumped against the Crown Stone, panting.

The battle was over quickly after that. Panting, bloodied baboons stepped back, swaying, some giving a last hard swipe at their defeated enemies. Around and between the trees, baboons lay dead and wounded. Groans of pain came from dry throats. Dawntrees baboons snapped their jaws and chittered in triumph.

The sun was rising, its rays piercing the trees of the forest, and above their heads, in the sudden quiet, the birds began to sing.

Dawn, thought Thorn. *And Dawntrees is victorious. If this isn't a sign from the Great Spirit, I don't know what is.*

He limped to the Crown Stone, where a stunned but still-living Tendril was being dragged roughly to her paws by the Crown Guards. Spider stared up at them wide-eyed. Berry squatted on the Stone, regal and angry, and stared down at her rival as her indignant troop gathered before her.

"Take the wounded of our troop, Goodleaves," was her first command. "Then I shall deal with this would-be infant-killer."

The Goodleaves rushed to do Berry's bidding; Dawntrees baboons were slapping one another's shoulders and hooting in triumph. The Crown Guard stood close around Tendril, their lips peeled back in menace. At last, an ominous quiet returned to the glade, and Berry still sat there, her face rigid with fury.

Thorn creased his eyes and peered closer. Berry was angry, of course, but her whole body quivered with what seemed an uncontainable rage. There was a visceral hatred in her expression as she studied the beaten Tendril.

Thorn's heart skipped with sudden realization: *She knows about her mother.*

Creeper stood at Berry's side with the rest of his Crown Guard colleagues. Thorn caught his single eye and saw its cold glint. He sucked in a breath.

Creeper had told her. He must have done it in the moments after the battle, Thorn realized with a sickening jolt. *That was not your right, Creeper!* Thorn was her mate, and Creeper knew it—and Thorn would have broken the news gently. He didn't

dare imagine how bluntly Creeper had imparted the news—
and he didn't dare predict how Berry might react.

Berry rose to her hind paws. As Tendril blinked rapidly
up at her, her face streaked with blood, Thorn saw a new and
unaccustomed terror in the enemy baboon's face.

"Swear allegiance to me, Tendril *Deeproot*."

There was a moment of heavy silence. "What?" rasped
Tendril.

"Do it," commanded Berry. "Do it, as is the custom for
defeated leaders. Take the one opportunity I give you for survival. *Swear me your allegiance*."

The whole forest seemed to go still, holding its breath.
Even the birds in the canopy paused their chorus.

Berry hopes she won't submit, thought Thorn suddenly. *She wants
to kill Tendril.*

"Yes." Tendril's voice, breaking the silence, was a hoarse
croak. She sagged in the grip of the Crown Guard. "I swear
you my allegiance, Berry Crownleaf, and . . . I repudiate my
former rank." She spat on the ground, as if the words tasted
like poisonous leaves in her mouth.

For a moment, a fleeting disappointment passed across
Berry's stern face. Then she nodded, once.

"I accept your submission," she declared through bared
fangs. "A Deeproot you will remain until you die. And your
absolute loyalty and obedience will be to me, and to Dawntrees Troop. Now get out of my sight. Crown Guard: find her
dung-clearing duties."

Tendril was dragged away by Viper and Grit. The troop

erupted in cheers and hoots of acclaim.

"*Berry! Berry Crownleaf!*"

"Long life to our Crownleaf!"

"May Dawntrees prosper under our wise leader!"

With the hoots and whoops ringing in his ears, Thorn loped toward Berry, shoving his way through the excited troop. He reached for her arm and clasped it gently.

"Berry. I'm so sorry about your mother. I—"

"Not now, Thorn. I'm busy." Turning brusquely away, Berry beckoned another baboon to stand at the base of the Crown Stone.

Thorn blinked in shock. He took an involuntary step back, feeling pain sting his heart. She'd never spoken to him like that, so cold and dismissive.

It was Spider who she'd summoned. He was looking at her with his bland, guileless gaze, fingers scratching at the pink, wounded palms of his paws. "What can Spider do for Berry?" asked the scabby baboon, a little nervously.

Berry smiled down at him. "You can accept my pardon, Spider Prickleleaf. Or whatever you're calling yourself now." She laughed, her rage all gone. "In fact, I believe you shall now be Spider Highleaf. You did save my life, after all."

Spider straightened abruptly, and his scrawny chest puffed out with delight.

"Spider thanks you, Berry Crownleaf! So kind, so kind. But." He shut one eye. "Spider doesn't care much about ranks, to be honest."

Berry's eyes glittered with what might have been amusement. "Then what does Spider want from me?"

Spider inclined his head humbly, and his eyes darted left and right.

"If there are any locusts around," he said hopefully, "I'm absolutely starving."

CHAPTER 22

The sun was melting into a line of violet and amber at the horizon, and silhouetted egrets flew lazily across its glow as Sky finished her tale. She felt more than worn-out; she felt empty, as if her whole body had been scraped hollow by scavengers. Boulder and his herd-brothers stood around her, watching in awed silence as she cleared her throat yet again.

"And since the death of the last False Parent," she finished hoarsely, "no true Great Parent has come forward. All of Bravelands is waiting, as you know, but there's no sign."

Boulder was gazing at Sky in wonder. "Sister, it's the most remarkable tale I've heard in Bravelands. This Stinger murdered Great Mother—and died himself in the jaws of crocodiles? Those reptiles do not follow the Code either—though at least they are honest about that—so it somehow seems fitting."

"Nor should you feel bad about your part in his death," said another big bull, sternly. "The False Parent deserved death, from all accounts. When you sent him to his doom, you saved all of Bravelands."

Sky remained silent. She wished she could truly believe it.

"And really: you count a lion, a baboon, and these little cheetahs among your friends?" said a young male admiringly. "You're an unusual elephant, Sky Strider!"

"I agree, Forest, that *is* astonishing," said Boulder. "And your visit to the vultures sounds miraculous, Sky. You carried the Great Spirit all that time since then? I am a proud brother! But how desperately sad about little Moon's death." His dark gray eyes drifted sideways to fix on a stocky bull with a pale, brown-gray hide.

Indeed, all the herd turned to look at the bull. He stood a little way back, and he stayed far quieter than the others. Sky thought she saw a dark depth of sadness in his eyes.

His head came up. "Brothers, I'll leave you for now," he rumbled. "I'd like to have some time alone to think. And to remember."

They all nodded slowly. "We understand, Dune," said Boulder softly. "Take all the time you need." He turned back to Sky. "Dune was Moon's father," he murmured.

"Oh!" Sky's heart ached for the grief-stricken elephant. He plodded slowly away, halting under a copse of trees with his head hanging dejectedly.

As the afternoon wore on, she expected the rest of the herd to mourn in sympathy; her own family would have taken time to grieve, to console one another. But the bulls seemed restless and boisterous. They split away in twos and threes, throwing up dust as they circled and stamped. Play-fights broke out, and a few of the sparring matches went beyond play; a thickset bull gave a sudden trumpet of irritation and stamped the ground hard, and that seemed to be the signal for another two to charge him, ears flapping wildly. Tusks were swung, feet thumped the earth, heads were flung back to give wild braying calls to the sky.

Dune stayed apart and alone, mourning in silence.

Boulder seemed to think nothing of any of it. He stayed close to Sky, talking calmly, but now and again he would half bolt toward one of the scraps and butt his head at the fighters as if he wanted to join in. Still, he would back away quickly as they tossed their tusks and raised their trunks, and then he would jog back to Sky, a little shame-faced.

When twilight began to dim the savannah, and the air grew misty and cool, it came as a surprise to Sky. The day had passed so quickly as she and Boulder caught each other up on all the news of their respective herds. All the hours of daylight, Nimble and Lively had played happily at her feet, ambushing each other into play-fights or pretending solemnly to hunt; now they were yawning, stretching out their forepaws to claw the earth and looking pleadingly up at Sky.

"It's time you rested," she said softly, extending her trunk to let them scramble up to her shoulders. Perhaps the cubs could have huddled under a bush again, but with so many enormous bull elephants milling around, it wasn't worth the risk. None of them would hurt the cubs deliberately, Sky was sure, but watching the high-spirited males scrap and challenge, she didn't have much faith that they would pay attention and avoid the tiny cats.

After all, I trusted Rock, didn't I? Too much.

"What will you do now, sister?" asked Boulder gently. "Will you try to rejoin the Strider herd?"

"I don't think so." Sky shook her head. "I miss them terribly, of course I do. Every moment I'm apart from them hurts." She sighed unhappily. "But I still feel such a responsibility toward the Great Spirit. Until the new Great Parent comes forward, I don't think I can go back to my old life."

"I can understand that," said Boulder sympathetically.

"And I understand the Great Spirit being hesitant." Forest, taking a break from sparring with his brothers, had wandered closer to listen. "Given all the impostors you say have claimed the role, it wouldn't surprise me if the Spirit has abandoned Bravelands altogether."

"That will never happen," said Sky firmly. "I trust the Great Spirit." Perhaps she had had her qualms of doubt in the past, but she couldn't allow herself to think that way again. Someone had to keep the faith.

"Well," said Boulder, "I wish you good luck, sister. You deserve to see the Great Spirit's return, after all you did for it."

"Thank you, Boulder." She butted her forehead gently against his. "I plan to travel as widely as I can across Bravelands. The Great Spirit still needs me for some purpose—I know it—so I'll look for signs of it everywhere I go. I'll talk to as many animals as I can. Now I have to—"

"Sky! Sky!" The little cheetahs on her back were wide awake again, bouncing with agitation. "There's shadows moving! Out there on the plain! Coming this way!"

Sky jerked up her head, peering anxiously out into the deepening twilight. "Don't worry, cubs. It's probably noth—"

Falling silent, she raised her trunk, scenting the air. Yes, there was a dark tang on the breeze that drifted over the rustling grass.

Lions!

She could make them out now: a line of dark, menacing shapes, prowling straight toward the bull elephant herd. The lions' shoulders were hunched, their heads low, their pawsteps light but deliberate. Even at a distance she could see their eyes beginning to glow pale in the oncoming night.

"Sky," whimpered Nimble, "I can't see. Are they lions?"

"Yes," she told the cubs gently. She swallowed hard. When she had so recently retold the story of Moon and his death at the claws of Titanpride, the approaching pride was an especially unsettling sight.

Boulder rumbled angrily, and his foot raked the earth. "Don't worry, little ones," he told the cheetahs. "Lions won't mess with a herd of bull elephants."

"Then why are they still coming?" asked Sky with trepidation.

Boulder furrowed his brow, staring. The other bulls were abandoning their play-fights now, shambling over to Boulder, and assembling behind him. They grunted and flapped their ears, perplexed, as the lions drew closer and their eyes glowed brighter.

"That's strange," said Forest. "I can see about ten or twelve. Males and females."

"And they're not turning back," remarked another male.

Sky shifted nervously. If she had been alone with the cubs, this might have been very bad news indeed. But with the bull herd ranged at her back, surely there was no threat? Surely the lions would never attack a herd of male elephants. . . .

Yet it was so *odd*. Why were those lions still advancing?

"They don't look especially hungry." Boulder shared a bewildered glance with his neighbor.

One of the lions halted, his posture stiff, his head held high and challenging, as the others walked forward. Sky narrowed her eyes, trying to study him in the rapidly dimming daylight. There was something about him: his size, his huge black mane, his arrogant stance.

She drew in a shocked breath. *It's Titan. I'm sure of it!*

Boulder, looking angry now, raised his trunk and bellowed: "What do you want here, little cats? Do you have a death wish?"

The lions only glared at him. One of the lionesses bounded forward faster, drawing ahead of the others; she was a plump and well-fed creature, but the way her belly sagged suggested more to Sky.

She's a nursing mother, Sky realized with shock. This grew stranger by the moment. A lioness with cubs to protect should not be taking such risks!

The lioness halted and drew back her muzzle to show her fangs. "We've come for the strongest elephant in this herd."

"Are they *mad?*" Forest muttered to Boulder.

Sky stared at the lions, her heart fluttering in her chest. *I'm with Boulder and his brothers, I'm safe, I'm safe. They're not afraid, nor should I be.* And sure enough, some of the approaching lions looked downright terrified.

But they weren't retreating. Closer and closer they prowled, their fangs bared in nervous but menacing snarls. What was going on?

From the rear of the bull herd, Dune strode abruptly forward. "I'm one of the strongest here," he trumpeted to the advancing pride. "And lions killed my son. Come for me, if you like."

"Dune," whispered Sky, "that's the very same pride that killed Moon. I'm sure of it."

He glanced at her, and the dull light in his eyes kindled to fury. He turned back to the lions.

"Come on, then, killers. You murdered my baby son. Now try to murder me!"

They took him at his word.

Sky could not believe her eyes. The pride was rushing forward, snarling, their paws thundering on the dry earth. The bull elephants stood stupefied.

The lions flung themselves on Dune, a mass of tawny, furred bodies, clawing and yowling and snapping. One clung to his hind leg; one was trying to haul itself onto his back.

Boulder gaped in shock. "I don't believe I'm seeing this."

He didn't move to help; he didn't need to. Dune was swinging his body from side to side, lashing with his tusks, lifting
his great feet and slamming them into the dust. Lions were
flung away, tumbling and rolling, some of them crawling in
pain into the long grass. But still they came, jumping up frantically at his huge body like squirrels trying to bring down a
great tree.

"Oh, I've had enough of this," snapped Boulder at last. He
waded into the fray, followed by his brothers.

But it was hardly a fight, thought Sky. The pride didn't
have a chance. Tusks flashed in the dying light, great gray
bodies slammed into small yelping ones. Even the wind of the
elephants' flapping ears sent lions cowering into the dust. Yet
the cats fought on, making increasingly desperate lunges at
the perplexed and angry Dune.

A shadow moved behind Sky; squealing in fright, she
turned and lashed out wildly. A lion, sneaking up on her flank,
was caught by one tusk and flipped in midair, tumbling to the
ground. Breathing hard, Sky stared at it, swinging her head
from side to side. Blood leaked from its gored hindquarters,
yet still it took a dragging step back toward her, its muzzle
wrinkling back to expose its yellow fangs.

"Sky!" yelped Lively in fright. "Chase it away, chase it away!"

Sky drew a deep breath. The lion was reckless and vicious,
but her brother and his herd were here! She lunged forward,
pounding her forefeet onto the ground hard enough to make
it tremble. At last the lion backed off, still snarling in disappointment, and fled back to its pride at a lurching run.

Sky stood very still for a moment, breathing rapidly. Then she shook herself and harrumphed in annoyance—as much at herself as at the lions. These creatures were not a threat; they never could have hoped to stand against these elephants! *This is not Moon, you cowards*, she thought contemptuously. *This is Moon's father, and all his father's brothers.*

Touching the two cubs with her trunk-tip to make sure they were still safe, Sky swung around to check that no more lions were close. But the bull elephants were keeping them thoroughly occupied. Dune seemed in a frenzy of violence, pursuing two young males across the grassland, bellowing and stamping. Boulder swung his tusks viciously to left and right, his eyes blazing at a lioness who cowered before him. Even the gentle-looking young male, Forest, was blaring his fury, thrusting his tusks with brutal force at a motionless lump on the earth at his feet. A tremor of apprehension rippled at the nape of Sky's neck. *Of course they're angry. But this?* The bulls seemed positively . . . *enraged.*

At last the lions were giving up, some bolting and some hauling themselves pathetically into the long grass by their claws; there were blood trails in patches of bare sand where they dragged themselves clear. A beaten rabble, they limped and slouched and lurched back the way they had come, heading as fast as they could for the distant ridge where their leader still stood, glaring at them with contemptuous disappointment. One straggler was too slow: Dune overtook him and halted with a trumpet of fury, then pounded his forefeet against soft flesh until the guttural whimpering of his enemy was silenced.

Sky could not feel triumph or pleasure; this had been a rout, and whatever she thought of Titanpride, she had no appetite for a massacre.

Shambling backward, her haunches touched those of a big bull; he turned with astonishing speed and blared a warning at her, his eyes blazing.

Sky froze in astonishment, then swerved as his tusks swung at her. She gave an involuntary squeal of terror and cowered. But despite the pounding of her heart, he did not seem to wish her particular harm; he was already charging aggressively in the other direction, toward his brothers. The lions had already fled, but now the elephants were brawling with one another. They jabbed their huge tusks, crashed their shoulders into their friends', trumpeted in high-pitched fury. Forest barged furiously at Dune; two big bulls clashed tusks and hollered with incoherent anger.

The Rage. Sky's heart chilled as she backed away from the herd. Boulder was close to her flank, and she edged behind him for protection.

"Hold on tight, Nimble and Lively," she called. "Don't fall now, whatever you do!"

Boulder spun around at the sound of her voice. Sky started. The hot glow in his eyes was the same light she'd seen in his enraged herd-brothers'.

"Boulder—?" she began.

He swung his tusks, driving her aggressively back. "Go, quick! Get out of here!"

Sky drew a shocked breath and tensed her muscles. She did

not wait for him to repeat the order. Turning, she cantered away as fast as she could. She could feel the cubs' tiny claws digging into her skin, and she hoped desperately that they could keep their precarious balance. Her head whirled with confusion and terror even as she fled gasping from the scene. So this was the Rage that had caused her beloved Rock to kill River: no one, not even her own kin, was immune to it.

She could feel the ground shaking beneath her, and was almost afraid she might lose her footing and trip. Her breath rasped in her lungs as she lurched up a shallow slope, and at the unexpectedly steep drop beyond it she gave a squeal of terror. Jamming her forefeet into the ground, she skidded to the bottom.

"Sky! Sky!" The cheetah cubs yammered in panic, and she felt the prickling of their claws dig deeper.

Don't fall, cubs! she thought desperately, but she didn't have breath to reassure them. Drawing a sharp breath, she cantered on.

Sky ran on, pounding through dry gullies and between acacia trees until her aching legs forced her to slow. She wasn't built for speed, she knew, but at last she seemed far enough away from the still-brawling herd. Turning her head, she cocked an ear. She could still hear them, trumpeting and bellowing as their huge bodies crashed against one another. On her shoulders, she could feel the cubs trembling violently.

She gave a shudder of her own. About to walk on, her eye caught a flash of golden fur at her foot. With a gasp, she halted and peered down.

A lioness lay sprawled and immobile, her fur torn in a great gash along her flank. Dark blood leaked from the corner of her jaws and stained her fangs as she bared them at Sky.

It was the lioness who had led the ill-fated attack; Sky recognized her mean face and plump belly. As Sky stared at her in pity, the wounded cat gave a feeble growl of threat.

"Don't waste your strength," said Sky, touching her side. The lioness winced and whimpered. "You have broken bones."

"Many of them," snarled the lioness. "My name is Artful, and I have been first lioness of Titanpride for many seasons. That is my legacy, elephant, and I want to keep it. So kill me. Kill me now, and I will be free from *him*."

Sky gaped. "Kill you? Of course I won't do that!"

"*I want it!* Please." The lioness's face was agonized. "*Please!* Kill me, I beg you! Free me!"

"What do you mean, *you'll be free?*" Sky blinked, stupefied. "Who is *he?*"

"Who is *he?*" Artful coughed a mirthless laugh. "Don't you know of him?" Painfully she twisted her head, peering with apprehension across the darkling plain. "Quickly! Please!"

Sky followed her terrified gaze.

It was locked on a lion. He was visible only as a dark silhouette, but Sky couldn't fail to recognize the great, black-maned creature who had stood back as his pride attacked. Titan. It was hard to see properly in the gloom, but Sky could scarcely believe what she thought she could see. Titan straddled the body of one of his wounded pride, his head leaning eagerly down.

Blood hammered in Sky's ears and raced in her body. Was it a trick of the twilight? As she watched, the great lion gave a triumphant roar and flung up his head. A shapeless chunk of flesh hung dripping from his jaws.

A sound broke through Sky's frozen shock; the thud of great feet. Dune was running toward her, black and huge against the last glow of sunset, his ears splayed, his tusks raised.

There was no more time to lose. "I'm sorry," Sky told the lioness, twisted around, and fled. *Even though you beg, I can't break the Code. Not again.*

Halting some distance from Artful, Sky turned to look back. Dune had not followed her after all. He stood over the motionless bundle that was Artful Titanpride, the first stars picking out his massive outline. Sky saw him lift one of those enormous legs and stamp his foot down hard.

So Artful had gotten her wish. In a way Sky was glad for her; the lioness had been wounded beyond hope and desperate for death. *Free me from him. . . .*

Another shudder rippled through Sky. Nothing she had seen, in all her dangerous adventures, had been quite so disturbing. The insane attack on the herd. Artful, begging for death.

And Titan, triumphantly ripping flesh from one of his own . . .

It was so unnatural, so against the proper order of Bravelands. The Code had been shattered back there in the darkness, over and over again.

Sky shook her ears hard, trying to dislodge her awful,

clinging sense of dread. Tiny claws were digging into her neck. *The cubs!* How had she forgotten them? "Nimble! Lively! Are you all right?"

"We're fine," chirruped a shaky voice from between her shoulder blades.

"You ran fast," piped up another, "but we hung on very tight."

She curled back her trunk to touch them gently. "Well done, cubs. It was too dangerous for us, and I had to run."

"What was that big lion eating?" mewed Nimble.

"He looked crazy," added Lively.

Oh no. They saw. Sky swung her trunk, unsure how to explain to the cubs what she couldn't explain to herself. But in the quietness of the night, with the insects just beginning to stir, she heard a sudden, querulous mewling.

"What's that?" She turned and peered around.

"There," came Lively's voice. "By that fever tree. With the forked trunk."

Apprehensive, Sky ambled cautiously toward the tree. The mewling was easy to follow; it was high-pitched, frantic, and constant.

She parted the grass with her trunk. A little lioness cub peered up at her nervously, her eyes wide in the starlight.

"Go away!" snapped the tiny cat, before Sky could speak. "I'm calling for my mother, not you!"

Sky blinked in shock. "Little one, I—"

"Who are *you*?" demanded the cub. "I want my mother! Where is she?"

Sky stared down at her. This baby was so small, and probably still nursing. . . .

With a sickening suddenness, Sky realized who she was. "You're Artful's cub?"

"Yes, I am! My mother is the first lioness of Titanpride," declared the cub proudly. She flattened her ears and glowered to left and right. "Where is she? Where is my mother?"

Sky took a breath. There was no way she could tell the cub what had happened. "Your mother . . . she's been . . . delayed," she said at last. Tentatively, she touched the cub's head with her trunk-tip; the cub winced and growled.

She was a prickly little thing, thought Sky. But she couldn't abandon Nimble and Lively, and she couldn't leave this cub either.

"Your mother can't be here right now," she told the cub softly. "She says you have to come with me. Just for a little while."

"Oh." The cub looked pensive. "Oh. All right, then." Getting to her paws, she pranced out of the grass and cocked her head. "I'm Menace Titanpride. Who are you?"

"I'm Sky Strider." Sky dipped her head; she was instantly annoyed at herself, but something about the cub seemed to demand a touch of respect.

"And we're Nimble and Lively," called Nimble from the crown of Sky's head. "Come on up here, Menace. It's comfy and it's quite safe."

Sky extended her trunk, and the little lioness scrambled up without a qualm.

It was black nighttime now, and the crickets and cicadas were in full-throated song. From a nearby grove of acacias, tree frogs piped a few experimental notes.

It was time to find shelter, Sky knew. She headed for the small copse of trees, glancing anxiously left and right. Yes, it should be safe here for tonight, she thought with relief. For her *and* her ever-growing "herd."

No living lions were in sight; except for little Menace, Titanpride had vanished. Even their crazy leader must have decided that, for now, discretion was the best strategy.

What was he doing? What was he thinking?

The attack itself had been ill judged at best, suicidally insane at worst. And as for what Sky had seen in the darkening twilight—she didn't even want to remember it. Had Titan really been doing what she'd thought? Would a rational lion tear at the corpse of one of his own?

Sky knew one thing with absolute certainty: her quest must go on. Rock had distracted her, and she had been weak; she must never again forget her duty to the Great Spirit. Bravelands needed its guidance more than ever.

CHAPTER 23

The night was almost unnervingly peaceful; in the distance a jackal bayed and yipped, but briefly. From even farther away, the grunting roar of a lion resounded across the flat grassland, but when Fearless flared his nostrils to catch the scent, it was not even detectable. The voice of a stranger, he realized: it came from some territory near the mountains, carried disconcertingly far on the night air. He, Keen, and Ruthless had wandered almost to the farthest fringe of Mightypride's territory, aimless and a little apathetic.

"Where are we actually going?" asked Ruthless, padding along between Fearless and Keen.

"I don't really know," admitted Fearless. "Far away from Mighty, that's all."

"At least we can make our own decisions now," said Keen

heartily. "Nobody to challenge you, Fearless. Nobody to make silly suggestions."

That was the trouble, Fearless thought gloomily. He wasn't at all sure anymore that Mighty's suggestions *had* been silly. Most of them had made a lot of sense. If only Mighty hadn't been so *arrogant* about it.

Except that wasn't quite true either, if he was honest . . .

"We'd be safer with the pride," he grunted. The admission hurt. "Three young and inexperienced lions trudging across Bravelands in the night?"

"We'll be fine. There are fewer of us," Keen pointed out brightly. "That means we can react faster!"

I could have listened more patiently, thought Fearless, as the row played out once again in his head. *The pride would have come down on my side eventually. If I'd given them a chance . . .*

Maybe he *had* rather let things get out of control.

"Lions," whispered Keen, coming to a sudden halt. "Nearby this time. I can smell them."

Shaking off his guilt and misery, Fearless stiffened and pricked his ears. His hackles sprang erect. "What lions?"

"I don't know," murmured Keen. Ruthless looked nervous, his ears twitching.

"You stay behind," Fearless told the cub. "Close, but behind. We'd better investigate."

"Carefully," warned Keen, shooting him an anxious glance.

Fearless nodded, and with Ruthless trotting on light and fearful paws behind them, the two bigger cubs prowled forward through long dry grass.

Keen halted, one paw raised. "Four of them," he murmured.

Fearless hunched his shoulders, creeping forward. The scent was very strong and sharp, and he could see them ahead: three lions and a lioness, their backs sagging as they plodded exhaustedly across the plain toward them.

"They don't look much of a threat," growled Fearless, one ear flicking forward. He mustn't make any more rash decisions or stupid moves, he knew—but he had to be strong, too. Maybe it had been a mistake to leave the pride, but his decision had been made, and there was no going back. He had to start acting like a proper leader. Taking a deep breath, he bounded forward into the path of the lions.

"Who are you?" he demanded. "Whose pride do you follow?"

They glanced up at him, startled, but their wary eyes held no aggression. They looked exhausted and miserable. Three of them were injured, with great bloody scrapes on their haunches and flanks, and even the uninjured lion looked too weary to fight.

"I know who they are!" Ruthless padded forward between Fearless and Keen, his eyes wide. "They're Titanpride lions. They joined when Father beat Steadfastpride."

"Titanpride?" snarled Keen, lowering his shoulders and prowling forward menacingly.

"Hello, Adamant," said Ruthless, his voice hard but quavering. "Have you come to drag me back to my father? Because I won't go!"

The strange lions only stared at all of them, wordless. At last the one called Adamant took a pace forward. Fearless tensed, but Adamant only ducked his head, opened his jaws, and swung his flank toward Fearless.

Fearless blinked in surprise. He hadn't done a thing, but Adamant looked downright cowed. As he watched, the big lion staggered awkwardly sideways, flopped to the ground, and rolled onto his back.

Fearless simply gaped. No full-grown lion had ever shown such submission to him before. He swallowed hard.

"All right, I won't attack you," he said, trying to sound as arrogant as he could. "But what are Titanpride lions doing approaching our territory?"

Adamant rolled back onto his flank and got to his paws. His head hung low. "We're not Titan's anymore," he growled. "And we're not trying to threaten anyone's territory. We're just looking for a new pride. One that isn't mad."

"You're deserters!" exclaimed Keen.

"No lion in its right mind would stay loyal to Titan!" snapped Adamant. He shot a glance at Ruthless. "He's gone completely insane. Sorry, Ruthless, but it's true."

"What's he done now?" mumbled Ruthless.

"Ha! His latest demand? That we bring down the largest bull elephant in Bravelands."

"What?" Keen sat back on his haunches and stared. "That's impossible!"

"Exactly. But he threatened us with death if we didn't try." Adamant narrowed his eyes. "Perhaps we should just have chosen death. Because plenty of us met it anyway. A lot of good hunters paid the blood-price for Titan's madness today."

Ruthless's eyes started wide. He took a pawstep forward. "My mother? Menace?"

"Both dead," said Adamant curtly. "They fell under the feet of the creature that Titan would have had us kill."

"No!" Ruthless's cry was desperate. His small body shook. "That can't be true!"

"Take my word for it, cub," growled Adamant. "And they're both better off now, so take comfort. Artful is free of your father's tyranny."

As Ruthless made a choking sound in his throat, Keen gently licking his head, a lioness limped forward. Fearless remembered her: Tenacious, a fine and fierce hunter. Now she looked beaten and dejected, and her beautiful lashing tail had been severed to a stump. Blood still leaked from the raw wound.

"Titan's been behaving strangely for moons," she growled. "But it's become far, far worse lately. He spends his nights alone, and when he comes back at dawn his fur smells sickly and odd."

"He's obsessed with killing," said Adamant, "and just for the sake of killing. He hardly ever eats the flesh of his prey."

"He has changed the Code," said Tenacious. "He says the old one no longer applies. His new Code is this: *Only kill to be strong.*"

"This has to be nonsense." Wrinkling his muzzle, Keen drew back in revulsion. "I don't trust these deserters, Fearless."

"Is that so?" Adamant sounded more weary than threatening. "You might be interested in Titan's next target, though, because I believe he's one of yours. A lion called Mighty."

Fearless's ears went back. "What?"

"The most powerful male in this area, Titan says. He wants Mighty's spirit."

Fearless's neck fur bristled. It might be Mightypride now, but that had been his pride only that morning! "If Titan wants to take over Fearlesspride, I will accept a formal challenge. Then I will have my revenge—"

"You don't get it, do you?" said Adamant with a sigh. "He's not interested in your pride. I told you, he simply wants to kill Mighty: the most powerful lion in this area."

It was dreadful news. Mighty may have ruined his life, thought Fearless, but the big lion was Valor's mate, and the father to her unborn cubs. He could not let this happen to his sister!

All the same, beneath the horror, Fearless couldn't help a ripple of resentment. *The most powerful lion*, huh? And what about you four?" he asked grandly. "Will you stay to resist Titan, then?"

"Not a chance," huffed Tenacious. She was trying to flick her tail, but the stump only wobbled. "We're heading far from here. We'll find a place where the Code is still respected. Where lions can still live as they should."

Adamant turned away with a nod, and one by one the others followed him. They limped away slowly into the darkness and were swallowed by the night.

Drawing a breath, Fearless turned to Ruthless and nuzzled the cub's head. "I'm sorry," he whispered, "about your mother."

The cub nodded, his head drooping. It was a hard blow for him to accept, Fearless knew. However Titan had made her behave lately, Artful and Ruthless had once been so close.

"You know," muttered Keen in his ear, "this may not be so bad. Mighty's a big lion. He might beat Titan."

Ruthless's ears pricked up a little and flickered hopefully. "Or could Mighty just run away? Then we could return to your pride."

Fearless shook his head. "Titan won't let him escape. By fair means or foul, your father always wins," he growled. "I've told you how he cheated to kill Gallant, haven't I? And he did the same to Keen's father."

"Yes. I'm sorry, Ruthless, but what Fearless says about your father is true." Keen's ears had flattened. "If Titan wins, there'll be no chance of Mighty simply being driven out. He'll be killed."

"I can't let Mighty go through that, whatever I think of him," declared Fearless, shaking his head. "I can't do it to *Valor.*"

The decision, after all, was an easy one. Swiveling his head back toward the pride he had abandoned, making sure of the direction and his own recent scent trail, Fearless set off at a loping run.

He could not keep up the fast pace for long, but even when he slowed, Fearless maintained a steady trot through the darkness. Behind him he could hear Keen's pounding paws and the lighter, more hurried tread of Ruthless as the cub panted to keep up. They had come a long way from the pride, but Fearless was surprised at how much farther it felt on the return journey, with his heart tense with fear for Valor. The plains seemed suddenly endless.

The night was so still, their pawsteps seemed horribly loud over the chirping of insects. *We have to be in time*, Fearless thought, his heart in his dry throat. *If something happens to Valor and her cubs, I won't forgive myself.*

As they passed a tangled acacia grove, its flat canopy edged in starlight, the sound of a wild cry brought Fearless up short. The sound came out of nowhere, a wild trumpet of distress. *An elephant?* Confused, he skidded to a halt, his ears straining.

There it was again, panicked and hopeless. *"Help! Help us! Boulder!"*

He didn't know who Boulder was, but he knew that voice. For a moment, Fearless was torn.

But he didn't know when Titan planned to attack Mighty-pride. Sky Strider was in trouble *right now.*

With a grunt he sprang off in a run to the left, down a shallow slope of cracked earth. His companions, unquestioning, followed his lead.

Slowing, he blinked, trying to focus. Beneath the thorny trees the night seemed even darker; their branches obscured even the faint star-glow that lit the grassland. Beneath his paw pads, the ground was growing softer; Fearless could feel its cool dampness.

Just ahead of him, the ground fell away. He stopped with

his protracted claws on the edge of a sharp drop.

And there, outlined in blue moonlight, he spotted the elephant.

Sky Strider was struggling hopelessly, her legs and belly mired in a thick patch of mud that was blacker than the night. Her glowing eyes caught and held his, and he saw her terror and panic.

"Sky!" he grunted in shock. Then his eyes drifted to something pale that moved on her back. "What is *that*?"

He did not need her answer; he recognized a lion cub when he saw one. The tiny creature was hunched with two small cheetah cubs between Sky's shoulder blades. They propped themselves desperately with stiff forepaws, staring in fear at the sucking mud that had almost reached them.

He shouldn't be surprised at anything where Sky Strider was concerned, but she could still take him aback.

"Hold on, Sky! We'll get you out of there." Fearless wished he could be as sure as he sounded.

"That's Menace!" Ruthless scrabbled to a halt at his side, gasping. "That's my sister. She's alive!"

"*Ruthless?*" A high-pitched, indignant squeal drifted from between Sky's shoulders. "I thought you were a deserter! What are you doing with those strange lions? Are they enemies of Titanpride? I don't think you should be—"

"Hush, Menace!" chirped one of the cheetah cubs crossly. "They're helping us!"

"Menace, hold on! These lions are my friends, they won't hurt you." Ruthless's voice was strained with fear as he watched

Sky plunge and struggle in the mire. "Fearless, what can we do? I can't lose my sister now!"

"We'll get them all out," growled Fearless. He placed a paw on the steep slope and began to inch his way down, but his paws slithered on the muddy surface. He dug in his claws, wary.

"Fearless, don't risk getting stuck yourself!" Keen called from behind him. He was peering down anxiously from the edge. "There are trees. That might be a way to help."

Fearless glanced up. Keen was right: the tangled branches clustered thickly above the mud hole. They were too high for Sky to reach, though.

"Maybe we can bring them lower?" suggested Keen in the silence as Fearless hesitated. "Somehow. Then the elephant can grab one. If you're *determined* to get her out."

"I am," said Fearless firmly. "She's as much my friend as Thorn Highleaf."

Sky's glowing eyes turned to him, filled with gratitude. She looked a little calmer. "I think your friend's idea might work," she gasped.

"How do we do it, though?" Fearless licked his jaws uncertainly. "Keen or I would break those branches, and then we'd all be in the same mud."

"I'm smaller," Ruthless piped up suddenly. "I'll make the climb."

Fearless turned his head to the cub. "Be careful," he growled. "Don't fall, Ruthless."

The cub set his jaws firmly. Without another word, he

leaped up to sink his claws into a sturdy trunk, then dragged himself up toward where the branches began to spread out over the mud hole.

The lowest branches were obviously too short; Fearless watched, his breath catching in his throat, as Ruthless hauled himself farther up the trunk. At last the cub stopped and placed an experimental paw on a higher branch.

"I think this one will reach," he called down.

"Be *very* careful," Fearless warned him. His heart skipped as he watched the cub edge out onto the branch, paw by paw. The bough dipped slightly, then a little more. Fearless could hear the wood creaking.

Fearless wanted to focus only on Ruthless—*If he falls, maybe I can spring out and catch him*, he mused doubtfully—but there was an itch in his spine that was distracting. His fur was rising all along his back, and he frowned.

Are we being watched?

Yes, that was definitely the sensation he felt. Fearless gave himself a light shake, but it did nothing to dispel that uneasy suspicion. He risked a glance over his shoulder, but he could see nothing moving in the shadows around the mud hole.

"Hurry, Ruthless," he murmured. Suddenly the chance of the cub falling didn't seem like the most pressing danger.

The branch was drooping dramatically now, as Ruthless crept farther and farther along it. None of the watchers seemed to be breathing, not even the frightened Sky or the cubs on her back.

Then, abruptly, Ruthless stopped. He raised his head

sharply, staring out beyond Fearless.

"Look out!" he cried.

Fearless spun around, just too late. A furred shape lunged for his hind leg, fastening sharp teeth in his flesh. With a roar of shock, Fearless lashed at it.

It fell back, but suddenly the shadows were full of them: quick-moving shapes with glowing eyes and glinting fangs. Fearless saw flashes of pale fur, the flick of bushy tails.

Hyenas? No, the tails were wrong, the outline of the ears too big. And these were smaller—though they seemed even more vicious than hyenas, their sharp snouts biting and tearing with glee. And these creatures were *faster.* Fearless spun and slashed, roaring with anger, as they darted in and snapped at his flanks. On the top edge of the slope, Keen too was under attack, growling and twisting as he tried to defend himself.

The air was filled with a cackling and a racket of sharp yelping howls. As soon as Fearless could fling one away, another two seemed to take its place, chattering and shrieking. Pain stung Fearless's flanks and haunches and shoulders as they seized mouthfuls of his flesh and shook their heads violently.

Are these little brutes actually going to kill *me?* he thought, a wave of panic flooding in along with the pain.

No. He couldn't let that happen, not now! *Valor needs me.* Shunting three of the creatures away, he roared and flung himself sideways, knocking another two off their paws. As sharp teeth sank into his shoulder again, he let himself fall, crushing his attacker beneath his weight.

They seemed warier now, backing off and circling. Fearless

shook himself and roared again.

They still surrounded him. Gradually they prowled closer once more, and individuals darted forward in a feint now and again, their movements fluid and confident. It was as if, thought Fearless, they were following some well-practiced plan to wear him down. *I mustn't take my eyes off them!*

But how could he watch them all at once? And they were so *fast.* Jackals? No, Fearless thought; they were *like* jackals, but somehow different. Their grins were lurid, their muzzles peeled back in spite, and now it was easier to make out the details: they were slender creatures with narrow faces, big ears, and bushy tails. In their glowing eyes was nothing but cruelty. Fearless knew instinctively that if he showed a single trace of weakness, they would fly for his throat.

From the corner of his eye, he saw one of them move. On quick, delicate feet, it raced to the edge of the mud hole. And then to his horrified astonishment, it tripped lightly *onto* the mud and trotted across as easily as if it had been hard sand.

It sprang up onto Sky's back and snatched Menace. The cub gave a yowling cry of terror.

The creature loped back to the bank, the cub gripped in its jaws, but Keen was in just the right position to intercept it. He shook off two skinny attackers, then plowed through a line of the rest and sprang on the one that held Menace. His jaws seized its scruff, and he shook it hard. With a yelp that was abruptly cut off, it fell to the earth, limp.

Menace tumbled away from its lolling jaws and scurried

back to the edge of the mud hole. She mewled desperately. By now Ruthless had bowed the branch low enough for Sky to grab, and the young elephant had managed to curl her trunk around it; she was dragging herself painfully slowly from the sucking grip of the mud, her upper legs and belly now exposed. They were black and dripping with the sludge, but she was still grimly hauling on the thick branch, inching herself from the lethal mire.

With an explosive splash, the mud released her, and she stumbled forward. Menace ran to her, scrambling onto her shoulders as Fearless and Keen prowled back and forth, glaring defiance at the jackal-like creatures.

But the attackers seemed to know that their advantage was lost. They backed away, howling and wailing, into the darkness of the trees. One was slower than its comrades; it snarled angrily at the lions, its hackles bristling. Fearless made a lunge for it, but his jaws snapped on thin air as it vanished over the edge of the slope. He bounded up, following, but the last he saw of it was a flick of its thick tail as it vanished into a shadowy burrow.

Fearless stood in the sudden silence, panting for breath. Cicadas chirped and a night bird gave a lonely cry. The mud sloshed and settled. It was as if the creatures had never been here.

"Thank you, Fearless," gasped Sky, as black mud slid and dripped from her hide. "And thanks to your friends, too. Thank you!"

Keen was glaring at the bank with narrowed eyes. "I don't

know what those things were. But the one that had Menace isn't quite dead."

He padded to its limp form, and Fearless loped to his side. Both lions stared down at the misshapen creature, its long legs jutting and its neck twisted. From the corner of its mouth dripped foam mixed with blood. Its flanks heaved.

"What are you?" snarled Fearless.

Its head lay immobile but one eye was gazing up at him, glowing with a dull, scornful hate. "We, Lion? We are the dogs of darkness, the golden wolves, the eaters of spirit." Its tongue caressed its teeth. "This goldwolf is Slash, Eater of Eighteen Hearts, and he *sees you.*"

"Don't talk dung," Fearless growled, repressing a shudder. "Where are you from?"

"We come from beyond." It cackled a high laugh. "But here we are. Here we stay now, and Bravelands will be ours. We do not stop until we have it."

Fearless stared at it for a moment, uncomprehending. "You're mad."

"And you . . ." It gazed at him hungrily, and its tongue flopped out to lick at its foaming jaws. "Your heart is plump and strong. Oh, how we might sink our fangs into its red oozing life. Ah, your spirit would taste fine and sharp and *gooood.*"

"Be quiet!" roared Keen.

"Haha. Haha, we do not *be quiet*! We are the golden wolves and we cannot be silenced!" It craned its head, twisting it impossibly, and howled into the night. "Brothers! Sisters! Come to me! Take my spirit, so I may run with the Pack forever! Let *me* be *we* for all time!"

Fearless started. Sure enough, the rest of the wolves were gathering once more, their shadows blacker than the night. They slunk between the trees and crept over the edge of the slope, their tongues lolling hungrily, their eyes alight.

"Let's get out of here," he growled.

His companions didn't have to be told twice. The lions bounded together away from the mud hole and up the far bank, and Sky climbed as rapidly as she could, her feet digging into the soft earth. Pausing at the crest, Fearless looked back.

The injured wolf was out of sight, hidden by a seething crowd of his pack-mates. Shoulders hunched, they shook and tore, and as their heads jerked up, Fearless could see lumps of torn flesh in their jaws. The night was filled with the sounds of snapping bones and ripped meat and gnashing, chewing teeth.

He shuddered and bolted after the others.

Sky was shaking and wide-eyed as she trotted at their side. "Oh, Fearless. What is this new terror in Bravelands? It's more important than ever to find the Great Parent—she has to be told! Or *he* has."

"What do you plan to do?" Fearless panted as he loped. "You've searched long enough without a sign of the Parent."

"I'll return to the mountain." Glancing back, Sky slowed her pace. "I need to talk to the vultures again. If anyone has an idea where to look, where to *start*, it's them."

"I'd come," he growled, "but I have another urgent mission. Will you be all right?"

She nodded. "Of course, Fearless. I'll *have* to be."

"You don't have to look after Menace as well as the chee-tahs," said Ruthless. "We'll take my sister."

"Oh, you will, will you?" put in Menace from Sky's back. She glared down at her brother. "And how do I know I can trust a deserter? Hmm? I know what Mother would say—"

Before the startled Ruthless could make any retort, Keen cleared his throat. "You know, Ruthless, I don't think that's a good idea."

"Nor do I," murmured Fearless. "Sky, your path has many dangers, but if we take Menace it'll be easy for Titan to seize her."

"Good!" snapped Menace.

Fearless ignored her. "I'm sorry, Ruthless, but I think the safest place for your sister right now is with Sky." If Menace stayed with them and things actually turned out for the best, she would have to watch her father die, just as he and Keen had—and he wouldn't wish that on any creature.

Ruthless looked agonized. He licked his jaws, but he nod-ded. "Will you do that, Sky? Can you keep Menace safe?"

Sky raised her trunk to touch the fluffy heads of the chee-tahs. "I'll do my best." She smiled. "I think I can handle three cubs."

"Then I wish you good luck," said Fearless solemnly.

"And I you, Fearless." She lowered her trunk to touch his head. "In our own way, we are all doing what we can to save Bravelands."

CHAPTER 24

"Thorn, wake up. Wake up!"

The voice seemed to come from far above Thorn, as if he was submerged in a deep dark pool. And the pool was so very warm and welcoming, and no one was fighting him, or attacking Dawntrees, or calling him a traitor. Thorn grunted in protest and wriggled himself deeper into his nest of leaves.

"Thorn, *please* wake up. It's important!"

Much against his will, Thorn blinked his eyes open. He was still groggy, but Mud shook his shoulder until he was at last awake and half alert.

"What *is* it, Mud?" Thorn growled irritably, and scratched at an itch on his neck.

"Listen," hissed Mud, "it's the stones. Thorn, you have to come. Something awful's going to happen, the stones are telling me so."

"Something awful is *always* happening," grunted Thorn.

"This is different." Mud crouched to gaze seriously into his eyes. "The Code is going to be broken. By a *baboon*."

"Well." Thorn got unsteadily to his paws. "Yes, Mud, that's bad." He shook the dregs of sleep from his fuzzy head. "But how? And when? We'd better tell Berry."

"That's just the problem." Mud looked agonized. "She's the one who's going to break it!"

That brought Thorn finally, fully alert. *"What?"*

"It's true. The stones are sure."

"I can't believe that." Thorn forced his spinning head to think. How could this be possible? Yes, Berry had been distant lately and a little cold, and he was still uncomfortable with the Crown Guard. . . . But Berry—break the Code? *Never!* "The stones are wrong," he said firmly. "That's not Berry, Mud. You know her!"

"Um." Mud's gaze shifted to the side, and he chewed his upper lip. "It's possible, I suppose. I mean, I don't *want* it to be true, Thorn. There could be any number of reasons they're falling wrong. . . . They have been a bit unreliable lately." He nodded, as if he was beginning to convince himself. "After all, they've been telling me that the Great Parent is close by, and that's *obviously* not true."

Thorn sucked in a breath. It *was* true, of course . . . so that must mean Mud was right about Berry. He rubbed his eyes, his head thumping. Berry, a Codebreaker. How could this be happening? When he lowered his paws he was shocked by

Mud's expression—his small face was twisted in an agony of self-doubt.

Thorn straightened and set his jaw. *I can't let this go on. Time to tell the truth.*

"Mud," he said quietly. "Could you do something for me? Could you fetch Nut and Spider? I want to talk to you all. Please?"

Looking startled and a little concerned, Mud nodded. He turned and scampered from the clearing.

Thorn closed his eyes. It felt like a terrible betrayal of trust, but he had to know: he had to find out for sure what Berry was thinking. If she *was* considering breaking the Code, it was only because she'd been deceived somehow, or . . . or she wasn't thinking straight. She'd regret it, he knew. For her own sake, he *had* to stop her.

Searching for her presence with his mind, Thorn locked onto her swiftly. *So easy. Because I know her so well.* He knew her, and he couldn't believe—

He blinked. He was inside her head, looking out through her eyes.

She was perched on the Crown Stone, and Viper and Creeper stood before her, their faces full of urgency.

"Berry, you know we're speaking the truth. It's hard, but decisions like this are hard."

"Viper's right," said Creeper. "Tendril can't be trusted. She'll always be a snake in the branches."

"We have to deal with her," Viper went on. "Think of all the baboons she

has killed already. Your own mother!"

"It's a dreadful decision." It felt for a moment as though Thorn was speaking himself, but he knew they were Berry's words. "But Tendril's presence in the troop cannot be tolerated."

"We agree," said Creeper.

"Nor can she simply be driven out. She'd be even more dangerous if she was out of our sight and our control." Berry shook her head. "It's a hard thing, to break the Code. That's all."

"No baboon likes to contemplate such things," said Viper soothingly. "But sometimes, for the good of the troop . . ."

"Yes," said Berry. "And in truth, you don't have to persuade me." She gave a great sigh. "It pains me to say it, but do what you must. Just . . . make sure there are no traces of the body."

Gasping, Thorn jerked himself free of Berry's mind. He stood alone in the glade once more. His whole body felt hot and panicky, and he had to part his jaws and pant for breath.

"Oh, Berry," he murmured, horrified. Had that been real? No, of *course* it was real: he knew his powers by now.

"What happened?" Mud had already returned to the glade; behind him, Nut and Spider eyed Thorn nervously as Mud loped hesitantly closer. "Thorn, what's wrong?"

"Thorn-friend looks as if he's seen a shrew eat a leopard," observed Spider, curious.

Nut tilted his head and frowned. "Do you need help?"

Thorn drew his paws down across his face. "I . . . I haven't got time to explain. . . . You'll see. I need to go and talk to Berry. Right now." He took a sharp breath. Would Creeper and Viper still be at Berry's side? "Mud, Nut, Spider—will you come with me? Because—yes, Nut. I think I might need some backup."

"Of course we will," said Nut, shrugging. "We're your friends."

Mud and Spider nodded in agreement.

"Thank you." Thorn clenched his paws and set his teeth. This was the last thing he wanted to do, but there was no putting it off.

He led the way with a heavy heart to the Crown Stone clearing. At least Viper and Creeper were nowhere in sight. Berry sat alone on the Crown Stone, her face creased in worried contemplation.

"Let me talk to her," he murmured.

Exchanging glances, Mud, Nut, and Spider held back at the edge of the clearing, their eyes wide with curiosity.

Thorn crept forward, his heart beating hard. "Berry," he said softly, and she glanced up. "Berry, is something the matter?"

She sighed. "Thorn. It's good to see you." Glancing over his shoulder at the other three, she lowered her voice. "I'm finding being Crownleaf harder than I expected. That's all."

Thorn bit his lip. "I'm always here for you if you need me. You know that, right?"

"Are you?" Berry straightened suddenly. She gazed at him with piercing brown eyes and raised her voice. "Are you *really*, Thorn? Because it hasn't felt that way lately."

A pang of hurt stung his heart. "Berry! How can you say that?"

"You've been so distant, Thorn." Her stare was accusing. "You've been drifting ever further from me since my father was killed."

Thorn gaped at her. "*I'm* the one who's been distant?"

"You're keeping something from me, I know you are! I'm your *mate*. What can be so terrible that you'd hide it from me?"

Thorn swallowed hard. "Berry. You need to call off the Crown Guard. You can't do what you're planning."

"*What?*" Her eyes widened, then flashed toward Thorn's companions. "You three. Leave us!"

"No!" Thorn flung out a paw, and they froze, exchanging apprehensive looks. "I want them to stay, Berry. They're my friends, and I want them to hear this too. Please."

"Hear what?" A cold light came into Berry's eyes. "What I'm *planning*? And what exactly is that, Thorn?"

He sucked in a breath. "Killing Tendril. You can't do it." He heard the three baboons behind him gasp in unison. "You know this is wrong, Berry!"

"How did you—what—" Berry's face grew tense, her eyes hard, but he noticed that she couldn't quite meet his gaze. *She's ashamed*, he thought. But she was angry too. Her glare flickered to Nut, Mud, and Spider. "Thorn, have you been *spying* on me? How dare you!"

"That's not the point!" blurted Thorn. "The Berry I know—the Berry I *love*—she'd never consent to a murder in her name!"

Her disbelieving stare became fiery with rage. "I had to! That's something you can't understand, Thorn—taking responsibility! I can't think only for myself—I have to think for the troop, as well. For all of you other baboons! You don't know what that's like!"

"I—"

"Don't you get it? The Great Spirit has left Bravelands *forever.* The animals who live here—we must adapt, find new ways of living. We haven't got a choice."

Heat flared within Thorn. "What, by following your father's example? By making your own Strongbranches?"

There was a moment of awful silence. Nut, Mud, and Spider didn't seem to dare breathe. Berry stared at Thorn, unblinking.

When she spoke again, her voice was low and cold. "Leading a troop is tough," she growled. "Tendril is malevolent to her bones. She killed my mother. She wanted to slaughter our infants in their nests! How can I spare her and risk her harming us again?"

"You mustn't listen to Viper and Creeper." He stretched out a paw, but she didn't take it. "They don't understand, they don't realize how terrible this choice would be—how there's no coming back from it."

"Viper and Creeper?" For a moment Berry stared at him, then slowly shook her head. "Do you understand nothing, Thorn? This has nothing to do with them. I listen to counsel, as any leader should. But the decision is *mine!*"

Thorn's heart plummeted in his rib cage. He felt sick, and for a moment his throat could not form words.

"But . . . the Code . . ."

"I have to make hard choices," she said curtly. "Maybe some of them are wrong, who knows? Certainly not you, Thorn. You and I may love each other, but you are not their Crown-leaf: *I am.* You may *not* sit in judgment on me. And you may *not* tell me what to do."

It was too much. Thorn's claws bore into his palms. "You think I know nothing about responsibility? You think I don't understand duty? *I am the new Great Father!*"

She actually, physically reeled back, her paw shooting out to steady her crouch.

Mud cried out in astonishment and clapped his paws over his mouth. Nut gave an incoherent yelp and stared at Thorn in awed shock. Spider simply blinked and furrowed his brow, in his perplexed way.

Berry recovered first. She opened her jaws, then closed them again. At last her eyes narrowed.

"Thorn, how could you? The Great Parent is not a thing to mock!"

"I'm serious!" he said angrily. "You wanted to know where I was after the battle with Tendril? *That's* where. The vultures took me to their mountain, tried to persuade me to assume my duties. And I refused. Because I didn't want it, I didn't think I was *fit* for it."

"Thorn," whispered Mud, "you *are.*" But then he seemed to run out of anything to say. He went back to gazing at Thorn, his eyes huge.

"But now I think I'm beginning to understand," Thorn went on, his eyes locked on Berry's. "Maybe there's a reason I was chosen. Maybe it's for moments like this. Maybe it's just so I can save *you*."

"I don't believe you!" growled Berry, her jaws tight.

"Then I can't convince you," Thorn said, more quietly. "But you could ask the vultures, if you understood Skytongue—*which I do*. They acclaimed me Great Father after the battle. Does that explain why I've been so distant? Do you understand now? I couldn't tell you! I wanted to, but I *couldn't!*"

Berry stared at him. She was trembling slightly, but her fangs were still clenched hard.

"I don't even know you anymore, Thorn Highleaf. Maybe I never did." She jerked her head away and stared into the shadows between the trees. "Get out of my sight."

Thorn stood immobile for a moment, disbelieving, stunned by pain. But Berry didn't look at him again.

"Thorn," murmured Nut, coming to his side. "Thorn, come on. There's nothing more to say, is there?"

Thorn stared at Berry for a moment longer, at her stiffly averted head. He felt Mud's paw touch his arm, heard the rustle of leaf litter as Spider wandered diffidently closer.

At last he turned, flanked by his friends, and stalked out of the Crown Stone clearing. Berry didn't call him back.

Heart aching, Thorn blundered through the undergrowth, not caring that prickles scratched his hide. He could hardly think straight. It had taken all his strength to make his confession to Berry—and she had rejected him. So far, the Great Spirit had brought him nothing but grief and trouble. *Is this what you wanted when you chose me?* Anger and resentment flared inside him along with his misery and doubt. *It's not fair, Great Spirit. You know I didn't want this.*

"Thorn," Mud murmured as they halted beneath a cluster of date palms. He still wore a look of sympathetic incredulity, and he swallowed hard before he could speak again. "It's true, then? What you said to Berry?"

Thorn halted, swamped by remorse and shame. His head drooped. "Yes," he muttered. "Yes, it's true."

"The stones," whispered Mud hoarsely. "They were right all along."

"Yes," said Thorn. "I'm sorry, Mud. Sorry I didn't say anything. But they were telling you the truth."

None of them expressed a word of disbelief, as Berry had. They just gaped at him. Nut and Mud looked overwhelmed, their expressions a mixture of awe, respect, and growing delight. But as Nut began to grin and Mud placed his paws over his mouth, Spider only tilted his head to one side and poked in his ear. Finding some parasite, he popped it into his mouth and chewed.

"Well, there's a thing," he said. "That's nice."

For some reason, it released all the tension in Thorn's body. His shoulders slumped, and he found himself on the verge of actual laughter.

But there was no time for that. "We have to stop Berry," he blurted. "If her Crown Guard harms Tendril, she's going to regret it bitterly. In the end, she will—I know it."

Mud, Nut, and Spider exchanged looks. "You're right," said Mud, nodding.

Nut frowned in thought. "One of my Deeproots said he saw the Crown Guard taking Tendril away, toward the south of the forest," he said. "That's where we can start to look for them."

"But what should we do?" asked Mud. "What *can* we do?"

A moment ago, he hadn't really known. But now Thorn felt something kindle inside him: a fierceness that began deep in his chest and radiated out to the tips of his paws. He was suddenly filled with certainty, and that gave him strength.

"We're going to stop them," he growled. "Come on!"

He turned and bounded from the clearing, the other three at his heels. He didn't feel doubt or hesitation anymore, and he wasn't afraid. Yes, the Crown Guard could hurt him, Great Father or not—but what he was doing was right.

Is that the Great Spirit talking? he wondered. *Because if so, it's suddenly got a lot louder . . .*

Once they broke through the Tall Trees boundary, it was easy enough to follow the fresh tracks of the Crown Guards. There were paw marks, scratches in the yellow earth from their claws—and signs, too, that a baboon had been dragged across the dry ground: broken blades of grass, paw scrapes in the dirt, smudges of blood. A sense of urgency seized Thorn, and he ran faster, bolting across the grassland toward the deep gash of a dry streambed. He knew it. It was the place where the Strongbranches had taken Frog Deeproot, their former colleague, when she began to doubt Stinger. It was where they had murdered her.

As he heard the sounds of a commotion, Thorn slowed his

pace and prowled more quietly to the edge of the gully, signaling with a paw to the other three to take care. Mud, Nut, and Spider crept up to his flanks as he paused and peered over at the fracas.

"I swore an oath!" Tendril sounded confused as well as terrified. She grunted as Creeper grabbed her shoulders and flung her against a slab of white rock. Grit stood to the side, grinning. "I don't understand! I'm loyal, I said I was!"

"Loyal to who?" snarled Viper, giving her a clout on the jaw that made Tendril's head snap back. "You think we'll take that kind of risk with you?"

"Hold her still, Viper, Grit." Creeper snatched up a jagged stone. "I'll make this faster than you deserve, Tendril Deeproot."

With a holler of rage, Thorn leaped down the bank and flung himself at Creeper's blind side. Belatedly, Creeper spun around, gasping; he dropped the stone as he flung up his paws to defend his face. Viper screeched in shock and began to run at Thorn, but Nut launched himself at her, and they rolled, kicking and scrabbling. Between them Mud and Spider were wrestling Grit to the ground; the big baboon snarled and lashed out, and the air filled with the panting shrieks of fighting baboons.

Creeper slammed a paw against the side of Thorn's head, and he tumbled sideways, dazed. But Thorn could already see Tendril fleeing up the bank; she was limping badly, but she vanished over the edge and was gone.

Creeper staggered to Thorn and dragged him up. Thorn

shook himself angrily, clearing his head, and snarled in Creeper's face.

"She got away!" howled Creeper. "You pack of traitors!"

"And we've stopped you from breaking the Code," yelled Thorn. "You should be thanking us."

Mud, Spider, and Nut were scrambling to their paws with the other two angry Crown Guards, brushing dust from their fur and growling. The fight was over, then; it had been brief, if savage. *And we did what we came to do*, thought Thorn with grim satisfaction.

"The troop's in danger now," hooted Viper, "because of you four!"

"We've upheld the Code," growled Thorn. "You lot were about to shatter it. Who gave you the right?"

"Our Crownleaf!" yelled Creeper. "That's who. We're defending Dawntrees—and you've ruined everything. You don't deserve to be Berry's mate, Thorn. You don't deserve a place in the troop at all."

"That's why you should never have come back," snarled Viper.

"Right!" shouted Grit, glaring at Mud and Spider. "Get yourselves away from Tall Trees for good. The lot of you!"

"Do as he says," growled Creeper, his one eye flashing dangerously. "It would be the biggest mistake of your lives to return to the troop. And the last."

Panting, Thorn stared at him. But there was no mistaking the serious intent in his glare, or the coiled menace that oozed from Grit and Viper.

"We're going back to report to our Crownleaf now," sneered Viper, padding away. "You'd better be far from here by the time we tell her what you've done."

Thorn watched them go, his heart wrenching. They were right; that was what hurt so bitterly. He'd done the right thing—but Berry wouldn't think so. Not right now, anyway.

Great Spirit, when does something good come of this?

"We'd better get away from here," he said dully. "I'm sorry I dragged you all into this."

"You didn't drag us," Mud corrected him, his eyes shining fiercely. "We came with you because we trust you. And we believe in you."

Nut shrugged. "You're the Great Father, after all. How could we say no?" He shot Thorn a cheerful grin. "Rot you, Thorn Highleaf, you keep making me do the right thing."

"As for Spider, he doesn't mind a bit about your Tall Trees." Spider scratched his armpit and yawned. "Spider's at home anywhere."

The enthusiastic support of his friends made Thorn feel a little less wretched. He gave them all a wry smile.

"But I have to go back to the mountain now," he said. "There's something I must do there. Something important."

"Then we'll come with you," cried Mud, slapping his fore-paws together.

"Of course we will," said Nut, and began to strut ahead toward the mountain range on the horizon. "We're with you all the way—Great Father."

CHAPTER 25

Fearless slunk through tall, wispy grass, his paws raising puffs of pale dust. Keen was at his flank, and Ruthless just behind them both; the cub seemed much more cheerful since he had discovered that his sister, at least, had survived the attack on the elephants. But all three of them padded on without speaking, keeping their bodies low; they were moving now across the plain between Titanpride's territory and Mightypride's. It wouldn't do, thought Fearless, to be spotted before they were ready for a confrontation.

Fearless came to a halt, breathing hard. The rising sun already beat down warmly on his back, and the trilling of bee-eaters sounded very loud. From a distance came the grunting call of a serpent-bird. He flicked his ears, tensing, and glanced around to find its quill-crested head, but there was no sudden roar of alerted lions. Relaxing a little, he turned to Keen.

"You stay here," he growled softly. "I'm going to go on with Ruthless and warn Mighty about Titan."

Keen laid his ears back in alarm. "I should come with you."

"No. I need you to stay and scout, let me know if Titan or his crew are approaching. Will you do that?"

Keen hesitated, then nodded reluctantly. "Be careful, Fearless."

He was going to be as careful as he could, that was for sure. Silently, Fearless beckoned Ruthless and slunk on once more, heading for the camp where he had last seen Mightypride.

That serpent-bird grunted again, loud and resonant. Fearless paused and glanced over his shoulder. Keen was well out of sight. Ruthless glanced up at him, his head anxiously tilted.

"This way," murmured Fearless, and set off at a sharp angle to their previous path.

"What are you doing?" Ruthless trotted after him, confused.

"Hush." Fearless frowned at him. "We're not going to Mightypride. We're going to intercept Titan before he can attack them."

Ruthless sucked in a shocked gasp. "Fearless, you can't. Keen would be—"

"I can and I will. If Keen doesn't know, he can't try to stop me. I'll have the advantage of surprise, Ruthless, so don't worry."

"Titan is still so much bigger than you," objected Ruthless. "I'm scared, Fearless."

"Don't be. You'll see, I'll take him by surprise—and he's

lame, you told me so." Fearless took a breath of the morning air. "Your father owes me a fight, Ruthless, for many reasons. And I'm tired of waiting."

"I still don't think this is a good idea." But the cub crept along with him, his small tail quivering with nerves.

Keeping his body low, Fearless prowled on, his nostrils wide and alert. The Misty Ravine was close to this point, he knew; there could be no mistakes, no accidental noises to betray him to Titan.

A low line of sandy rock became visible through the grass, and Fearless slowed his steps, his shoulders stiff with tension. That was the edge of the gully; he recognized the jagged crest of the stones.

"Stay here, Ruthless," he growled. "And keep your head down. This is my quest, and mine alone."

"Be careful, Fearless," whispered the cub. "I don't want anything to happen to you."

Leaving the youngster looking forlorn and anxious, Fearless bounded up over the crest and began to stalk down into the gully. Its slopes were horribly steep and high, but there were ridges he could follow, leaping down from one to another. True to its name, the ravine lay shrouded in a pale gray mist, and as Fearless descended, skittering rocks beneath his paws, it only grew denser. As the sun rose, he knew, the mist would burn away; now was his best chance to catch Titan unawares.

And Titan was here, he knew. The big lion's hot and bloody scent was distinctive.

Paw by paw he crept on, ignoring the tremors that rippled

through his fur. There was something deeply unnerving about pressing on down into this gray cloud, his own paws half obscured as he placed them carefully on the narrow rocky ridges. But he could not afford to obey his instinct to run. Not now, when he was so close to the thing he had wanted for so long.

Vengeance, he thought. *Justice.*

Ahead, a great dark rock loomed through the mist on the almost-sheer hillside. As Fearless paused, one paw raised uncertainly, the rock moved.

It was a mane. And that was no rock: it was a lion.

Titan crouched on a flat, broad ledge, hunched intently over some motionless thing beneath him. As Fearless drew closer, he realized his enemy was gnawing and ripping at a carcass.

Fearless halted. Tendrils of mist drifted between his fore-paws as he stared down at the massive beast. Titan did not even glance up.

As Fearless watched, Titan threw back his head and gulped down a lump of dark flesh, his throat jerking once, twice. He licked his jaws, slowly and lasciviously.

"Ah, Fearless," he drawled at last. "I smelled you in the air. I knew you would come."

Fearless had to clear his throat; the dampness of the morning seemed to have affected it. He took a pace forward. "Then you know why I'm here."

"You are here as a lion should be." Titan's growl was distant, unconcerned, and it seemed to rebound from the mist itself, echoing oddly. "A son must avenge. Sometimes, a son must die. Such should be the way of the lion."

"I won't die today," said Fearless.

"Every lion dies," murmured Titan, "except, perhaps, those who learn the truth. Those who draw their life from the land itself. Such a lion may live forever."

"You're mad," said Fearless. It wasn't that he had an urge to insult the great lion; it simply struck him, with the force of a falling tree, that it was true.

Still Titan did not rise to his paws. Slowly, methodically, he rasped his tongue along the spine of his prey. *An antelope?* wondered Fearless. *A zebra?* It was impossible to tell. It didn't matter.

"You have grown *powerful*," murmured Titan, his voice lingering on the last word. "I compliment you, young lion. You bring yourself to me in strength, fit for sacrifice. I thank you."

A tremor juddered along Fearless's spine; he couldn't repress it.

Titan at last stretched his forepaws, lazily and slowly. He rose to a standing position and shook out his great mane. He took a pace toward Fearless, then another.

For all his determination, Fearless quailed. Ruthless had been wrong. There was no longer a sign of Titan's limp from the wound he'd taken at the Great Battle; the huge lion looked as powerful and remorseless as ever. His fur gleamed palely in the misty dawn, and his eyes were brilliant.

Had he been too rash, wondered Fearless, too impatient? Sudden doubt clenched his heart, and his blood raced. *I don't know if I can beat him.*

But this was what he had prepared for, all his life. As Titan stalked toward him, Fearless was reminded of the first time he'd seen this brute: on the day he'd come to kill Gallant and take his pride. Fearless had been so small then, so helpless for all his youthful bravado. There had been nothing he could do to stop Titan.

That wasn't true anymore. And what he was about to do now: that was for Gallant. And it was for Loyal, too, his true father. It was for his mother, Swift, blinded and ruined by Titan's cruel mate. It was for Valor, deprived of her family and forced to work for a pride she hated. It was for Keen, whose father, Dauntless, had suffered the same murderous death as Gallant. It was for all the lions Titan had warped and brutalized and terrified.

Fearless still didn't know that he could beat him. But he could no more back down now than he could sprout wings and fly.

"I, Fearless of Fearlesspride," he roared, scraping his claws across the rock, "challenge Titan of Titanpride. For the honor of my father. In memory—"

Titan's onrush was so sudden and brutal, Fearless almost fell back out of sheer shock. The huge lion bore down, his jaws wide and dripping. For a fraction of a moment, all Fearless could see was those long yellow fangs, still stained with the blood of prey: those, and a gaping ridged throat, and the billowing black mane, and Titan's freakishly bright eyes.

Staggering, dodging the worst of the blow, Fearless rolled and sprang back to his paws, snarling. Titan's claws had raked his shoulder, but the wound was shallow. Titan landed with a crash that shook the hillside and then turned once more, his movement slow and lithe as a python's. Muscles rippled and contracted beneath his glossy coat.

Clenching his jaws, Fearless feinted, swerved, and slammed into Titan's body. Striking out with his claws, he felt them dig hard into fur and flesh, and he ripped with all his might. Before Titan could strike back, he rolled again and leaped upright, his flanks heaving.

Titan stood calmly, eyeing him. He barely seemed out of breath. And he did not flinch or growl, even though a flap of flesh had been ripped from his flank by Fearless's claws. The raw wound dripped blood down his torn hide, and Fearless saw the gleam of exposed white ribs.

Yet Titan only stood, quite still, and watched him.

The huge lion sprang again, without warning. This time his forepaws smashed into Fearless's chest, tumbling him back-ward off his paws. Fearless hit the rock with a grunt of pain and felt Titan's claws tear at his belly; panicking, he squirmed and kicked, dislodging the brute at last. He rolled up and stag-gered back, just managing to stay on his paws. Pain bit into his soft underbelly, and he could feel his own blood dripping. He could hear the sound of it on the bare stone.

The repeat attack came out of the mist, overwhelming and inexorable. He had barely seen Titan move, but the great lion flung him onto his back and straddled him. Hot slaver dripped onto Fearless's face and neck from those gaping jaws.

"You fought me bravely," growled Titan, his voice breathy and uninterested once again. "But now: now it is time to die. I thank you for your tribute of battle, Fearless Fearlesspride. Be glad, be proud. A moment's agony, and then pain will be as nothing to you, ever again."

Gently, almost dreamily, the jaws began to close on Fearless's stretched throat. Terror had seized him; for a hideous, agonizing moment, Fearless did not know which way to move, how to strike back. Cold terror stung the open wound on his belly.

Something shot through the mist from the slope above them, barreling into Titan, flinging him aside. There was a grunt of surprise from the black-maned lion, and then Fearless found himself staring up at Keen.

Keen's muzzle was peeled back in fury. "You idiot!" he snarled, then jumped and twisted swiftly to face Titan again.

Fearless rolled hurriedly, staggering to his paws, only just catching his balance on the precipitous rock. Beyond Keen he saw the figure of a smaller lion, rooted to the spot and trembling.

Ruthless! He fetched Keen! I told him not to, I told him—

Panting, both Fearless and Keen stared at Titan. He watched them from a short distance, his body wreathed in that eerie mist. For a long moment, they faced one another in tense silence.

Fearless took a step forward, and Keen matched him. On

Fearless's other flank, Ruthless suddenly bounded forward too. Together the three young lions bared their fangs and growled.

Titan's stare darkened. He tensed, his muzzle curling, a growl rumbling in his throat; he seemed torn between rational wariness and the overpowering need to kill them all.

Then, with a single fluid motion, Titan swiveled and sprang out over the edge of the precipice. The dense gray murk swallowed him, and he vanished.

Fearless gasped and took three quick running bounds to the spot where Titan had jumped. Shivering, he stared down.

He knew this ravine, knew its gaping width and the height of its precipitous walls. Had Titan really been so determined to escape that he'd jumped to his death? There was an eerie stillness to the fog-bound air: no rattle of stones, no yowl of pain, no distant thud of a body on rock. All was gray, damp silence.

"He can't have made it," muttered Fearless. "The ravine's too wide. No lion can fly!"

"He's fallen," said Keen crisply, padding carefully to Fearless's side. "He'd sooner leap to his death than be beaten by three young lions. You told me he was a coward."

Fearless shivered. "He was, but he's changed," he murmured, half to himself. "And not in a good way."

Nothing was visible beneath them, not even the next rock shelf. It was impossible to make out Titan's body on the ground below. And as Ruthless crept forward, shivering, Fearless realized he was glad that they couldn't—at least in these first shocked moments—see the corpse. *Titan was monstrous and mad*, he thought, *but he was still the cub's father.*

All the same, they had no choice but to seek it out. "I know you're right, Keen," he growled softly to his friend. "Titan can't have survived. But I have to be sure. I have to see his body with my own eyes." He turned to Ruthless, kindly. "You don't have to come with us—"

"Yes I do," said Ruthless, quietly but firmly. "I'll come with you, Fearless. I have to see this to the end."

Fearless nodded, and with painful caution, the three young lions began to creep toward the foot of the slope. They sprang lightly from outcrop to outcrop, slithering on patches of scree and sending rocks rolling and tumbling to the gully floor. The mist was beginning to burn off in the sun as they jumped down to safety at last.

"I'm sorry, Fearless," muttered Ruthless. "You told me not to tell Keen where you were going, but I was so afraid for you—"

"With good reason!" interrupted Keen. "What were you *thinking*, Fearless? You didn't have a chance against that enormous brute! What if you'd been killed?"

Fearless didn't have the energy to answer. A dull misery had settled over him, now that the danger of the sharp cliff was behind them, and his gut felt hollow. He had dreamed of Titan's death so many times—but not like this! *He should have died at my jaws. I needed to avenge Gallant and Loyal and all the others, and Titan took even that from me.*

Methodically, sniffing at every rock and crevice, the three

lions patrolled the valley floor, hunting for any sign of Titan's broken corpse. Mist still lay thickly in a few sheltered hollows; that must be where the body had fallen, thought Fearless, scraping aside patches of brush. *He landed in some kind of deep hole. He must have . . .*

Keen was prowling at his side, snuffling under rocks. With a glance toward Ruthless, who was a little way away, he brought his muzzle close to Fearless's ear.

"I saw what Titan was eating," he growled. "Not a zebra, not a gazelle. A lion."

Fearless took a breath. But even that horrible news didn't have power to shock him deeply, not now that he'd stared into Titan's crazed eyes. "Bravelands is well rid of him," he muttered. "Though I wish it had been me who ended him. But *where is he?*"

"Somewhere in this ravine," said Keen. "I hope it's us that finds him, and not Ruthless."

But it was none of them. The young lions searched until all three of them were exhausted and their paw pads ached. At last, Keen halted and flopped onto his belly, growling with frustration. The sun was high and hot, the mist dissipated, and despite their frenetic and slightly irrational hunt, there was no rock, no patch of scrub here that was big enough to hide Titan's massive body.

"He's not here," said Keen.

Fearless remained on his paws, trembling with frustration. He gazed up and around, angry and despairing. The ravine was too wide to jump; it *was*. The slopes were too steep and high for any lion to survive the fall.

But Titan was gone. Fearless's vengeance had disappeared with the mist.

Tipping back his head, he let out a roar of grief and rage. It reverberated around the barren stone of the ravine, echoing back to taunt him.

CHAPTER 26

"This is no fun for Spider." The eccentric baboon glowered at the rocky trail as he stomped on up the hillside. "Spider is bored."

"Spider will have to be patient," said Nut dryly. "And Spider needs to stop whining before I knock him on the head."

"Nut-friend has been whining *much* more than Spider."

That, thought Thorn, was actually true. Spider was the only one of them who didn't seem hungry and tired and footsore, and he was in fact a lot less grumpy than Nut. He spent most of his time chatting to a bright pink-and-blue agama lizard on his shoulder. At least, Spider was chatting, making little hisses and clicks to try to persuade it into a conversation. The lizard just perched there, staring at the baboon's face with amiable incredulity.

"Cheer up, everyone." Nut squinted into the hot blue sky and pointed at black specks that were circling lower. "When we finally collapse, the vultures will finish us off nice and quickly."

"Thanks for that cheery thought," said Mud sarcastically. "Honestly, if the stones had told me my paws would ache this badly, I'd never have trailed after Thorn. Great Father or no Great Father." He shot Thorn a wry look.

"I don't think it's far now," said Thorn, though he found it hard to remember. The long, dusty slope didn't have many distinguishing features: a twisted acacia here, a big craggy boulder there. It just seemed to rise, endlessly, toward the lilac haze of the higher mountains.

"You've been saying that for ages," pointed out Mud gloomily. "It's always *not far now.*"

"I'm starting to think he made the whole thing up," said Nut. "Don't look at me like that, Thorn, I'm joking. But *how much farther?*"

"I'm honestly not sure," Thorn sighed. He clambered up a ridge of steeper rock, the pale dust crumbling away under his paws. "I seem to remember this bit—*oh.*"

He rose onto his hind paws, staring as hope surged in his chest.

He *did* know this tall crag of rock. It rose before him, a pale golden bluff with one tenacious juniper clinging to a crevice. He was sure now—

Dark shapes stooped swiftly from the sky above them, and behind Thorn, Nut gave a gasp and squeaked, "I knew it!"

Thorn dropped to all fours, tensing.

The vultures tilted their wings into the still air, the tips of their feathers flaring. The largest of them landed, with a hop and three quick steps; her companions followed, and suddenly Thorn was surrounded by the birds, and separated from his anxiously chittering friends.

"Thorn, look out!" shouted Nut. "Leave him alone, you carrion-munchers!"

Ignoring him, cocking their bald heads, the vultures studied Thorn with glittering black eyes. Windrider—he recognized her—stretched her wings, then folded them.

"Why have you come?" she croaked.

"Thorn, what are they saying?" cried Mud, jumping up and down beyond the ring of vultures. "Can you understand them?"

"Yes. Yes, I can." Thorn reared up on his hind paws again and met Windrider's gaze. "I'm ready to accept my destiny."

The vulture said not a word. With a flurry of black wings, the flock lurched into the air around him. Thorn felt Windrider's powerful talons grip his shoulders, and abruptly the ground was gone from beneath him. Cold air rushed through his fur, stung his eyes. Once again, he was flying, lifted effortlessly through the sky in the claws of a vulture.

Cries of shock erupted below him, but they grew fainter and more distant with every moment. Mud was jumping up hopelessly, screeching into the air.

"Thorn! Thorn! Let him go, you crazy birds!"

"We'll rescue you!" hollered Nut. "We will!"

"It's fine!" Thorn tried to shout, his voice caught and whipped away by the wind of the vultures' wings. "Don't worry! I'll be all right. . . ."

His friends' cries faded to nothing as Thorn was carried over the crest of the rockface. Below him the mountain, so recently an aching slog of rock and scree and heat, became a majestic series of points and jutting crags, with slashes of dark shadow lying in its sharp crevices. The sight of it made Thorn's heart leap and stutter, but more in awe than in fear.

The serried peaks rose before him like storm-whipped waves on a river. Thorn craned his head around, desperate to see everything as these birds did. Beyond the lowest foothills, the mountain's flanks swept down in every direction to the boundless plains of Bravelands: green and gold and infinite, splashed with patches of dark forest and streaked with silver rivers. Tiny with distance, great herds moved, golden and black and brown. Thorn could not tell what creatures they were, but from up here their movements seemed slow but purposeful, as if they were taking part in some ancient, Spirit-ordained procession.

The rocks below him reached a jagged summit, high vertical crags that circled a flat crater. With a breathtaking swiftness Thorn was borne down into it, and with a gentleness that surprised him, Windrider set him down in its center.

He clambered to his paws, smoothing his fur nervously. The pool lay before him. Bubbles rose and popped on its surface, and Thorn smelled again that thick, sharp under-earth reek. He raised his eyes to its far edge.

Grayfeather was already waiting, his creased ancient eyes fixed on Thorn's.

"Thorn Greatfather," he rasped. "Will you truly commit to your destiny, once and for all time?"

When he put it like that? Thorn swallowed.

For a horrible instant, he wasn't sure at all. He stood in a place that was as strange and dangerous to him as the blue arc of the sky, among creatures whose language he should never have been able to comprehend. If he did this, he was committing to honor, serve, and advise all those great herds and packs and clans of Bravelands—when frankly, he wasn't sure he could do that for himself and three friends. He was offering Bravelands his entire *life*.

Thorn stared around at the sheer walls of rock. He remembered the sight of the mountain from above, and the eternal plains spreading out beyond its roots to the gleaming horizon.

"Yes," he said, quietly and clearly. "I will."

Grayfeather nodded once; Thorn thought he caught a spark of satisfaction and delight in the old bird's milky eyes.

"Then drink," said Grayfeather, and hobbled back.

Thorn crouched at the pool's rim. The water stank, and his gut recoiled at the thought. *I have to do this.*

He stepped forward into the pool, its coldness making him draw a sharp breath. Then he cupped his paws and scooped up water. It glinted and glittered in the sun. Droplets of it fell on his chest fur, sparkling in the light. Bringing his paws to his muzzle, Thorn drank.

His first thought was that the taste wasn't so bad at all. It was nothing like the odor; it was sweet and fresh and keen, and it tingled through his body and cleared his head in an instant.

Well, that was easy enough. It—

And then the visions swamped him.

He was a gazelle, pronking and leaping, outmaneuvering a cheetah with a thrill of energy and triumph. He was the cheetah, his lungs aching and his legs faltering, the disappointment swiftly fading before a new determination. He would hunt again.

He was a hyena, lifting his paws lightly as he trotted, a hunger stirring inside him to feed the cubs of his clan. There—an unwary dik-dik . . .

He was a serpent-bird, launching himself into flight, his black-and-white wings riding the warm breeze, his long legs trailing behind him. He was a bee-eater, swooping and flashing his fine colors, darting after insects for the sheer fun of it.

He was a lion, his heart dark with madness, loping across the plains with nothing but immortality on his mind. Powerful, remorseless, murderous.

He was a shrew, scuttling panicked through tall, tall grass. He was the serval cat, his movements so graceful and lithe, that leaped on it with joy.

He was the agama lizard on Spider's shoulder. What was this strange creature trying to say, chittering and clicking its nonsense? He tilted his head, curious. Well. He liked the baboon. He liked his perch up here. There were tasty flies buzzing around that bristly brown ear, and he could reach them easily. It was a happy place to be.

Now he was the baboon. No, he was another *baboon, not Spider. He was himself. He stood in a glinting pool, high on a mountain, the cool water lapping around him, and his heart brimmed with certainty and joy.*

Thorn blinked and took a breath. He stood motionless, the

visions still drifting at the edges of his mind. He was staring into the wise, worried eyes of a young elephant.

"Thorn? Thorn!"

"Sky Strider." His voice seemed to come from far away; from a hyena, a serpent-bird, a lizard.

"Thorn . . . what's happening?" It was no vision; this truly was Sky, standing real and solid on the opposite side of the pool. She flapped her ears in bewilderment. "I've come to find the Great Parent. I have to speak to him. It's important, *so* important."

"Then," said Thorn, "you've come to the right place. And the right creature."

Sky's eyes widened. She stared at him for a long, wondering moment. He heard her take a soft, deep breath: it held surprise and relief and intense gladness.

Her head dipped, and her eyes closed.

"There is a terrible new menace in Bravelands, and you are the only one who can thwart it." Sky's eyes flickered open once again, gazing into his; for all her obvious anxiety, they sparkled with solemn happiness.

"Please help us. *Great Father.*"

EPILOGUE

"Night is falling, little ones." *Darktrill* the nightjar felt excitement mounting in her small breast. "It's time for me to hunt. But I have something to tell you before I go."

Her chicks trilled eagerly beneath her wings.

"We'll miss you, Mother."

"But you'll be back soon!"

"And we're hungry, Mother!"

Fondly Darktrill gazed down at them, so well concealed in the litter of bark and leaves beneath the cordia tree. "Stay safe in the forest-shadows until I come home, my dears."

"What are you going to tell us, Mother?" The biggest and oldest of her chicks blinked up at her.

Darktrill paused, so full of happiness that for a moment she was lost for words. She glanced up through the branches at the deep lilac twilight, where the other birds of Bravelands flew toward their roosts. White egrets flapped lazily homeward, the last light of sunset glowing on their wings. A lugubrious marabou stork, high in a nearby kigelia, folded its massive wings and hunched its head sleepily into its shoulders. Their day was ending for now; her time was only beginning.

But it was the finest day she could remember, one that had lightened her heart and brought it new song. Darktrill stretched her wings in sheer joy and sang up to the settling egrets.

"Good night, Purefeather! Good night to you all! Thank you for your news!"

"*What* news, Mother?" cried her oldest chick again.

"That hunting will be good now, Sweetsong, and my dear chicks will thrive, and that all will be well once more. The egrets say the Great Parent has come at last!"

The chicks trilled and chattered with delight.

"The egrets? They said so?"

"It's exciting!"

"We've never had a Great Parent!"

"No, little ones." Darktrill preened their feathers gently. "For too long, all Bravelands has been without one. But now you will live in the time of Great Father Thorn, Baboon of the Dawntrees!"

Sweetsong's eyes were huge and dark and bright. "A baboon? I thought the Great Parent was an elephant! Are you sure, Mother?"

"Of course, my chick!" Darktrill gave a rippling, churring laugh. "Egrets tell no lies. A baboon may not be as strong as an elephant or as swift as a cheetah, but he is clever and wise. He has brought the Great Spirit back among us all. And it is not for us to question the Great Spirit's choice, Sweetsong!"

"Of course, Mother." Sweetsong's eyes shone.

"Now, stay quiet and hidden until I bring you fat moths and beetles and spiders. There will be many of them, I know, because this news is a wonderful sign! Now Bravelands will thrive again, and there will be peace and plenty and—"

A cracking noise split the darkness, and Darktrill froze.

She swiveled her head, staring into the almost-black forest. What was this? Night had fallen so quickly, even one of its own creatures could be astonished.

And out there in the trees, there was something darker than night; she knew it instinctively. Darktrill felt her feathers rise in fearful apprehension.

"Mother?" whispered Sweetsong.

"Quiet, my dears," she breathed.

Pawsteps. Heavy, deliberate, and ominous, their slow thunder made the ground tremble beneath Darktrill's breast. For a long moment, she was immobilized by terror.

Then the scent flooded over her, a hot tang of earth and blood. This time, the fear was sharp and urgent, and she twisted back to her chicks, her big eyes widening with desperation.

"Hide, my little ones. Hide!"

They scurried back as she urged them with her wings. She watched them, her tiny heart thrashing, as they nestled deeper into the forest litter. When she was sure they were as well hidden as they could be—when only their fearful trembling could possibly give them away—Darktrill backed into the shadows with them. Turning her tail on her chicks, she crouched there in the dried leaves, her feathers prickling. She would, she thought fiercely, be a living barrier between them and the oncoming menace.

Rigid with anxiety, the mother bird gazed into the darkness. All was silent: even the crickets and tree frogs seemed to hold their breath and still their bodies. The marabou stork, high in its nest, clattered its huge bill in alarm; then it too fell quiet.

And then the lion came.

Massive, black-maned, its eyes glowing red as blood, it padded out of the shadows toward Darktrill's cordia tree. Slow and deliberate, its paws struck the earth with a thunder like falling rock. Darktrill, huddled between the roots, could only stare up in awe and terror as the huge lion came closer. Her head seemed filled with the stench of blood and death, and for a moment she feared her small heart might stop.

The shadowy lion strode on right above her, oblivious to the tiny birds beneath. Darktrill shivered, cowering close to the ground, until it had passed. A flick of a powerful tail and it vanished into the forest, swallowed by night.

It felt like a very long time before the crickets began to chirp once more, hesitant and subdued. Darktrill shook out her feathers, trying to dislodge the terrible, cloying sense of dread.

"Mother?" came Sweetsong's voice behind her, feeble with panic. "What was it?"

Darktrill could not answer. Her voice, usually so strong and beautiful, failed her.

She knew little of lions, but she knew enough. That oozing malevolence, that dark power, that aura of blood-soaked evil: it was not the spirit of a normal lion.

Thorn Greatfather, she thought, trembling, had brought the Great Spirit back just in time.

Now more than ever, Bravelands needed its savior.

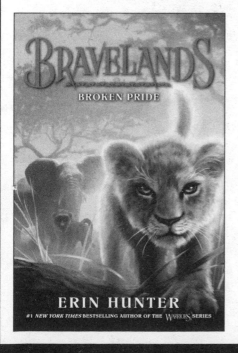

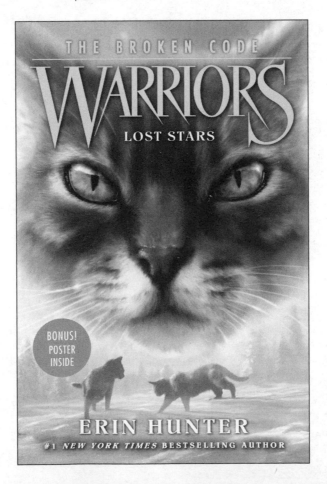

WARRIORS

How many have you read?

Dawn of the Clans
- ○ #1: The Sun Trail
- ○ #2: Thunder Rising
- ○ #3: The First Battle
- ○ #4: The Blazing Star
- ○ #5: A Forest Divided
- ○ #6: Path of Stars

Power of Three
- ○ #1: The Sight
- ○ #2: Dark River
- ○ #3: Outcast
- ○ #4: Eclipse
- ○ #5: Long Shadows
- ○ #6: Sunrise

The Prophecies Begin
- ○ #1: Into the Wild
- ○ #2: Fire and Ice
- ○ #3: Forest of Secrets
- ○ #4: Rising Storm
- ○ #5: A Dangerous Path
- ○ #6: The Darkest Hour

Omen of the Stars
- ○ #1: The Fourth Apprentice
- ○ #2: Fading Echoes
- ○ #3: Night Whispers
- ○ #4: Sign of the Moon
- ○ #5: The Forgotten Warrior
- ○ #6: The Last Hope

The New Prophecy
- ○ #1: Midnight
- ○ #2: Moonrise
- ○ #3: Dawn
- ○ #4: Starlight
- ○ #5: Twilight
- ○ #6: Sunset

A Vision of Shadows
- ○ #1: The Apprentice's Quest
- ○ #2: Thunder and Shadow
- ○ #3: Shattered Sky
- ○ #4: Darkest Night
- ○ #5: River of Fire
- ○ #6: The Raging Storm

Select titles also available as audiobooks!

HARPER
An Imprint of HarperCollinsPublishers

www.warriorcats.com • www.shelfstuff.com

SUPER EDITIONS

- ○ Firestar's Quest
- ○ Bluestar's Prophecy
- ○ SkyClan's Destiny
- ○ Crookedstar's Promise
- ○ Yellowfang's Secret
- ○ Tallstar's Revenge

- ○ Bramblestar's Storm
- ○ Moth Flight's Vision
- ○ Hawkwing's Journey
- ○ Tigerheart's Shadow
- ○ Crowfeather's Trial

GUIDES   FULL-COLOR MANGA

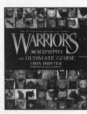

- ○ Secrets of the Clans
- ○ Cats of the Clans
- ○ Code of the Clans
- ○ Battles of the Clans
- ○ Enter the Clans
- ○ The Ultimate Guide

- ○ Graystripe's Adventure
- ○ Ravenpaw's Path
- ○ SkyClan and the Stranger

EBOOKS AND NOVELLAS

The Untold Stories
- ○ Hollyleaf's Story
- ○ Mistystar's Omen
- ○ Cloudstar's Journey

Tales from the Clans
- ○ Tigerclaw's Fury
- ○ Leafpool's Wish
- ○ Dovewing's Silence

Shadows of the Clans
- ○ Mapleshade's Vengeance
- ○ Goosefeather's Curse
- ○ Ravenpaw's Farewell

Legends of the Clans
- ○ Spottedleaf's Heart
- ○ Pinestar's Choice
- ○ Thunderstar's Echo

Path of a Warrior

HARPER
An Imprint of HarperCollinsPublishers

www.warriorcats.com • www.shelfstuff.com